Season For Murder

ANNA A ARMSTRONG

.

Season For Murder

Published in the UK in 2023 by The Cotswold Writer Press

Paperback ISBN: 978-1-7394217-4-8
eBook ISBN: 978-1-7394217-5-5

Cover design and typeset by SpiffingCovers

For Richard,
Thanks for all the fun.

I believe in an aristocracy of the sensitive,
the considerate and the plucky.
Its members are to be found in all nations and classes,
and all through the ages,
and there is a secret understanding when they meet.
They represent the true human tradition,
the one permanent victory over cruelty and chaos

E. M. Forster

Chapter 1

Vivian Plover liked graveyards, especially this one in Little Warthing. She approved of the magnificent medieval church at its heart, famous for being the finest in all of the Cotswolds. The graveyard was a benign resting place, neatly measured out by Victorian railings on three sides and flanked on the fourth by a burbling river, on which glided a pair of swans enjoying the autumn sunshine. The graves were politely placed side by side. Vivian found it comforting that their respective size denoted the social importance of each occupant.

Even in death, breeding will out.

Vivian shifted her miserly weight on the bench beneath the giant yew tree which looked out at the sea of graves. Her uninspiring hair and features were groomed to the point of stiffness and her painfully appropriate clothes added to her air of rigidity. Only her thoughts were original.

It's reassuring that on my whim anyone I choose can end up here. She smiled. *I will deal with any obstacle that gets in my way in the same calm efficient manner that I dealt with Mrs Jenkins.*

She shuddered as she thought of the noisy, rounded lady who had scrubbed and polished the grand house that Vivian shared with her husband, Christopher, for the last twenty years, until …

Amazing how simple it was – a syringe of saline solution with an air bubble straight into a vein and that was it; one dead cleaner on the kitchen floor, still wearing her Marigolds and with a mop in hand. That took care of Mrs Jenkins' snooping.

Vivian surveyed the majestic turrets of Little Warthing's ancient church. Its soft, sandstone mullions and arches had stood firm for centuries. It had seen plagues come and go, it had witnessed the Civil War, the First and Second World Wars, the

Falklands War and all the skirmishes in between, and now it was going to observe the greatest triumph of Vivian's fifty-five years.

Of course, there will be causalities – deaths – but one expects that in war. There are no battles without bloodshed.

She looked content in the way a cat does as it languidly watches a trapped and terrified mouse.

In twelve weeks at the Michaelmas Ball, I will be declared the wife of the next Lord-Lieutenant, no lesser person than the monarch's representative in the region.

She sighed as practical considerations invaded happy daydreams.

Of course, between then and now I'll have to deal with one or two things. Sebastian Rivers, for a start – he's bound to be in the running, then there's Jim Stuart, not to mention that annoying Jo Roper.

Her planning was interrupted by the sound of happy whistling. She looked up to see Dee FitzMorris virtually skipping down the Michaelmas daisy-strewn path. Neat, petite and invariably happy, Dee was offensive to Vivian. With disdain, she took in Dee's slim-cut tan trousers and copper cashmere top which toned so well with her auburn hair with its chic pixie cut.

Mutton dressed as lamb. Ghastly woman.

Vivian pasted on a smile that didn't reach her eyes as Dee spotted her.

Dee paused and smiled warmly. 'Vivian, how lovely to see you. Isn't it a glorious evening? I love early autumn. Can't stop now, I'll be late for Taekwondo.'

As Vivian sourly watched her disappear through the side kissing gate she thought, *Whoever heard of a pensioner doing martial arts? And why is she always so jolly? She'll have to go too!*

'Just tell me again exactly why we are trailing up the M40 to stay with your godparents?' enquired Emily Laddan, wrinkling up her pert freckled nose and tossing back her short blonde curls.

'Isn't it quite natural for a godson to leave London on a long weekend to visit his godparents in the Cotswolds?' replied Tristan Plover suavely as he changed lanes to avoid a large lorry.

'Yes, but it's hardly normal to take a fake fiancée. I'm not even your girlfriend.'

Tristan smiled, his vivid blue eyes alight with mischief. 'You, my dear old thing, are much better than a mere girlfriend. You are a mate and as such I can rely on you not to let me down.'

Not for the first time, Emily had the feeling she should have said an emphatic 'No!' to Tristan's request, but then he'd turned those blue eyes on her, and his mop of black hair had tousled over his forehead like a forlorn school boy or a lost puppy and … well, here she was speeding along the M40 posing as his fiancée and about to meet his godparents.

'Don't change the subject,' she said severely. 'Why couldn't I just be your girlfriend? Why fiancée?'

She glanced at his profile and just caught the tell-tale clench of his jaw before the strain was masked by a laugh.

'Come on, it will be a lark,' he coaxed.

That was the problem, Tristan's larks were usually just that – fun.

'There must be more to it than that.'

He swallowed, changed lanes to overtake a lorry and replied, 'It's Vivian.'

'Your godmother?'

'Yes.'

There was a pause.

'Go on.'

'She's always on at me to get married and I thought this would be a good way to get her off my back.'

'Married? Well, I suppose at thirty-one you're almost over the hill,' she teased. 'But surely you could just say, "Give it a rest Vi!"?'

'You haven't met Vivian – and if you value your life, don't call her Vi!' Tristan's laugh was warmer now; more relaxed.

They skirted Oxford and were soon heading down the A40.

'Right, so if my job is to charm the godparents, give me some pointers. What should I talk to them about?'

Tristan shrugged; he was getting frustrated by a slow-moving caravan and there was no opportunity to overtake. 'The usual stuff.'

'That's not a lot of help. What are their hobbies? Actually, thinking about it, let's start with, what are their names?'

'Christopher and Vivian Plover.'

'Plover? The same as you? Relatives?'

'Yes, distant cousins. Same great, great grandfather – I think.'

He put his foot flat down on the accelerator and gleefully overtook the caravan.

'Given that you lived with them when your parents were killed in that car crash, you must be close to them.'

Again that tightening of his jaw; his parents were one of those subjects Tristan didn't like to talk about. 'I was fifteen, so virtually an adult, and away at boarding school.' There was an awkward silence then Tristan put on the radio and with rather implausible enthusiasm, started singing along with Ed Sheeran. He only turned the radio off half an hour later to say, 'Here we are – Little Warthing.'

He turned off the main road and almost immediately they were cresting a steep hill.

'Let me start the tour,' he announced in a parody of a bus tour guide. 'First, we have the outer circle of the village. Note the large recently-built houses all in their own landscaped plots. You live here if you have a bit of money but not much class.'

'*Tristan!*' shrieked Emily in disapproval.

He guffawed. 'It's my godmother Vivian's description, not mine.'

He paused to let a mum push a pram across the road, leaving Emily to admire all the surrounding trees turning gold.

'Next, we have the unfortunate 1970s bungalow – ugly!' He sighed. 'But it has a historic point of interest: Mrs Jenkins lived in that one.'

He indicated a small, bland bungalow on the left.

'Mrs Jenkins? That poor cleaning lady your godmother found on her kitchen floor?'

'Yes – jolly inconvenient for Vivian as she hadn't finished cleaning it.'

'*Tristan*!' reprimanded Emily.

Undeterred he carried on, 'And here we have the village proper.'

They twisted down the tree-lined hill and modernity gave way to a soft crumpling antiquity. Squashed-together houses tumbled down the hill in assorted sizes and dates, medieval nestled next to Georgian with every age in between. Lattice windows and sturdy, studded oak front doors abounded and almost every home boasted twin pots with regimented bay trees or window boxes with overflowing autumnal orange plants. At its heart lay the majestic spire of St Mary's Little Warthing.

'It looks like a scene from one of those historical dramas. Cranford or something from Austen, you know the thing, where all the female characters are in muslins and wearing a fetching bonnet,' gasped Emily.

Displaying a wide grin Tristan playfully nudged her. 'So do you fancy me in breeches and a scarlet cavalry coat?'

Before she had time to answer he was waving at a couple walking up the hill. They were arm-in-arm and had a fluffy dog on a pink lead. The man was middle-aged and sombrely dressed whereas his younger female companion was wearing a bright pink fit-and-flare dress topped by a mass of blonde Shirley Temple curls.

'And speaking of dressing up, there are our resident clowns.'

The couple recognised Tristan and smiled and waved as they passed.

'*Tristan*! That's mean!' scolded Emily.

Tristan was laughing as he replied, 'No, honestly, they are clowns! Ken and Julia. Their stage names are Joseph Popov and Blossom Bim Bam and they really are clowns when they're not being actuaries.'

'Really? No! You must be joking!' spluttered Emily, twisting in her seat to get a better view of the couple, but they were lost from sight as Tristan turned onto a little side road. He pointed to a low double-fronted building that sat between a small cottage and a rather smarter, equally ancient, home. Its window boxes were a riot of flowers, a neat ramp led to the bright red front door and on either side of the door were square tubs planted with twisted bay trees. Above it, hung a witty sign showing a comic pheasant.

'That's my local, the Flying Pheasant. We'll go there one evening – I'd love you to meet the Rossellinis who run it. And that's their daughter, Alex.' He waved at a pretty girl with a Mediterranean complexion and a mane of almost-black hair, in a wheelchair but she didn't notice.

Giving up trying to get her attention, Tristan conversationally added, 'She's an accountant but I know her and her brother through tennis. They're quite good.'

'Coming from you, that's high praise,' smiled Emily.

'And there's the best bit of Little Warthing – well, at least my favourite part.'

Grinning, he pulled the car into the curb next to where a slim petite lady was walking briskly along. Emily judged her to be in her sixties. She had flame-coloured hair threaded with silver and was wearing a chic autumnal-toned sweater and slacks combo. What struck Emily most about her outfit were her shoes; as someone who lived in her worn-out trainers she was surprised to be drawn to a dainty pair of flat pumps – these were tan in colour with a pointed toe.

Tristan jumped out of the car and enveloped the lady in a bear hug. Emily unclipped her seatbelt and got out of the car to the sound of Tristan and the lady's mingled laughter. Her face was alight with happiness as he put her back on the ground.

Leading his friend by the hand he announced, 'Come on! I want you to meet Emily. Emily, this is Dee; she saved my sanity when I was younger and stuck here for the hols – and it was she who got me into Taekwondo.'

Dee had an open smile and her green eyes were warm as she gazed directly into Emily's.

'How lovely to meet you. Can the pair of you come for a late lunch tomorrow? Say one-thirty? Nothing fancy, just mushroom soup in the garden. Zara and Amelia will be there. Emily, they're my daughter and granddaughter and I know they'd love to meet you.'

The date was readily agreed and Tristan drove Emily another hundred yards or so to his godparents' house.

'Brace yourself, we're here,' said Tristan, with a tight edge in his voice.

'Home!' said Emily with enthusiasm as she surveyed an impressively large Georgian house set back from the road and hidden from sight by an immaculately trimmed hedge. The gravel in front of the house looked freshly raked. As Tristan neatly parked his car next to a pair of highly polished Range Rovers, Emily caught sight of the vast garden beyond.

'Gosh, I've never seen a lawn with such precise stripes!' she exclaimed.

'It's my godfather's pride and joy. Come on, we'll go in by the kitchen door,' said Tristan, bundling both their bags out of the boot of the car and leading the way around the back of the house and in through a split farmhouse door with not so much of a porch, more an overhang.

The kitchen was one of those spacious affairs, too shabby to appear in a glossy mag but nonetheless boasting a double Aga. At the door, they were greeted by a chocolate working cocker spaniel. It was larger and sleeker than a normal cocker but its eager tail-wagging was typically spaniel.

'Hello Bramble,' cooed Tristan who dropped the bags and knelt to give the dog a proper greeting. Delighted, Bramble rolled over to have her tummy tickled. When Tristan finally stood up Bramble happily trotted over to Emily and gave her hand a wet sniff.

Emily was about to introduce herself to the dog when a tall thin woman wearing tweed walked in. Tristan stepped forward and gave her a polite peck on the cheek.

'Tristan, why didn't you use the front door? And for goodness sake tuck your shirt in.' Then she spotted Emily and with icy eyes she surveyed Emily's trainers, ripped jeans and a baggy sweatshirt.

'Who is this?' she asked in a tone that made Emily wonder when the next bus back to London was leaving.

At that moment a tall but distinctly rotund man bumbled in. Like his wife he wore tweeds but they were tatty and he had on a pair of leather Wellington boots. The small amount of hair he had was grey and his bulbous nose was pink, whether from too much gardening sun or an excess of port, Emily could only guess.

'Tristan, my dear boy, you're here! And who is this delightful young lady you've brought with you?'

'That was exactly what I was asking and for goodness sake, Christopher, don't wear your muddy boots in the house.'

Tristan made the formal introductions. 'Vivian and Christopher Plover, allow me to present Emily Laddan.'

Emily offered her hand to Vivian. 'How do you do?'

Vivian hesitated but Christopher swooped in, clasped her hand in his own and vigorously shook it.

Vivian was eyeing their bags or, more precisely, Emily's Union Jack roller bag, a relic from her student days. 'Where are you staying?'

'Here!' declared Tristan with false brightness.

'Impossible!' said Vivian crisply. 'Victoria is down for the weekend to check on the renovations to her family home and with all our other rooms being decorated we simply don't have a spare room.'

She turned to Emily and added with a glacial smile, 'I'm sure you understand. Really, Tristan should have warned us.'

Emily glowered at Tristan and wondered how soon she could get him alone.

How dare he put me in this situation? How could he not even tell his godmother I was coming? Surely he should have asked Vivian if he could bring a guest?

She was about to nod and murmur profuse apologies while simultaneously backing out of the door when Tristan grabbed her by the waist and pulled her close to him. For a second Emily was surprised by how muscular his torso felt as she was squashed against it and how pleasant his cologne smelt, but all such thoughts were driven out by his proclamation, 'It's fine, she'll sleep in my room with me. Actually, she's my fiancée.'

There was a stunned silence.

Vivian's nostrils visibly flared, something that previously Emily had only read about in books. Emily's mouth went dry and suddenly she was perspiring. She could feel Tristan's heart beating fast.

When Vivian spoke, her voice had a deeper tone and slightly shook. 'What about Victoria?'

'What about Victoria?' replied Tristan.

Emily could tell he was attempting to sound flippant but that actually he was scared. He came across as a sheepish teenager and Emily noticed his eyes were fixed on his shoes rather than his godmother.

Christopher and Bramble both looked from Tristan to Vivian and silently slunk from the room.

Pink cheeked with anger, Emily thought, *So that's why he needed a fake fiancée, it's to get him out of some sort of a jam with this Victoria person.*

'I'll just show Emily our room,' he declared and, grabbing her by the hand, he dragged her through a spacious hallway peppered with portraits of Plover forebears in dark, ominous oils and heavy gilt frames. He gave her no opportunity to speak as he hurried her up the oak staircase and along a corridor before pushing her into a bedroom. As Emily took three calming breaths she noticed that it was very different from her childhood bedroom. Her mother maintained her room as a cross between a museum of her childhood and a safe womb that she could retreat to if adult life got too hard. There were no photos of happy childhood holidays with smiling faces and buckets and spades, no cuddly teddies still lovingly placed on the pillow and definitely no posters of teenage crushes stuck on the wall.

Right at that moment Emily was too furious to contemplate the implications of Tristan's impersonal room. She yanked her hand free of his grasp.

'What the hell do you think you're playing at?' she demanded to know, glaring up at him, her fists clenched and her eyes blazing.

Hastily he clamped his hand over her mouth. 'Keep your voice down!' he hissed.

This action only made her even angrier and as she struggled to free herself they both overbalanced and toppled onto the double bed with Tristan slightly on top of her. Not caring if she hurt him, Emily kicked and thrashed around until she was free of all physical contact with him.

He was laughing as he sat up and whispered, 'Alright! Alright! I had no idea you were such a wildcat but keep your voice down.'

She knew she shouldn't waver – what she should do was march straight out of the house and refuse to ever have anything to do with Tristan in the future. However, friends made in Freshers' week at uni are not so easily discarded, especially when they had eyes as big and soulful as Bramble the spaniel's.

Emily's heartbeat was slowing and her breathing returning to normal. All she managed by way of reproach was a stern, 'This isn't funny.'

He did at least look contrite as he murmured, 'No, sorry, but I really am in a tight spot.'

'Who is Victoria?'

'Victoria Pheasant. It's a bird thing – plover, pheasant?'

He looked hopefully at Emily but she wasn't smiling at his lame joke.

'She's another of Vivian and Christopher's godchildren. I've known her all my life. Her family lives nearby in a great pile of a place. She grew up there when she wasn't at school in America – her mother's American, her father's English. Actually, he was in the Guards with Christopher.'

'If she has a place nearby why isn't she staying there?' Emily's freckled nose wrinkled in thought.

'There was a fire, so at the moment it's being renovated and as her parents are off on some exclusive cruise, Victoria is overseeing the work.'

Emily was still looking thoughtful. 'Why is Vivian so keen for you to be engaged?'

Tristan sighed and flopped back on the bed, his hands pillowing his head as he gazed at the ceiling. 'The old Lord-Lieutenant is retiring – he's turning seventy-five and Vivian's grand ambition is for Christopher to be the next Lord-Lieutenant. Normally the announcement is all done initially by discreet letters but we have a local quirk and it's announced at the Michaelmas Ball which this year just happens to be taking place here. Quite a social coup for old Vivian to be hosting it – it's always a grand affair in aid of some charity. It's usually pretty amazing. You should come – it'll be fun.'

He looked at her expectantly but she wasn't interested in balls, Michaelmas or otherwise.

'What's a Lord-Lieutenant?'

'It means they are the monarch's representative in the area and they report directly to the throne about local goings-on. They also accompany any royal who happens to drop by to open a hospital or chat with the locals.'

'Is it well-paid?' asked Emily who was getting more confused by the minute.

Tristan snorted. 'It's voluntary, though I think you might get your expenses paid.'

'I don't get why Vivian is so keen for Christopher to get appointed; it sounds a bit archaic.'

Tristan laughed. 'Don't say that in Vivian's hearing. It's very prestigious and in her world that counts for a lot. What you need to understand about her is that she's from a noble Saxon family that has never quite gotten over the Norman Conquest.' He smiled and his eyes had a twinkle in them.

She threw a pillow at him which he caught and sat up, still holding it.

'There must be more to it than that,' she said.

Tristan shrugged and laughed, adding, 'Perhaps she fancies Christopher in uniform.'

Emily persisted and with her brows pulled down in confusion

asked, 'I still don't see what Victoria and you have to do with it.'

Tristan put the pillow behind his head and lay back down with his eyes shut. 'We're a perfect match. She's tall, blonde and attractive, an excellent hostess, and smart too. She's a hedge-fund manager and has excellent connections so Vivian has always been keen on it; but with the old Lord-Lieutenant retiring it's taken on a new urgency. Candidates for the post are recommended to the monarch by the prime minister and Victoria's parents just happen to be very chummy with the PM. Although I think Vivian is scheming in vain, there are some very strong candidates. Sebastian Rivers is a bit of an old buffer but he's reliable and knows his stuff – his son went to my old school but he's way younger. Then there's Jim Stuart who's a very successful businessman, but if I was placing a bet I would put my money on Jo Roper – she's frighteningly efficient, runs the family hospitality business as well as every charity board that comes to mind.'

'All sounds a bit odd,' said Emily, lying down next to him.

She rolled onto her side and stared at Tristan who turned his head and opened one eye as she asked, 'Why can't the pair of you just tell Vivian you're not interested?'

Tristan's pale skin flushed and he rolled onto his back and looked up at the ceiling. He clasped his hands over his stomach and started twiddling his thumbs.

Emily sat up and in a tone that was both teasing and accusatory declared, 'She likes you!'

He nodded.

Emily observed his lack of ease and thought, *There's more to it than her just having a crush on him.* Then the penny dropped, 'Tristan, you didn't …'

He hastily sat up and blushed. He looked at Emily and spluttered, 'It was only a kiss – well actually it was a pretty long kiss, but I was very drunk.'

'Oh, Tristan!' sighed Emily, not sure if she was angry or amused.

Chapter 2

Dee FitzMorris liked mornings, especially early autumn ones such as she was enjoying now. There was a rich earthy scent in the air; it was a heady mix of fallen leaves, burgeoning fruit and mist that you only get at this time of year.

'We must make the most of this, Cat. There won't be many more mornings I can have my first tea of the day outside.'

As usual, her large Persian pet was totally uninterested in anything Dee might say and simply flicked her luxuriant cream tail as she stalked away to investigate one of the borders. Dee watched her go and pulled her bright paisley shawl closer to her; it was a reminder of backpacking around northern India with her daughter, Zara, and granddaughter, Amelia. The shawl was cashmere and the perfect comforter to protect her from the nip in the air. She took another sip of her hot red-bush tea and savoured its vanilla undertones. She settled back in her garden chair to admire the garden in its autumn glory and to mentally run through the day ahead.

The garden was what had first made her fall in love with her home. It was vast, a great strip of land that had remained attached to the modest medieval cottage for hundreds of years. It was a relic of bygone years when this portion of land had had to feed a whole family throughout the year. Now it boasted vivid orange, gold and tan dahlias as well as a magnificent elegant acer whose delicate leaves fluttered in the breeze, burnished and brilliant in the early sun's rays. There were still reminders of the garden as a provider of produce; a couple of lamented apple trees on whose lower branches hung a profusion of bird feeders, alive with finches and tits, and beyond an arch. Just visible from Dee's perch was her portage, laid out in neat geometrical beds and overflowing with exuberant nasturtiums and vegetables. Dee avoided thinking about the deceased clown she had discovered there at the start of the summer; instead, she focused on her upcoming day.

So as soon as I finish my tea it's on to my morning Taekwondo routine – I feel like a good stretch. Then a shower – I'm looking forward to trying the sandalwood gel Zara gave me, so seasonally scented. Breakfast – I'll have some of that apple, cinnamon and blackberry compote I made yesterday.

The thought of breakfast always spurred her through her daily exercise and grooming routine.

It's lucky I made flagons of mushroom soup, as there will be plenty for Amelia and Zara's lunch as well as Tristan and Emily's. I can't wait to hear all of Tristan's news and Emily looks delightful. I'll need to go to the deli for some more bread and cheese. It won't take me a moment to rustle up a crumble topping for the apple and blackberry compote so I should have plenty of time to pop into Robert's interior design shop and chat with him about getting my bedroom refreshed – it's always a delight to browse around there. And haven't Robert and Paul got a big anniversary coming up? I'll ask about that.

Her attention was momentarily taken by shrieks from the bird feeder where two brilliant gold-and-red-plumed finches were squabbling over a peanut. She smiled.

It's such a gloriously busy time of year. I need to put my summer clothes away with plenty of lavender – Mother Nature is so clever to provide a gloriously fragrant way to deter the clothes moths. I need to make some pies for the Harvest Lunch – I wish I could remember what it's in aid of this year. Of course, half of the proceeds will go to the local food bank but is the rest going to Shelter Box or Save the Children? Still, it doesn't much matter as long as I remember to make my pies.

She took another sip of her tea.

It will be fun to see everyone at the lunch on Sunday. I can't believe Oliver is about to retire as Lord-Lieutenant; still, Justine will be relieved not to spend another year having to dress up for endless smart do's – she can live in her riding togs. I wonder who the next Lord-Lieutenant will be? I hear Jo is in the running, she'd be excellent. Oh, that reminds me! I must check my diary – I can't remember when we're meeting in the woods at dawn to do our bird count. Jim Stuart will be at the lunch too – I'd like to get to know him better. I trust he'll be active as a governor at the village school. I wonder if I can press him to donate more books for the kids' library – some of the books are getting rather tatty, though that's only to be expected with all those grubby little fingers.

She sighed as she happily thought of all those grubby little fingers and their adorable owners. She enjoyed volunteering at the little village school. Reading with the children was great fun; it reminded her of when Zara was little and wide-eyed, rather than a glamorous estate agent, or when Amelia was cute and cuddly rather than a Goth who was studying psychology at university.

Now who else will be at the harvest lunch? Of course dear old Sebastian Rivers – amazing that he's my contemporary but has a son at uni with my granddaughter. Oh my goodness! I totally forgot I'd promised Sebastian some of my blackberry jam! She checked her watch. *If I drive, I'll have time later this morning.*

Cat languidly walked past on her way to the kitchen.

'Right, Cat, I must get going or the Michaelmas Ball will be upon us and I'll still be in my PJs.'

Cat ignored her and as Dee followed her indifferent pet into the house her thoughts turned to the Michaelmas Ball.

I'm glad Vivian and Christopher are getting to host the ball this year. Their home and garden will make a wonderful setting and Vivian does so enjoy that sort of thing.

Dee's bright morning smile was replaced by a concerned frown.

I do hope Vivian won't be too upset; she's bound to be expecting Christopher to be announced as the next Lord-Lieutenant at this year's ball, but with Jo and Sebastian – not to mention Jim Stuart – in the running, I think it's highly unlikely.

Meanwhile, at Vivian's house Tristan and Emily had more pressing problems than the Michaelmas Ball.

They were both carefully avoiding eye contact as they nibbled on their croissants and sipped strong black coffee. Neither could think of anything to say, so the only sound was Bramble's tail rhythmically beating against the kitchen flagstones as she gazed up adoringly at Tristan.

Emily was confused. *I can't think what happened! Last night started off so well. Of course, I couldn't let him sleep on the floor and the bed was enormous – quite big enough for two adults with a row of pillows in between.*

She took a sip of her coffee and braved a peek at where Tristan was sitting. His black hair looked even more dishevelled than usual and he hadn't shaved so there was a hint of stubble, and his shirt was neither ironed nor tucked in – all of which Emily suspected Vivian would disapprove of. He seemed to be finding his croissant utterly fascinating.

The last thing I can remember thinking before I fell asleep was, 'What fun this is, lying side by side in the dark and chatting about odd things. This must be what it would have been like to have a brother to go camping with instead of two sisters.'

She took another mouthful of coffee to fortify herself for what was coming.

So how did it go from that to waking up this morning with us cuddled up together?

She felt herself going hot remembering how wonderful it had felt to have his strong arms around her, holding her tight. She recalled his delicious hint of aftershave. Their breathing had been perfectly in sync and their bodies had fitted together so perfectly.

It had all been quite dreamy until I woke up properly and realised just who I was snuggled up to. How I got out of bed and into the shower without waking him, I'll never know. Thank heavens he doesn't know what happened.

Tristan may have been unaware of the compromising way they had spent the night, but he was quite troubled enough by his own thoughts.

How could I not have noticed that good old Emily is a girl?

He thought of how she had looked wrapped in only a towel

coming out of the shower. Her hair had been wet, the curls lengthened so they caressed her bare shoulders and sent rivulets of water over her milky flesh.

Well, a woman really – and quite a curvy, attractive one at that.

He smiled and then felt embarrassed – actually more confused than embarrassed.

And what could I say when she asked me what I was staring at? I would have seemed a right twit if I'd blurted out something about her being a babe.

He swallowed and casually glanced over at her; she was looking at Bramble.

She must be finding it a bit warm in here with the Aga, she's a bit pink – that flush is rather – well – attractive. I wonder if she looks like that when—

He gave himself a strong mental shake and looked back at his croissant.

Get a grip of yourself, Tristan! Emily is a mate, just a mate, and you don't want to screw that up by complicating matters.

Upstairs, Vivian was fighting her way through a fog of sleeplessness and nightmares. With difficulty, she rolled over to look at her bedside clock but her eyes refused to focus. She had that all-consuming hungover sensation that heralded an upcoming migraine; she would just have to take a tablet and stay in bed and hope for the best.

Bloody, bloody Emily Laddan! It's all her fault. Well if that scheming witch thinks she's going to stop my plans she has another thing coming!

Thank goodness the engagement hasn't been made official yet. No announcement in the Times or Telegraph, so I can deal with the situation and no one will be any the wiser. I wonder what the time is? It must be late as Christopher is up. She sighed. *At least the oaf didn't wake me when he got up – miracle of miracles, he's usually so clumsy.*

The heavy floral curtains were still drawn but even the few

rays of weak sunshine that found their way inside burnt straight through her brain. She was beginning to feel nauseous.

Bloody Emily Laddan!

The grandfather clock in the hall downstairs bonged nine o'clock.

Bloody, bloody Emily Landon!

If only I'd married George instead of Christopher ...

She didn't consciously think of George often, but he haunted her dreams. He was Christopher's older brother – his taller, slimmer, brighter, more charming, older brother. An older brother who had left the Blue and Royals as a Major and had then made a fortune in the city while Christopher had only made it to the rank of Captain. Christopher had followed his brother into the city and ... well, what could you expect from Christopher? He had tried, really tried to make money – to make her happy, but well ...

Vivian hadn't married George, her older, blonde, blue-eyed sister Venetia had. And now it was Venetia not Vivian who was chatelaine of the Plover estate and more importantly *Lady* Plover. Vivian screwed her eyes up and clenched her fists beneath the bedclothes.

I just know they laugh about us, and joke to their friends about how useless Christopher is and what a waste of space I am. Venetia was always doing that when we were children – ignoring and belittling me, making me the butt of her jokes when her glamorous friends came around. 'Just look at what a fright Vivian looks! That party frock is an old castoff of mine – but of course, on me, it looked sensational!' Venetia would give her admiring cohorts a wicked smile and how they would laugh!

Bloody Emily Laddan!

Vivian was trying not to cry – even all these years later those childhood memories made her—

Bloody, bloody Emily Laddan!

She swallowed and a tear trickled down the groove of her crow's feet.

But this time it will be different – at this year's Michaelmas Ball, Christopher will *be announced as the next Lord-Lieutenant!*

Despite her dizziness, she allowed herself a smile. She could see the admiring, even awed, faces of those she knew. There would be applause, and champagne toasts – finally, she would get to look modest and humble in the way only the truly victorious can.

The greatest satisfaction wouldn't be the hats and clothes, the events or even the possibility of meeting the monarch – the supreme gratification would be in knowing that her sister and all those poisonous girls from school would feel the same burning envy that had been her constant companion since early childhood.

The night before had been haunted by nightmares. It had begun well enough; her first dream had been about her first ball that balmy summer's night when she had just turned seventeen. She might be wearing a second-hand dress but she had felt almost attractive. It had been the first time she had worn lipstick; she had known it wasn't quite the right shade but she didn't have any so she'd borrowed some from her mother. She'd crept into her mother's room, somewhere she'd only entered before on rare occasions. Her mother's dressing table captivated her with the awe of a worshipper at an altar; there on a pristine square of white linen, surrounded by mirrors, were a set of silver brushes, an extravagant soft powder puff and several lipsticks in gold cases. Vivian had seized one and scuttled away.

How different it all was from Vivian's memories of her older sister Venetia's first ball – there'd been trips to London for the dressmaker, there had been makeup lessons and further visits to London to the hairdresser, who had made Venetia's curls gleam.

But when it came to Vivian …

Her mother had looked at her over the lunch table and laughed. 'What's the point?' And her father, Venetia, and some visiting neighbours had all joined in gazing at Vivian, taking in her skinny proportions, her pale skin and undistinguished features, her spots and her lank mouse hair. They had then all joined in the mirth while Vivian had stared at her uneaten salad and wished that she could die – or at least that they all would.

Triumph crept into Vivian as she had proved them wrong. By dint of an ancient curling iron she had forced a kink of a curl into her bob – true, in her efforts she had singed it a bit, but that was easy to cut out and it didn't smell too badly.

Then came the pinnacle of the evening, she had danced with George Plover! It was this moment that she had dreamed of on the previous night. It was as if she had actually been there and all her hopes were still alive and possible. He had looked dashing in his full dress uniform; its narrow cut and embellished front set off his figure to perfection, while the dark, almost black, colour looked dramatic with the broad red stripe on the trousers. As he swirled her around the ballroom she could see all the faces of the other girls wishing they were in his arms, not Vivian.

But then she had awoken with a jolt and it was Christopher – not George – Plover in the marital bed with her. Vivian was left with this lump of a man. It must have been his snoring that woke her. He let out another rasping snore that shook the bed and Vivian elbowed him. He snorted, spluttered and rolled over.

She thought of Venetia who at this moment would be many miles away nestled up to the still-lithe and athletic George, surrounded by the family acres. What's more, she had a title.

I have been cheated! But not any more!

She gripped the bedsheets till her knuckles ached and eventually as the first rays of the sun crept through and the murmurs of the dawn chorus swelled, she fell asleep again, only to be tormented by vivid nightmares of school.

School! Vivian shuddered.

Venetia had loved that rambling old mausoleum of a place and still sang all three verses of the school song when she was a little tipsy. She'd been captain of lacrosse and Head of House.

Vivian had arrived one rainy September, clumsily clutching her lacrosse stick, feeling sick with apprehension. Venetia's old brown tunic didn't fit and she couldn't have been there for more than twenty minutes before two of the mistresses had walked past and commented, 'She's nothing like her sister!' To be nothing like Venetia was the most damning comment anyone could make at

Thorneycroft. It was often repeated throughout her time at school.

The incident that invaded her sleep the previous night had been from when she was twelve.

Of course, I took the necklace – it was a pretty, blue enamel swallow on a silver chain. The enamel shone in the sun like pictures I'd seen of the brilliant Mediterranean Sea. I so wanted – needed until I ached – something, anything pretty. And Frankie had lots of fetching things: books, bracelets, a pink sponge bag tied with a satin ribbon ... Why shouldn't I have just one special thing? I didn't think she'd even miss it but she did and no one would have known it was me who took it if that sneak Janet hadn't seen me in the dorm when I was meant to be at music practice.

Snapshots of the incident played out in her dream while she tossed and turned in her sleep, vainly trying to escape her emotions. She could see all the girls from her dorm encircling her, accusing her. The dream was in black and white, like an old movie, but that only made the raw feelings more intense. Over forty years later she could still feel their disdain and dislike and her own quivering terror of rejection.

Then came the image of the house mistress searching her room. She could hear her own terrified, tearful denials and the sick apprehension of inevitable discovery.

Finally, she was before the headmistress. Slim, neat and saddened, the headmistress had shaken her head and murmured, 'You are nothing like your sister.'

Vivian had awoken with a start.

Bloody Emily! Well, I won't let it stop me. By the time Victoria's parents get back from their cruise, I'll have taken care of Emily. Victoria will be part of our family – or as good as – and what could be more natural than for them to drop a discreet word in the prime minister's ear about what an excellent Lord-Lieutenant Christopher would make?

The thought didn't bring her ease. This new development – the arrival of Emily Laddan – had uncovered her deeply buried fear of being out of control: at the mercy of others.

I have to take back control! If I don't look after myself no one else will! I have *to take action.*

She had already been pondering what was to be done with the other obstacles – Sebastian Rivers, Jo Roper and Jim Stuart. Emily would take some thinking about.

But I need to do something now. Today. I want ...

She recalled that delicious sense of power that had surged through her as she had coolly observed Mrs Jenkins dead on her kitchen floor, with one stocking wrinkled and the bottom of her ample knickers peeping out of her crumpled dress.

Dee FitzMorris! It's quite simple; I will deal with the potential stumbling blocks one at a time. It's just the same as ticking off household tasks. Taking care of Dee FitzMorris will be a confidence booster. Having accomplished my immediate goal, I'll experience that delightful surge of power I felt with Mrs Jenkins and then there'll be no stopping me.

Of course, Dee is not an obstacle per se – thank God standards have not fallen to such an extent that persons such as that FitzMorris woman could be considered for the esteemed role of Lord-Lieutenant but her constant jollity is so *annoying, besides which she might get in the way of the grand plan – she is always interfering in people's lives.*

Finally, Vivian felt calm and peaceful and she could sleep.

The day was already warm as Dee, with a vast basket in her hand, headed out of the door.

A real Indian summer – perhaps I shouldn't put away my summer clothes just yet, she thought happily. She was wearing a navy linen dress which she'd picked up years ago in Provence and with her tan cropped cashmere cardigan – soft with many loving washes – she was comfy and cosy. She strode purposefully in her ballet flats and even let the basket swing in rhythm to her strides. Her Moroccan bangles jangled as she walked; they were another reminder of happy travels.

She glanced at the modern bungalow that neighboured her seasoned cottage – a 1970s anachronism, the result of a fire that had destroyed the previous home and was now an ugly eyesore that jarred against the charming soft sandstone of the surrounding homes.

I wonder how poor Mrs May is getting on? Still, the sold sign is up so I'll have new neighbours soon. I wonder who they'll be? It would be lovely to have a young family – perhaps I could babysit.

She heard retired Police Chief Paul Wilson before she saw him.

He won't be able to sit out on his front lawn in that deckchair for many more days – at least then we won't have to suffer the sound of him listening to heavy metal.

As usual she smiled at him while he, resplendent in his MCC tie and ponytail, scowled at her.

She reached the end of her road and was on the village high street with its quaint shops, tearoom and pub, all beloved by the tourists who flocked here in the summer but, like the swallows, departed as winter beckoned.

The venerable church bell chimed nine.

I must get a move on. Deli first, I think – it's the closest.

She turned left up the steep hill, past an ironmonger – *that reminds me, I must put my order in for some more logs, so handy it being so close* – past a clothes boutique – *what a pretty sweater in the window, I must pop in and try it on when I have more time* – and she was at Sophie and Son, the deli.

The gold lettering on the navy background looks so smart and I do like how they wear navy aprons with their logo on. And there is Sophie looking as lovely as ever. Amazing how with her blonde hair in a simple ponytail and just in her jeans and white shirt under her apron she can look so stylish.

'Morning Sophie.'

'Dee, we've some more of that goats' cheese you love.'

'Excellent. I need a few things as I've got both friends and family for lunch.'

Sophie beamed. 'Then you've come to the right place. You just have a browse and call me if you need me. I'll just be in the back; I've had a delivery.'

'And no David to help?'

David was Sophie's son, a tall gangly boy who Dee thought was rather sweet in his shy reserved way.

'College – typical, just when I could do with a bit of muscle,' smiled Sophie as she disappeared into the back room.

It was always a joy to visit this deli. Sophie – or perhaps it was David – had a knack for displaying produce so it looked as attractive as it tasted. Dee invariably walked out with more things than she'd intended on buying, but she never regretted it. Today some pickled walnuts called out to her.

And who could resist that quince jelly? It looks like a jewel and will go perfectly with the cheese – such a treat. Oh! And just look at those olives, I can't remember when I last saw some so plump, they'll be perfect to nibble on.

From the baskets of loaves, she picked a walnut one, still warm from the oven. *Oh, the smell –* she took a long lingering inhale and savoured the scent *– how will I resist having some before lunch? Perhaps I should get two? And I must get some of the sun-dried tomato rolls – Amelia loves them.*

She resisted the tempting rows of olive oils – largely because she knew she couldn't cram any more into her kitchen.

Sophie re-emerged just at the time to help her with the cheese. 'Do you fancy a bit of Geoffrey's?'

'Ooh, yes please. I'd love all of that round of Geoffrey's goat cheese, I don't know how he gets it so creamy.'

'He says it's because his meadowland has never been sprayed so it's full of herby goodness,' commented Sophie as she handed a wrapped package over the counter.

Dee took it and laughed. 'He told me it's because he has a fine tenor voice and he sings Puccini to his ladies while he milks them.'

Sophie smiled. 'Well that would work as well; most ladies appreciate a bit of Puccini. A hard cheese? This Cantal is excellent – would you like to try a sliver?'

'I'll take your word for it.'

'This much?' asked Sophie, showing where the wire would cut. Dee nodded and Sophie carefully cut and wrapped the chunk in greaseproof paper and secured it with a round navy sticker with the deli's logo on it.

'I need something blue for Tristan. I'm not that fond of blue cheese but he has a passion for it.'

Sophie paused. 'I didn't know he was down. I must tell David although they'll probably run into each other in the pub. How about a small slice of Colton Basset Stilton? He'll appreciate that.'

'Excellent – it'll be a treat for him. He's got a rather sweet-looking girl with him, but unfortunately, I don't know what her favourite cheese is,' mused Dee.

Sophie stopped her meticulous cutting and wrapping to stare at Dee.

'No! A girl? But what about Victoria?'

Dee blinked, half-shook her head and wished she hadn't said anything. 'I really don't think Tristan and Victoria have ever been anything but friends,' she stammered and refrained from adding, 'whatever Vivian would like to think.' Instead, she said, 'I mustn't forget some Black Bomber for Zara.'

Sophie laughed. 'I can imagine her reaction if there was no Black Bomber on the cheeseboard.' As she cut through the black wax coat to reveal the pale cheese within she said, 'Do send her my love. We're overdue a catch-up; I'll give her a ring.'

As per usual the bill at the end of this little foray was astronomical, but Dee valiantly managed to smile rather than wince as she bid farewell to Sophie. Once she'd left the shop she glanced at her basket laden with inviting brown paper packages. *Perhaps I should have called into the deli after I'd walked up the hill to Robert's.*

Bravely she headed up the steep hill, nearly colliding with Blossom Bim Bam. Blossom was in a tizzy, her daisy-splashed skirt swirled and her dog yapped in an excited fluffy sort of way.

'Oh Dee, I can't stop. I'm meant to be at work but I had to take the little one to the vet's. Nothing serious,' she added hastily as she saw Dee's look of concern. 'See you at the Harvest Lunch; I'm looking forward to your pie for pud.' She hurried off down the hill.

Dee arrived at Robert's interiors shop without any more interruptions. She always thought it was an exceptionally attractive storefront. An impressive front door was marked by two perfectly matched bay trees with ivy spilling artistically over the rims of the lead planters. The door was flanked by a pair of large windows and Robert had changed the window displays since the last time she'd been in. Then it had been high summer, and floral fabrics and bright lampshades had been displayed over white, iron garden furniture with an antique croquet mallet as a prop. Now Robert had embraced autumn; in one window there was a leather armchair with a cosy plaid rug in rusty tones and in the other was an attractive small table with accompanying chairs. The table-top was a chessboard with a beautifully crafted chess set depicted mid-game.

The wooden name board was newly painted with a dark-blue scroll font against a blue-grey background that proudly announced, 'Robert Rye-Richardson's Interiors'.

As Dee admired the exterior and mused, *I wonder if he regrets that there's no possibility of 'Robert Rye-Richardson and Son' although of course, it could be 'and Daughter'. Shame they haven't had children – both Robert and Paul have such dazzling blue eyes and they have film-star good looks.*

A gleam came into Dee's eyes. *I wonder if there's still a possibility – after all Robert is only in his forties.* She frowned. *But then Paul must be at least fifty, he just looks younger what with all that jogging and army training. But they are rather happily set in their ways and babies do tend to disrupt things.* She almost laughed out loud as it occurred to her that it was none of her business. *But I can ask whether I'm right that they have a significant anniversary coming up.*

The door's old-fashioned bell jangled as Dee pushed it open and Robert looked up to smile and nod. He was dealing with a female customer whom Dee could tell at a glance was down from London.

I'm sure she has some wonderful weekend retreat and Robert is just the man to give it that effortless rural chic. These London types always look so groomed but I can't help wondering if any of the women ever eat a square meal – it can't be good for them being that skinny.

Dee checked her watch. *If Robert is busy for more than five minutes I'll have to go or I won't have time to hop in the car and drop off my blackberry jam at Sebastian's before lunch.*

But Robert was already finishing with the lady and showing her to the door with a well-practised smile. 'Don't worry about a thing. We'll easily have your delightful home ready by Christmas. Your husband and children will love it; nothing beats a traditional Christmas in the Cotswolds.'

As the lady walked past her, Dee got a whiff of Chanel No 5, then Robert was embracing her and the scent of Chanel was replaced with something discreet from Trumper's. He beamed at her with those wonderful blue eyes and Dee noticed that his shirt complemented his eyes to perfection.

I do like a man who dresses well – Robert is always a pleasure to behold, and to sniff, for that matter.

'Dee, my darling, is this a social call or are you here to see me professionally? Only I'm due at Jim Stuart's place in half an hour.'

'Ooh, I'm longing to have a look at his place. People say it's quite extraordinary – a newly-built grand house, no less. I'm planning on getting to know him a lot better – did you know he's just been appointed as a governor of the village school?'

Robert smiled. 'And you want to get him enthusiastic about the library?'

'Exactly.'

He checked his stylish watch. 'I hate to rush you but—'

'Of course, actually, I'm pressed for time, too. Could you possibly pop in sometime next week to measure up my bedroom? It needs a bit of a refresh and I'd love to get your ideas. We can have a catch-up over a cup of camomile.'

When he smiled, the delicate lines around his eyes only made his eyes all the more attractive. 'I'd love that. I'll text you possible times and dates.'

As she was heading out of the door, with Robert following,

car keys in hand, Dee suddenly remembered, 'While I think of it, am I right that you and Paul have a significant anniversary coming up?'

Instead of the happy smile she was expecting from him, she noted a tightening around his eyes and a stiffening in his stance.

With a distinct flatness of tone, he muttered, 'Yes, it will be thirty years since Paul and I became partners.' He nodded to his assistant in the shop as he shut the door then, more to himself than to Dee, he muttered, 'Amazing how a neighbour can remember and see it as significant whereas …'

The normally impeccably mannered Robert strode off to his car without actually saying goodbye to Dee. She watched his slim, well-dressed figure as he walked away. Everything about him was well put together, from his Italian shoes to his discreet but co-ordinating briefcase, but…

Oh, dear! It looks like Paul's head is rather too full of matters of national security or perhaps it's his ghastly daily commute into Cheltenham. Could it be that years of military service have drummed all sense of romance out of Paul's ramrod spine?

Dee shifted the weight of her basket, wishing she'd left shopping at the deli until after her foray into the world of interiors.

Now how can I hint to Paul that he needs to pay a bit of attention to his home security? She took a few more steps down the hill before pausing and smiling as a new thought struck her. *Who are you kidding, Dee FitzMorris? When have you ever hinted at anything? I'll just collar Paul at the Harvest Lunch and say, 'Hey Paul, wonderful that you have your thirtieth anniversary coming up – such a significant date in a relationship. Have you thought about taking Robert off to celebrate on the Amalfi Coast? He always talks about it fondly as somewhere you went on your first trip away. And practically speaking there won't be all the tourists, not to mention it being cheaper off-season.'*

The church clock rang out the passing of another hour.

Goodness, is that the time? I must get a wriggle on if I'm to deliver the jam to Sebastian and get lunch ready.

And with that, she sped down the hill and home.

Dee just missed the removal van drawing up at Mrs May's old grey box of a bungalow, so she had no opportunity to greet her new neighbour, Winston Charter-Fox.

He was a small, slim, older man, dressed in a battered grey mac, rather reminiscent of the sort that Michael Foot, that left-wing politician of the eighties, used to wear. Winston Charter-Fox's hair was from the opposite end of the political spectrum – it was a grey Boris Johnson quiff.

With alacrity, he sprung from his beaten-up, beige, 2CV and set about energetically directing the movers as to where they were to put the functional sofa and his other austere furnishings.

Emily felt unsettled. Now it wasn't Tristan who was on her mind but his godmother.

'Honestly, Vivian is warming to you,' Tristan chirruped throwing a stick for Bramble. Overjoyed the spaniel ran over to the water meadow to fetch it back.

It was a glorious morning, the sun shone but there was just a hint of crispness in the air. The few trees dotted around these fields shimmered with golden leaves and there were dots of red hawthorn berries in the hedgerows. There was an enticing earthy freshness in the air that was so different from her smog-filled walks on Clapham Common. The sounds were contrasting too, here the noisiest things were the birds chirping or a melodious blackbird warbling away with an occasional gentle moo from one of the black and white cows languidly grazing in a corner of the field. This all played out to the relaxing backdrop of the river as it twisted though the countryside in no particular hurry to get to its destination.

All this was a far cry from the red buses and endless cars jostling and hooting for their place on the road, and the frantic commuters and mothers on the school run. Everyone in London seemed to be running late for important meetings, and Emily found other people's stress, even if they were strangers, to be more contagious than the flu. Walks like this made her wonder why she was living in London.

Bramble had rushed back and sat obediently at Tristan's feet, stick in her mouth, tail wagging and dark pools of eyes full of adoration. Obligingly, Tristan took the stick and threw it again, this time into the river. Delighted, Bramble crashed through the reeds; there was a splash and a squawk from an outraged moorhen. Tristan laughed, he looked very boyish and relaxed. His dark mop of hair was totally windswept; his pale skin had a glow to it. The country kit – junky knit sweater, jeans and boots – was a look that suited him. Emily was pleased that after the awkwardness of breakfast, they had fallen back into their normal camaraderie.

She was also pleased that she'd thought to bring her wellies, as the grass was damp. Wellies are always so bulky to pack but were really a necessity outside London's paved walkways. She liked her wellies; they were jolly – navy with white spots – but the look that Vivian had given them had definitely implied they were not quite the thing.

Of course, Emily could be just imagining it – after all the poor woman was obviously in a bad way. Migraines are the very devil. She glanced down at her wellies and then over to Tristan's. Emily had to admit that hers were rather more exuberant than his subdued green Hunter wellies and definitely more flamboyant than the brown leather ones Christopher had been sporting as he headed out to his potting shed. But since when had happy wellies been a crime? Emily felt there was a lot she didn't know.

'Like I said, Vivian is definitely warming to you.'

'Uh?'

'Come on, it's Vivian – she's not the touchy, feely type. Her saying that you must come too next time I'm down is tantamount to her rolling out the red carpet and kissing you on both cheeks.'

'Hmm.' Emily wasn't sure how to explain that it wasn't so much Vivian's words that bothered her as her body language. Fortunately – or perhaps, unfortunately – Emily was not privy to Vivian's inner thoughts.

That morning they had just been taking Bramble out for a walk. The spaniel was overjoyed at seeing Tristan reach for her lead and was slipping and sliding around the kitchen floor, her nails making a scratching sound on the flagstones.

Christopher lumbered in from the larder. He was wearing some tatty trousers which had obviously once been a smart twill and his sweater was patched at the elbows. His boots had left a trail of mud and he was holding some string in his chubby fingers. He was preoccupied but looked up and smiled when he realised that Tristan and Emily were in the room.

'You taking Bramble for a run? Excellent! Excellent! Run out of string in my potting shed and I've one or two things that need tying back so I just popped in to get some more.'

He gestured to the string he was holding. He might have said more but at the sound of Vivian's sensible square-heeled courts on the hall floor and approaching the kitchen, he made a dive for the garden door.

Vivian did not look well; she had a deathly pallor, her hair was lank, her blouse was buttoned wrongly and her movements were shaky. Her squinting gaze went straight to Emily's jolly blue-and-white wellies.

Through painfully narrowed eyes she peered at Emily. *Emily Laddan! The cause of my lack of sleep and this migraine. The person who's deliberately thwarting my plans.*

Emily smiled. *How bad can she be?*

Vivian caught the look. *That bitch won't be smiling for long – I'll take care of her and those naff wellies.* Weakly she smiled, 'I'm afraid I've got one of my heads, so I won't be able to spend as much time as I would like getting to know you this weekend. You must come back next time Tristan is down.'

That will give me enough time to read up and prepare the old oyster trick – offhand I think you bury an oyster until it's gone off and is suitably lethal, then you just let a few drops fall on the fresh oysters and serve with lemon and a garnish of frisée. Et voila! No more unsuitable fiancée!

Emily was finding Vivian's smile chilling and she was also disconcerted by Tristan's inane grinning as he said, 'No sweat, Vivian. Dee's invited us for lunch and we'll go to the pub for supper – what time will Victoria be arriving?'

'About seven.'

'Great, she can join us there. I hope you'll be up for the Harvest Lunch tomorrow.'

'I'm sure I'll be fine by then.'

Vivian blinked. *Thank goodness all the Harvest Lunch tickets are sold out or that scheming girl would get herself invited and insist on meeting everyone and charming them with that bloody winsome smile of hers.* She mustered another feeble smile and with all the sincerity she could muster murmured, 'It's a shame all the tickets are gone – it would have been so lovely had the pair of you been able to join Christopher and me, and meet everyone.'

'Don't worry; I thought we'd take Bramble and hike over to the Swan at Swinbroke.' He glanced over at Emily. 'They do an ace Sunday lunch.'

He took Emily's hand, an odd gesture for Emily who hadn't quite got used to her role as fake fiancée.

As they were walking out of the kitchen door she looked at Vivian and enquired, 'Can we do anything for you while we're out?'

She noticed the way the woman's knuckles showed white as she gripped the back of a kitchen chair and the tight lines around her eyes and mouth. She felt a wave of sympathy. *Poor thing, she's obviously feeling dreadful.*

'I do have one or two errands to run.'

'Can't Tristan and I do them so you can rest up?'

Not unless you know how to drive a puncture hole line into Dee FitzMorris' brake line without anyone noticing!

'That's sweet of you but they're jobs really only I can do. Off you both go and enjoy your walk.'

And leave me in peace to find my sharpened screwdriver!

Chapter 3

At least lunch will be restful, thought Emily, clutching a bouquet of copper chrysanthemums and seasonal red berries. The flowers were a gift for Dee. *The little I saw of Dee she seemed like a nice, normal sort of person.*

All looked promising as Tristan and Emily approached Honeysuckle Cottage on Witney Way. The cottage was the gentle sandstone the area was famous for. Centuries of rain and sun had mellowed it to a natural simplicity, giving the impression that the cottage had been there since the beginning of time. The sandstone pots on either side of a crooked oak front door overflowed with plants. Tall silver-grey rosemary stood at the back and Emily caught a pleasing whiff of their sweet savoury scent. With the herb were purple-veined ornamental cabbages, whose thick curly-edged leaves were a darker silver-grey and finally, there was a profusion of joyous purple-and-white pansies.

She was struck by how many windows this small cottage boasted. All of them had the time-honoured small wooden frames and were painted a traditional Cotswold green, a subtle grey-green that goes so well with the colour of the sandstone. The two largest windows were on either side of the front door with two slightly smaller ones the next floor up, then, tucked into the low roof with its tiny old-fashioned tiles were three windows marked out by Lilliputian gables.

Emily was only slightly taken aback when their knock on the door was answered by a Goth. A very pretty Goth but nonetheless a Goth.

'Amelia!' said Tristan. 'Great to see you, it's been ages! How's uni? I should think growing up in this village has given you a good foundation for studying psychology.'

The Goth called Amelia laughed and returned Tristan's warm hug, giving Emily an opportunity to get a good look at her.

She was petite and her laced black corset showed off her wasp waist. Beneath the corset, her stiff black tutu crackled as Tristan hugged her. Her dainty figure contrasted with the biker boots she wore with her fishnet stockings. On her long white neck, she wore a black leather choker and her delicate ears had multiple piercings outlining their edges. A simple gold stud adorned each piercing and as they had been meticulously chosen in size order, with the largest at her lobe, the overall effect was an elegant splay of gold against porcelain skin. A cascade of saffron curls tumbled down her back and spilled over her shoulders. The extraordinary colour of her jade eyes was emphasised by theatrically thick eyeliner and her black-purple lipstick and nail polish had been expertly applied.

'Emily, this is Amelia – Dee's granddaughter,' explained Tristan as he released the Goth.

As she looked at Emily, Amelia's smile was as warm as her grandmother's had been the night before when they had met on the pavement. 'Emily, lovely to meet you. Are those flowers for Granny? She'll adore them. Do come in. Granny got into a spot of bother this morning so the police are here. Thank God they are our tame ones, Chief Inspector Nicholas Corman and his sidekick, Josh Parks.'

'Police? If it's bad timing we can easily take a rain check on lunch,' said Emily rather alarmed at the prospect of being an unwanted guest both here and at Vivian's.

Amelia laughed. 'Not at all – come in! Granny has been looking forward to getting to know you and quite frankly, if she cancelled her social dates just because someone had tried to kill her she'd never see anyone!'

Amelia led the way into the house and Emily breathed in the pleasant scents of beeswax and lavender. The ceiling was low and the wooden beams had been stripped and polished to a natural brown, rather than an oppressive black. This sense of light was further expressed by the walls being painted a light colour while the art was bright and contemporary.

The stairs led straight off the front hall and, as they entered, a magnificent white Persian cat with eyes as green as Amelia's stalked past a side table with its earthenware jug of delicate brilliant orange Chinese lanterns. With her tail erect and an air of disdain, she ignored the visitors and slunk upstairs.

'Don't take it personally. Cat is objecting to her garden being taken over by people, even if it is just Nicholas and Josh. She generally dislikes people unless they are criminals. Come through to the kitchen.'

The kitchen was a surprise; it was obviously a later addition to the cottage with a high-pitched ceiling and wraparound windows. There was a profusion of lush green pot plants, and on the large kitchen table, there were more paper-thin ethereal Chinese lanterns, along with a basket of crusty bread, an impressive cheeseboard and a generous fruit bowl. Further colour was added by green herbs and golden squashes adorning the window sills.

At a compact Aga, a lady was stirring a saucepan which was emitting mouth-watering smells of mushrooms, onion and garlic. She was small and slim, in a green wrap dress with shining saffron hair expertly cut to skim her shoulders. On her narrow wrist was a chunky gold bracelet and Emily glimpsed coordinating drop earrings.

'Mum, Emily and Tristan are here,' explained Amelia unnecessarily.

There it is – the same genial smile, thought Emily.

'How lovely!'

And 'lovely' is obviously the FitzMorris family's most used word.

She hugged them both and Emily breathed in her light citrus scent.

'Now Emily, I'm Zara – Amelia's mother and Dee's daughter. Your timing is perfect as I think my mother, Dee, could do with rescuing. She's had quite enough of police questioning. It may just be Nicholas asking informal questions in her garden with Josh taking notes but still it must be wearing.' She glanced out of the window to some distant figures in the garden. Emily observed a wistful look about her eyes and a pensive half-smile. 'Nicholas is rather endearing when he gets all serious and professional.'

She seemed to give herself a mental shake and in a lighter tone added, 'Mother must be on her fourth camomile tea – it's high time she had some food to soak up some of its potency!' She pulled the saucepan off the hot plate before turning her attention to the tasks at hand. 'Emily, can you manage to carry the breadbasket and those wonderful flowers? Tristan, if you can take the tray with the water jug and the bowls and bits on – careful though, it's heavy. Amelia, if I entrust you with the cheeseboard, do you promise not to nibble at it en route?'

Amelia laughed and led the way into the vast garden with its abundance of flowers, shrubs, trees and garden birds. The table was in full sun and at its head sat Dee. She was rather pale with a brown plaid rug over her knees. In front of her stood a beautiful glass teapot where delicate camomile flowers floated in water infused with gold, and she held an oriental glass teacup.

As they walked out into the sunshine a distinguished-looking man with greying temples, blue-grey eyes, immaculately pressed trousers and very shiny shoes was just saying, 'Dee, think! Who might want you dead badly enough that they mess around with your brake line?'

The man's eyebrows were drawn together in concern and he was looking intently at Dee. Emily regarded the man and instantly thought, *He looks just like Cary Grant.*

Dee was obviously perplexed by the question. She tilted her head to one side and glanced around for inspiration. 'No, I really can't think of anyone ...' Her voice trailed away.

An attractive young man with a notebook put his pen down on the table as they walked into the garden. He was obviously pleased to see them.

Well to be more accurate, he seems delighted to see Amelia, thought Emily as she stole an admiring glance at the young man's lithe and compact figure. He was casually dressed in jeans, trainers and a hoody. His dark oriental eyes shone as he looked at Amelia. Springing to his feet he took the cheeseboard from Amelia with, 'Here let me help!'

Highly relieved by the interruption, Dee beamed at them and exclaimed, 'Emily, Tristan, how lovely! And what a wonderful bouquet – thank you. Amelia, could you possibly pop the flowers in a vase? They'll be the perfect finishing touch for the table. Nicholas, Josh, meet Emily and Tristan. Now let's have lunch and talk about something else. Josh, can you please get the soup?'

Nicholas sighed deeply and clenched his teeth.

Dee gave him a fond smile. 'Don't be like that, Nicholas, dear! I've got a small gift for you to remind you of our holiday in the Isle of Blom.'

Amelia, coming out of the kitchen with Emily's chrysanthemums in a vase, roared with laughter. Placing the flowers on the garden table she exclaimed, 'Honestly, Granny, with all those dead bodies and all that chasing around the island, I hardly think Nicholas is going to forget that so-called holiday.'

Nicholas was still stiff and serious. 'Dee, someone tried to kill you this morning – we need to get to the bottom of what's going on. You were lucky today, but another time you might not be so fortunate.'

Dee leaned towards him and patted his hand comfortingly. 'I'll tell you what, let's enjoy our meal and you can open your present, then I'll go over everything again when we've had our coffee and chocolates.'

Nicholas leant back in his chair and held his palms up and out as a gesture of defeat. 'Alright, you win!'

Cheerfully, Amelia chipped in, 'It's a compromise – besides which Granny always thinks better after she's eaten. By the time she's got through this lot, she'll probably have a list as long as your arm of people keen to bump her off.'

She indicated the feast laid out on the table. It all looked so inviting Emily could hardly wait to tuck in. An enticing variety of cheeses, ranging from soft white goats' cheese to blue-veined Stilton and a hard cheese that Emily couldn't identify had been artfully arranged on a wooden board. The wood's naturally knotted grainy beauty displayed the cheeses to perfection. Then in the fruit bowl, Emily was intrigued to see at least four different types of apples, all differing in size, shape and colour. As for the breadbasket, well, what could she think but *I do hope they serve the soup quickly so we can eat.*

As if on cue, Josh appeared with a vast soup tureen and ladle. 'This smells ace; I'm starving.'

The three FitzMorris females, Nicholas and Tristan erupted into gales of laughter.

There's obviously some in-joke, thought Emily as she looked from one happy face to another.

'You're always starving!' spluttered Amelia.

'At least, for once, you can't make your hunger an excuse to grind junk food into poor Nicholas' immaculate car,' added Zara and Nicholas winced at the mere thought.

Josh made a comic grimace. 'Don't make fun of my childhood trauma!'

There was another round of helpless laughter and Emily was more bewildered than ever. She was just beginning to feel like an outsider when Amelia swooped in to explain. 'Sorry Emily, it's just that Josh claims he was scarred by having two doting Korean grandmothers who insisted on feeding him endless Korean banquets with endless side dishes.'

Josh exaggerated his tragic expression and sighed. 'So now you're mocking my cultural heritage as well as my childhood trauma.'

There was more laughter and Emily joined in.

After it lulled, Dee wiped her eyes and said, 'Josh dear, while you're up please get the little package wrapped in brown paper and string – you can't miss it, it's on the kitchen table and has a sprig of an acorn tied to it. If you put it next to Nicholas I'll make sure Zara gives you a double serving of soup while you're away.'

Emily enjoyed the next hour or so. The sun had a faded warmth while the soup was both warming and filling. For Emily, the most enjoyable part was the easy conversation.

Dee was an attentive hostess. 'Emily do try some of this goats' cheese! The farmer – or does one say, goatherd? – anyway, whatever his title, he's a friend of mine and he makes amazing cheese.'

Emily took the board. 'It does look inviting, but so do all of them.'

Amelia popped a beautifully baked roll onto her side plate; it was peppered with rich red sun-dried tomatoes and pitch-black olives and it smelt of fresh bread and rosemary. 'Oh Granny, you got some of my favourite rolls. Hey, Emily, you must try one; they're heavenly.'

It occurred to Emily that Amelia's harsh Goth appearance was definitely at odds with her rather sweet nature. *Perhaps I've misjudged the Goth world or perhaps she's an exceptionally nice one.*

There were general comments of appreciation as the breadbasket went around the table followed by much mirth as Amelia dashed into the kitchen and came back with a tray laden with different olive oils and dipping bowls.

Even Nicholas relaxed enough to exclaim rapturously, 'Quince jelly! I haven't had that for years.' His classical good looks were transformed and he looked like a happy schoolboy getting his first penknife.

Zara, elegantly poised on her garden chair, passed on the breadbasket and only took a modest amount of quince jelly, but she became animated over the cheeseboard.

'Black Bomber! Thank you, Mother! Someone pass me the fruit bowl – which variety of apple do you think would best go with it?'

'Any, I should think dear. By the way, Sophie sends her love and says she'll call you.'

Zara nodded but was really focused on her cheese, her gold bangle glinting in the sun and her red bob shimmering as she kept her head down.

No one dared touch the Stilton until Tristan had had his fill.

Emily was intrigued by seeing him in this setting. *He's not being brash, no cocky one-liners – he's just ...* She glanced over to see him savouring a morsel of Stilton, his eyes half-closed, his black hair windswept, his face fair but relaxed and glowing with health. *He's just Tristan at his best.*

He was laughing now at something Josh had said; the sun glinted on his white teeth, and his chunky knit sweater heaved as he indulged in wholehearted happiness.

Funny how I never noticed before how attractive he can be – I mean it's always been pretty evident that he's good-looking, what with those blue eyes and the straight nose coupled with the classical jawline. She smiled. *And if I hadn't noticed for myself Tristan does have a habit of pointing it out.*

She glanced over at him again. Now he was solicitously passing Dee the fruit bowl and she noticed his eyes were warm with affection and his head tilted on one side so he could catch every word she was saying.

But this isn't just his looks; he's attractive as a person.

As the thought registered in her brain she felt a jolt of panic in the pit of her stomach. To cover up her discomfort she took a sip of water which went down the wrong way and she started to choke.

Much to her embarrassment, all conversation stopped. Tristan started to pat her on the back, which didn't help. Crimson with shame, she was relieved when everyone resumed their conversations. She didn't feel as if she was being interrogated or as if she was being interviewed for a job, but somehow as the meal progressed she realised she'd revealed quite a lot about herself.

Zara: 'So you're a vet and not a lawyer like Tristan? Oh! You shared halls at uni? Being a vet must be fascinating. Do tell me what you enjoy most about it?'

Amelia: 'Your parents sound lovely. What are your sisters like? They always say that middle children are easy-going and very good at getting on with everyone. What do you think?'

Dee: 'I can quite see, dear, how London's glamour would start to wane after a while and you'd long for lots of muddy walks. You can get such jolly wellies these days.'

Zara: 'What are you reading at the moment? Do you have any recommendations? I've just finished a novel and am looking for my next read.'

Amelia: 'Oh, you like the Proms too? Granny has been taking me every year since I was tiny. Don't you just love the Albert Hall? It's worth buying a ticket just to enjoy the building.'

Dee: 'Ooh! So you're a ballet fan! Yes, we adored Woolf Works too. I so agree, Wayne McGregor is a brilliant choreographer and Richter's music was inspired. Next time Zara, Amelia and I plan to go to Covent Garden, you must come too.'

The blackberry crumble was sublime added with some local cream – Dee said, 'I know the farmer – she does Taekwondo with me and is passionate about all things organic' – and there was much-heated debate on where the best local blackberry bushes were to found. Emily was slightly surprised by how passionate each individual got defending their own pet bramble patch.

Finally, they were onto coffee and chocolates.

'So, Dee!' announced Nicholas, suddenly looking serious and very much the policeman. Reluctantly Josh reached for his notebook.

Dee smiled at him, the faint lines around her eyes crinkling in delight. 'Of course, dear, but open your present first.'

Nicholas sighed and set about unwrapping the parcel of brown paper and string by first removing the acorn sprig. With meticulous care, he soon had a beautiful shiny model steam engine in front of him. All eyes were on him. He looked pleased but Dee noticed a flicker of concern in his blue-grey eyes and she laughed.

'You've already got this model haven't you?' she said. 'No problem. I left the receipt in the box.'

He gave her an apologetic smile.

Zara said, 'I bet it was your mother, Myrtle, who gave it to you.'

Amelia added, 'And I bet she said something about it reminding you of our time on the Isle of Blom and the steam trains there.'

Nicholas nodded and once again Emily was reminded of Cary Grant.

'Okay, Dee, now I really must insist you tell us exactly what happened,' he said.

Dee gazed around the table with a furrowed brow. 'Well, I'm not sure what you want me to tell you.'

'Why don't you just start with the beginning of the day?' suggested Josh gently.

'I had my morning tea in the garden then I did my Taekwondo forms and a fifteen-minute yoga flow – so important to stretch and breathe in the morning. Then I showered – by the way, Zara, I love that shower gel you gave me, it smells quite—'

'Okay, can we move on a bit?' interrupted Nicholas.

'Well I went to Sophie's to get the cheese – which reminds me, Tristan, Sophie said David will probably see you in the pub tonight.'

Nicholas coughed and Dee took the hint.

'So I next called in at Robert's.'

This time it was Zara who interrupted. 'Ooh! What are you planning on getting done?'

'I fancy a bit of a bedroom refresh.'

Amelia exclaimed with a squeal. 'Granny, you can't! I love the butterflies! Emily, you must have a look – Granny's bedroom is so pretty, it's in the eaves and she has sort of swooping-down curtains over the bed with butterflies all over them. When I was little I used to lie on the bed and imagine I was in a beautiful forest glade.'

Dee nodded. 'It is a rather fun bedroom. I love it when it rains – it's just like being in a tent.'

'Can we please focus?' Nicholas sounded stern in a resigned sort of way.

'Why don't we skip forward to when you were actually in your car?' proposed Josh.

'Yes, well, I had to take my car as I was running short of time and I did want to give Sebastian his blackberry jam. Normally I would have taken my bicycle – it's such a lovely ride and I do think it's so important to stay fit.'

'Sebastian Rivers?' queried Amelia. 'His son is doing a course with me this term on narcissistic disorder. We've only had the introductory lecture but it's quite fascinating. A narcissist's world view is so distorted, they really can only see things from their own point of view and they are so driven by fear and low self-esteem they are capable of anything.'

'How sad, they must be so lonely,' mused Dee.

'*Dee!*' Nicholas was beginning to get exasperated.

'Going back a bit – did you notice anything odd about the car when you first got into it? And where was it parked? Oh, and did you notice the time?' Josh had his pen poised.

Dee blinked at the rapid-fire questions then she took a breath. 'No, everything seemed normal. I couldn't find parking right in front of the cottage so I had left it in that secluded pull-in at the back of the road; it was nicely tucked away. And the time was eleven, the church clock was chiming so I knew I needed to hurry.'

Josh pulled out his phone and requested a forensic team to come and check the lay-by. 'When we finish here I'll go and tape it off so no one else parks there. You were saying Dee?'

'As I was saying, I was a bit pressed for time so perhaps I was driving just a touch faster than normal, but everything seemed fine, right up until I reached that sharp bend just before Sebastian's house. Suddenly a pheasant flew out of the hedgerow. I tried to brake but nothing happened and somehow I swerved and the next thing I knew I was in a ditch and you two were there.'

'You weren't concussed were you?' asked Zara anxiously.

Nicholas answered for her. 'No, the paramedics said she was fine.'

Josh added, 'It was fortunate we happened to be driving just behind her.'

Nicholas looked at Zara, blue-grey eyes seeking out green ones, his body tilted slightly towards hers. 'If it had been anyone but your mother I would have put it down just as an accident but Dee being Dee, I got Josh to check under the car.'

Josh took over. 'It'll have to be confirmed by the science buffs but I'm pretty certain I smelt brake fluid and I think there was a drop of it on the brake line.'

Zara sat back in her chair. Her thick saffron hair fell away from her face as she rolled her eyes and said, 'Here we go again!'

Vivian had been dismayed when she spotted Dee. She had hoped that the next time she would come across her would be in a silk-lined coffin. She shuddered. *Knowing that woman she would probably opt for one of those ghastly eco-friendly willow things.*

But Dee hadn't been in any sort of coffin, she had been very much alive and in the company of what Vivian thought of as *those interfering policemen.*

Instead of the much-anticipated rush of adrenaline and elation, Vivian felt crushed. With a pit in her stomach, she felt those old-school walls closing in. *You are nothing like your sister.*

And when she saw Emily, pretty and smiling, taking a magnificent bouquet of chrysanthemums into Dee's cottage all she could think was, *I knew it. They're conspiring against me. Well, they won't win! Dee FitzMorris might have Emily Laddan on her side but I, Vivian Plover, soon to be the wife of the next Lord-Lieutenant, have Victoria Pheasant as an ally.*

She took some more migraine pills and returned to her darkened room. She lay there tortured by the migraine and her thoughts.

Chapter 4

For the most part, Emily had been enjoying their evening at the pub right up until the moment Victoria Pheasant walked in.

The pub itself was a clever blend of classic but trendy, so the pictures were rural but quirky; around the wall were numerous large paintings of pheasants, one running from a hare, another comically squaring off against a sparrow and a third looking surprised at a small chick. The décor was blue-grey walls with an accent colour of deep red in the cushions. The tables and chairs were a simple Shaker style painted to tone in with the walls and on each table there was a jam jar with hedgerow berries and foliage. A large black Labrador lay in front of the crackling fire near the bar.

Emily and Tristan walked into not just a pub but the middle of a heated argument. Judging by Tristan's expression and that of a couple of locals leaning against the bar, passionate debate by the Rossellini family at The Flying Pheasant was a regular event and not to be taken too seriously.

Alex Rossellini swung her wheelchair around, her mane of dark hair thrown back and her black eyes blazing. 'Tristan, come and tell the padre that he can't go wild buying truffles just because Nona loved them. This is a business, not some ...'

Fury had robbed her of her words.

The small, slim older man, presumably the padre – her father – turned to Tristan and with a quick movement towards his daughter, exclaimed, 'Tristan, tell this accountant that she has lost her Italian soul in balance sheets.'

A voluptuous lady of a certain age, who looked so much like Alex that she had to be her mother, smiled at Tristan and Emily. She was wearing jeans and a silk blouse and lost no time in saying,

'Hello Tristan, and who is this?'

'I'm Emily,' said Emily hastily.

'And I'm Gina. Just ignore both of these two hotheads, sit down and have some cider and perhaps something to eat?' She gave them a wink and with a straight face said, 'I recommend the truffle risotto. Francesco, come with me to the kitchen!'

Alex was still fuming, her chin was held high and she glared at her parents as they turned to leave. With an audible breath, she attempted to calm herself. Looking at Tristan and Emily she said, 'Sorry about that.' Then in a louder voice so that the words would carry to her parents, she added, 'But they should be thinking of their pensions, not bloody truffles!'

With a faint whirl of her electric chair, she manoeuvred herself closer and held out a hand to Emily. 'I'm Alex.' Then she nodded to a young man, barely more than a boy, who in the family hubbub had gone unnoticed. He was small, dark and wiry like the rest of the Rossellinis but he seemed remarkably quiet and self-contained, and only nodded politely when Alex said, 'That's Marcello.'

They were joined by another young man who was tall and gangly with blond hair and a shy demeanour. He smiled at Tristan and glanced at Emily before quickly looking away. 'Mum said you were here this weekend.'

Tristan clapped him on the back. 'You must remember to thank Sophie for the excellent Stilton I had at Dee's. Emily, this is David – you have him and his mum Sophie to thank for a good part of the delicious lunch we had. David, this is Emily, my fiancée.'

Emily flamed hot, she'd momentarily forgotten her role as a fake fiancée. She registered the shock on Alex, Marcello and David's faces which hastily changed to smiles.

Alex declared, 'The cider is on me.' She called over to her mother who was now at the bar, 'Mum, Tristan is engaged!'

Emily wished she was back in London; no amount of Cotswold charm was worth this degree of embarrassment. She saw shock and surprise on Gina's face.

Gina stared at Emily, then Tristan, a pint glass and a bar

towel in her hands. Her immediate, 'What about—?' was hastily changed to, 'Great news! Cider on the house!'

Francesco, now with an apron around his waist, joined his wife behind the bar and exclaimed, 'Truffles on the house!'

'Ignore him – he has bills to pay!' cut in Alex and everyone laughed.

Emily relaxed; she liked Tristan's friends. *It's going to be a fun evening*, she thought.

'Let's get our usual table,' said Alex, leading the way to a large round table fitted snugly by a bay window overlooking the picture-perfect village.

Everyone was smiling and general news was being exchanged as the chairs were sorted and people worked out where they were going to sit.

Then Tristan said, 'Leave a chair for Victoria.'

Silence descended. Alex, Marcello and David stopped what they were doing and glanced from Tristan to Emily then back to Tristan.

Alex spoke first. 'Does she know about …?'

She didn't actually say Emily's name but the keen look she was giving Emily said it all.

Emily coloured and it was then that a tall girl with impossibly long legs in tight jeans walked in. She had luxuriant long golden hair, thick and wavy. Her makeup was perfect from the subtle eyeliner that showcased her stunning large blue eyes to the glossy shine on the pouting lips. She wore a funnel neck cream thick-knit sweater.

That's the woolly I saw advertised from Ralph Lauren – it costs the same as my monthly car payments! I didn't think anyone actually wore stuff like that apart from on photo shoots!

She glanced down at her faded red hoody, a relic from her rowing days at uni. *Perhaps I should go shopping. Why didn't I put some makeup on before coming out? I'm sure I packed some lip balm.*

The newcomer scanned the group with a languid smile. 'Hello all!' she drawled. She had an upper-class accent with just a hint of

America's Deep South that made Emily think of Scarlet O'Hara and crinolines.

So this is the fabled Victoria Pheasant, thought Emily, realising that if she was Vivian she'd probably want her godson to marry this vision elegance rather than ... *I really must get to the shops!*

Tristan stood up to up to greet her and now he was enfolded in long elegant arms and held unnecessarily close.

Who does she think she is? An octopus? And I may only be a fake fiancée but I am sitting right here!

'Tristan, darling, I hear congratulations are in order.' She slowly freed him from her grasp and turned her megawatt smile on Emily.

Dazzled, Emily could only wonder, *Why are Americans' teeth so white? Perhaps I should go to the dentist as well as the shops.*

She took in Victoria's perfect eyebrows and nails and the way her glossy hair flowed around her as she moved.

And a beautician and a hairdresser ... I need to check my bank balance and my diary!

'Why you must be Emily Laddan – aren't you just the dearest little thing?' She let the question hang in the air.

Patronising cow!

'Delighted to meet you,' she continued. 'I'm Victoria Pheasant and Tristan and I go way, way back.'

She evidently felt that this piece of information warranted her entwining her body around Tristan again. He was looking torn.

What young man wouldn't like having someone who looks like a Victoria Secret's model drape themselves all over him?

Victoria continued to smile at Emily while preferring to fondle her husband-to-be rather than offer Emily her hand to shake. 'I just know that we're going to be the best of friends!'

Sincerity dripped from Victoria's every syllable. Tristan had an inane smile on his face and he seemed to have started hugging her back. Emily felt a wave of hopelessness but wasn't sure why. *It's not like he's my real fiancé. He's not even my boyfriend and we only go 'way back' not 'way, way back'.*

Emily was staring at Victoria with all the sophistication of a drowning goldfish. Fortunately, Alex dived in. 'So Victoria, how are the renovations going?'

Victoria sat down on the vacant chair next to Tristan and pulled in a couple of inches closer to him so that their knees touched. 'Simply a nightmare. I had to come down hard on the contractor. Still, I'm getting there.'

She leant across Tristan and took a sip of his cider. Her face was inches from his as she brushed his thigh with her hand and huskily murmured, 'Tristan darling, be an angel and get me a half of whatever it is you're drinking.'

Emily stared at Tristan – he'd gone glassy-eyed but still had enough wits about him to get up and go to the bar.

'Robert's been a great help – at least he's professional – but he doesn't chase the tradesmen as hard as he needs to.'

'When are your parents back?' asked Alex.

'Soon – about three weeks before the Michaelmas Ball. I've got the sweetest dress for it.'

Again she turned that dazzling smile on Emily and glanced at the baggy, faded sweatshirt. If anything her smile gained wattage. 'What will you be wearing?'

Tristan came back to the table just in time to hear Victoria's question. He patted the top of Emily's head and said, 'Emily isn't really into clothes.'

Victoria smiled serenely. 'No, I didn't think she was.'

I am so going shopping!

Marcello spoke for the first time. 'How's Monty getting on?'

Emily glanced over to the quiet young man, in his understated jeans and sweater.

With his dark hair and complexion, Marcello looks a bit like his sister but he lacks her fire. Right now I could kiss him for changing the subject.

Tristan chimed in, looking at Victoria with rather more intensity than Emily liked. 'Yes, how is Monty doing?' He gave Emily a fleeting glance and added, 'Monty is from the same litter as Bramble.'

'Famously. You know Bramble would be a good gundog if you and Christopher didn't mollycoddle her. For a start, she should be in a kennel, not curled up by the Aga.'

'Gundog?' queried Emily.

'Yeah, you know for shooting.' Tristan sounded dismissive.

Emily *didn't* know, she felt it was another 'jolly wellies' thing. 'What with real guns? Don't tell me Christopher has real guns in the house?' she stammered.

Everyone but David started to laugh. He simply gave her a sad, compassionate look with his blue eyes, which was somehow worse than the guffaws of laughter.

Marcello was the first to stop laughing and when he spoke, his voice was gentle. 'Shooting is a big part of the local economy. A lot of people are involved; my dad has a couple of Labradors he works.'

'But guns? This is the Cotswolds, not New York.'

For some reason this was even funnier; even David smiled.

Tristan actually had to wipe away a tear as he said, 'It's all highly licensed, with police checks and guns in special locked safes. You don't need to worry. Besides which, Christopher wouldn't hurt a fly.'

Emily glared at Tristan; somewhere deep in the recesses of her mind she was aware that she was angry with him not about Christopher and shooting but about Victoria, but she had no intention of being analytical about it.

'He might not hurt a fly, just a load of innocent pheasants!' she snapped.

Surprised, Tristan looked directly at her for a second, then his mood changed and he quipped, 'Only in season. Anyway, you can't talk – I've seen what you do to a steak! You're not exactly a vegan!'

Only Victoria laughed at his joke.

Gina called to Marcello to carry the risotto to the table.

Smells heavenly, thought Emily as she inhaled its rich aroma but she didn't comment. *I'm not exactly sulking it's just ...*

There was a welcome silence as everyone enjoyed their food.

Alex tackled the eating experience as a true connoisseur. Emily observed her examine the visual presentation with approval: soft risotto rice with dark truffle shavings set off with a vibrant green herb garnish. When she took her first creamy mouthful she closed her eyes to fully savour the myriad of tastes and textures.

When she opened her eyes she was smiling. 'Don't tell Dad, but this is sensational.'

This time everyone laughed except Victoria who didn't get the joke.

Alex went on, 'Changing the subject – Tristan, do you fancy making a donation to the tennis club?'

Tristan put down his knife and fork. 'Wow! Alex, aren't you meant to be more subtle about getting the begging bowl out?'

'As the club's accountant, it's my duty to keep the money rolling in. We need to raise funds for the roof.'

David ran his hand through his blond hair and quietly said, 'Mum and I are donating a cheese hamper for a raffle.'

Victoria sighed. 'I wouldn't bother, David. I'll just have a word with Daddy and he'll cover the lot.' There was a silence which didn't seem to have any impact on her. 'Do you play tennis?' she asked with a suspiciously friendly smile at Emily.

'No,' replied Emily.

'I didn't think you would,' drawled Victoria still smiling at her.

Emily was about to chip in with a defensive explanation of that she rowed, but she checked herself. *I may only be Tristan's fake fiancée but I do think he could say something. Can he really be so dim that he doesn't realise Victoria is being a right bitch?*

She regarded the vacant way he was staring at Victoria's full pink lips and long fluttering eyelashes and concluded that he could.

This assessment was confirmed when they were leaving the pub. Tristan hugged Victoria and brightly asked, 'We're walking over to The Swan at Swinbrook tomorrow for lunch – can you join us?'

'Sweet of you, Tristan, but no can do. Tomorrow I'm meeting the architect, the decorator and the plumber.'

'On a Sunday?'

She glanced coquettishly at Tristan, head tilted, blue eyes flashing beneath long lashes and lips provocatively pursed. 'I had to use all my southern charm.'

I just bet you did! thought Emily sourly.

That night she put an extra layer of pillows down the middle of the bed and put on her biggest sweatshirt. Without looking at Tristan she climbed into bed and lay on the very edge of her side of it, turning her back on him.

'You'll bake,' he commented.

That's better than risking ...

After a bit of lying stiffly in the dark with sleep eluding her, she said, 'Victoria is …'

'Yeah, she's great – so efficient. She certainly gets things done.' He paused and Emily could hear the rhythmic sound of his breathing. She was just drifting off when he added, 'She's looking rather well at the moment.'

Emily stiffened.

'You know she makes a packet – I mean an absolute bomb – she works in hedge funds with her dad.'

Emily didn't know what a hedge fund was.

That same evening Zara FitzMorris had been having her own doubts.

So has Jim Stuart invited me over for supper at his place for romantic reasons or are his intentions purely commercial? she wondered as she drove along the winding country paths to his new home.

She didn't know him well enough to guess. She had met him both socially and professionally but only on a handful of occasions. He had made his fortune in property, but it was commercial properties – warehouses, a racecourse, a shopping centre – whereas Zara dealt with residential properties. Admittedly she tended to be involved with exceptionally large homes but still, there wasn't much of an overlap with Jim's line of business.

There was a rumour that he had recently purchased an option of a swathe of land designated for housing, so it could be that he wanted to discuss, but then again there had been a glint in his eyes when they'd chatted at the charity champagne gala last week, hosted by Oliver and Justine.

Thinking of Oliver and Justine naturally led her mind in another direction.

With Oliver stepping down as Lord-Lieutenant I wonder who'll get the post? I rather like the odd quirk of history that the new Lord-Lieutenant is announced by the outgoing post-holder at the Michaelmas Ball. It may be a very odd custom but it does give the evening a delightful 'game show' element.

She paused to let a car pull in front of her. Vaughan Williams' *Lark Ascending* was playing and she relaxed as she enjoyed a soaring bar or two before allowing her thoughts to reengage with the upcoming ball.

I must get a new dress – I'll check my diary and see when I can next get into London. Rather fun that Nicholas Corman has asked me to go with him.

She brushed over how she had cornered him after mushroom soup at her mother's and more or less forced him to ask her.

He's such a good dancer – it will be a fun evening.

Her thoughts strayed to a sultry salsa in the Cuban club and a more recent electric tango in the Isle of Blom and she started humming happily along to Vaughan Williams.

She took the turning for Jim's place. You could hardly miss it as two imposing gate pillars flanked an impressive iron gate. Zara leant out of her car window and pressed the electric intercom.

Magically the gates swung open.

The drive was long and winding so she had time to muse on her host. Newly-planted beech samplings had been planted at regular intervals along the pristine drive.

This must have been what Pemberley was like when Darcy had done a few improvements – somehow I can't see myself as an Elizabeth Bennet – still, you never know!

I wonder what Jim's chances are of him being the next Lord-

Lieutenant? His business record is impeccable and his charitable work is impressive. With a wry smile, she mentally added, *And so well-documented – you can hardly open the local paper without seeing him plant a tree or opening a hospital wing.*

Which reminds me, Dee wants me to put in a plug for the library at the local school – I'll have to play that one by ear; after all, he has only just been appointed as a governor. I'm not sure how good he would be either as a school governor or as a Lord-Lieutenant.

She ran through a checklist of necessary qualities:

Charming – yes,

Efficient – yes,

But warmth ...?

The tarmac gave way to thick gravel and the newly-built mini Pemberley was in sight.

She sighed. *It will all look wonderful in two hundred years when the stone has weathered down and the trees have grown up.*

Jim was on the doorstep smiling.

So what's it to be? An evening of romance or negotiations?

She had played it safe, wearing one of her many wrap dresses and long high boots with a bit of a heel, so she looked professional but feminine and then as she was driving there could be no question of drinking.

Jim Stuart was dressed in his version of smart-casual: blue suede loafers and no socks, *more à la South of France than Gloucestershire in the autumn,* with jeans – *they look expensive,* a shirt – *has he forgotten to button it or is it his idea of seduction? And naturally, he has a cashmere sweater draped over his shoulders!*

Jim welcomed her in with a neutral peck on the cheek – *no hint of his intentions there!*

'Thank you for coming.' His voice was deep with a hint of an East End London accent.

She knew he was a wine connoisseur and had chosen the bottle with care. He received it with grace, smiling as he carefully examined the label. When he next looked at Zara his eyes were alight and it occurred to her that he really was quite attractive.

She was whisked through a spacious hall with its ubiquitous grand staircase and into a vast kitchen which boasted a lot of white marble lit by subtle lighting – *that will have cost him a fortune but it's so worth it* – and a great many cathedral candles – *so flattering for one's looks.*

He led her over to a round table in an alcove. The table was set attractively and had a fine view of the garden.

She gazed out of the window. Inwardly she sighed.

Why has he got the garden lit up? Doesn't he like the stars? There's a full moon tonight! It would be so romantic to gaze out of the window at the moon and stars.

'Looks good, doesn't it?' He was confident and Zara murmured something non-committal.

Moving to the colossal work island in the centre of the kitchen he put on an apron and said, 'I hope you like steak.'

'Love it!' lied Zara.

Steak? The universal choice of chaps in a hurry. Why do middle-aged bachelors never think to serve soup? So much more seductive than steak. After all who can feel sexy with half a pound of cow in their stomach? It must be something to do with their inner caveman.

'What can I do to help?' she asked, taking in his array of chefs' knives and the heavy steak pan.

'It's all done,' he said happily as the steak hit the hot oil with a satisfying sizzle.

Over supper, the conversation ranged over many topics while Zara tried and failed to gauge his intentions:

Theatre, musical and latest releases – *romantic?*

His company – *professional?*

A passion for opera – *I hope he doesn't think I'd find that romantic.*

The bit of land he was hoping to develop – *professional?*

By ten o'clock she decided to give up trying to read him and simply enjoy his company.

Nicholas Corman was finding his evening equally confusing.

His home was like him – immaculate – and no room represented this impeccable order more than his model train room. Here he had taken systematisation and cleanliness to a whole new level.

He selected a small watercolour brush from a set which was lined up in his tool cupboard. It was a matter of great pleasure to him that he had an allotted place for every tool in his custom-made cupboard. It hadn't just happened by chance, it had taken him hours of puzzling over precise dimensions and plans. He had painstakingly measured every tool, from his wire cutters to his many spanners, but the results were well worth it.

With his brush, he set about methodically dusting the tracks, the minute trees, the built-to-scale station and finally his two new steam trains. With a pang, he realised he wouldn't be able to part with either train as he was exceptionally fond of both his mother, Myrtle, and Dee. He sighed as he knew that having duplicate trains would jar his sense of order.

Normally time in his train room was a period of total peace and serenity but now as he dusted Dee's gift he couldn't help thinking of Zara FitzMorris. She had looked so relaxed but also so alive when he had bumped into her fresh from her ride on one of the famous Manx steam trains, her saffron hair tied back, her eyes hidden by chic sunglasses and her trim figure showcased by her belted chinos and fitted top.

How come I didn't know she had a passion for steam trains? But it's probably better not to dwell on it. After all, I do like my life being ordered. Zara is vibrant, passionate and vivacious – she always complicates things. When I'm with her my life is anything but ordered, I am bewildered but then again ...

His mind wandered to feeling her body against his as they tangoed – he swallowed and fiddled with his collar.

Of course, that tango we had together was all in the line of finding out who the criminal was. It wasn't an emotional tango; it was purely professional.

Gosh, this room is hot – I think I'll just open the window.

Yes, our relationship is purely professional — brought about by Dee's habit of finding dead bodies.

That dress Zara wore for the tango was ...

He coughed and tried to think about something other than the way the dress had caressed her curves.

That sensational gown had been procured for Zara by his mother, Myrtle, who was an avid ballroom dance competitor and even owned her own dance academy.

That's one good thing – Myrtle adores Zara; they really get on very well. Unlike ...

He thought of the frosty, uncomfortable times he'd had when his ex-wife and Myrtle had been compelled to be in the same room.

He resumed his dusting, rather vigorously as thinking of his ex-wife always made him angry.

Ridiculous the way she was always accusing me of being OCD! Me? Obsessed with organisation and cleaning? Absurd!

Zara is very different from her.

He paled.

Zara could possibly be messier.

He took the engine to the window and examined it in the sunlight. *Not even a speck of dust on it.* Satisfied he replaced it on the track.

His mind strayed back to a picnic he'd had with Zara on a sunny beach in the Isle of Blom.

It was the first time she'd mentioned what it had been like losing her husband, Freddie, in that car crash when Amelia was still at primary school. No wonder Dee, Zara and Amelia are so close. They obviously all adored him. If I ... if we ... do I really want to compete with a ghost?

His mind switched to a steamy salsa in a Cuban club. *Of course, that salsa was solely professional too – we were gathering clues around those clown murders but still ...* Vivid shockwaves of electricity shot through his body as he recalled them moving rhythmically together in a darkened room while the saxophone throbbed. He swallowed again and checked the window was still open. *Yes, it was purely professional but it does indicate that we are* – he swallowed once more – *compatible.*

And now the Michaelmas Ball. I would like to waltz with Zara, an elegant dance with an elegant lady. But how did I end up asking her to go with me to the ball? I remember the mushroom soup and Dee being evasive, then Zara's eyes – mesmerising – and her lips very close to mine and her voice was suddenly husky and the next thing I knew she was delighted to accept my proposal that she went to the Michaelmas Ball as my partner.

He firmly put the brush back in its proper place and closed the cupboard door.

It's like that when I'm with Zara, there is a disturbing fervent confusion. No, much better to avoid complications. Peaceful order suits me much better!

He left the train room, thinking, *I'll just check that my black tie is in order for the ball.*

'Jake Rivers, will you please concentrate! This is turning into a total waste of an evening! I could have spent it at the Flying Pheasant with my mates instead of here!'

Amelia waved a slim white hand with deep purple nails around the airy room that the River family referred to as the library, due to the centuries-old leather books that lined the walls. The sofas sagged as if they were as old as the books. Various fat black Labradors slumped and snored on the sofas. The beautiful antique tables were obscured by discarded copies of The Times and various sporting magazines. The worn rugs and the thick elderly carpets would have made the room feel bleak if it hadn't been for the tremendous fire that crackled in the vast fireplace, giving the place both warmth and a delicious cedarwood scent.

Jake, who looked like a beanpole with sandy hair and the distinguished nose of the Duke of Wellington – reported to be the result of an extramarital liaison by his great, great, great grandmother – sat up and smiled.

'Okay, so back to, '*The effect of childhood trauma to the development of narcissistic personality*'!' said Amelia.

He leant his iPad on his knee. 'I'll copy and paste that long list of research papers.'

Horrified Amelia exclaimed, 'You can't do that!'

'Why not?'

'It's sloppy, besides which Dr Ibin will fail us both. I don't know how you always manage to get top marks.'

He laughed. 'Natural genius, I guess.'

There was a pause. Amelia fiddled with her stylus and iPad and Jake scanned the required reading. She glanced at him and it occurred to her that both his jeans and baggy sweater were as old and tatty as his home.

As he read, his forehead crinkled. 'The trouble is, who hasn't?'

Amelia, having sorted out her stylus, shifted her tutu into a more comfortable position and looked at him. 'What?'

'Who hasn't had childhood trauma? We don't all go on to become narcissistic, though.'

'Uh?'

'Your dad died in a car crash and my mum experienced one English winter in this draughty pile with a screaming baby before flitting back to Brazil, never to be seen again. So both of us have experienced childhood trauma but we are still well-balanced psychology students.' He tilted his head to one side and scrutinised Amelia. 'Well at least I am; the jury is still out on you. Did I mention that I'm thinking about doing a paper on, '*Is Goth culture a way to escape from adult reality?*'

Amelia threw a cushion at him; it hit him in the face.

Laughing he exclaimed, 'Hey, mind the iPad! You've no idea how difficult it was for the old man to scrape together the readies to buy this.'

'Perhaps it works for them.' Amelia was staring thoughtfully at the fire.

'Uh?' queried Jake.

'Narcissists. It's a pretty effective way of getting what you want.'

Jake nodded slowly. 'I read somewhere that they experience low levels of stress.'

Amelia grinned. 'If you were more diligent about citing your references, you would know exactly where you read it.'

He smiled back. 'Although I believe they experience extreme stress when thwarted.' He laughed and added, 'So if you are going to be a narcissist you need to be thorough – totally ruthless.'

'But what about the greater good?' enquired Amelia getting earnest.

The greater good was left unattended as Jake's father, Sebastian, walked in. He was wearing an old pair of slippers with his family crest embroidered on the top. He had his glasses perched halfway down his Wellington nose. His sandy hair had silvered with age and his beanpole figure had filled out. He looked surprised to see Jake and Amelia.

The dogs all started to wag their tails at his arrival. He patted the nearest one affectionately on the head while saying, 'Amelia, my dear child – no, no, don't get up. I was just looking for my reading glasses. I can't get the hang of varifocals but perhaps I should persevere as I spend half my life either looking for my distance glasses or my reading ones.'

'Here they are, Pops,' said Jake handing them to him.

'Thank you, my boy,' he said, giving Jake the same affectionate pat on the head he'd given the Labradors.

He smiled at Amelia but she thought there was a certain heaviness about his eyes. 'Send your granny my love and tell her I'm looking forward to her blackberry jam.'

Amelia watched him shuffling towards the door; she had not mentioned the whole failed blackberry jam delivery and the damaged brake line episode. She saw no reason to worry him, besides which Little Warthing was a hotbed for gossip and where Dee was concerned, Amelia had learned a long time ago it was better not to say anything about her activities.

As Sebastian reached the door he called over his shoulder, 'And I can't wait to have a large slice of her pie at the Harvest Lunch tomorrow.'

When he left Amelia asked, 'Is your dad okay?'

Without looking up from his iPad Jake muttered, 'Yeah.'

'It's just that he seems a bit … well a bit off, not his usual jolly self. Is he worried about anything?'

Jake thought for a moment. 'Could be this whole Lord-Lieutenant business. He wants it – well, I don't think he really wants it but he feels he has to have it to uphold the family name. His father and grandfather were both the local Lord-Lieutenant.'

'Oh dear – and he doesn't realise that times have changed? The role no longer goes with just having a big house and having been to the right school?'

'Exactly, his profile is all wrong; nowadays it's much more likely to go to someone dynamic and successful like Jim Stuart or Jo Roper.'

'I think Vivian Plover has the same impression.'

Jake nodded. 'And poor old Christopher would hate it. He really just likes pottering around his veg patch.' He glanced back at his iPad for a few moments before adding, 'Of course, it could be all the bills – we never have any money and keeping this pile going costs a fortune.' He glanced at his watch, a beautiful old Patel Philippe, a gift from a long-deceased godparent. 'Let's settle down to work, I'd like to get this done tonight.'

'Suits me, so back to, '*The effect of childhood trauma on the development of narcissistic personality disorder'*.'

Sebastian would have been delighted to know that at that moment Dee was putting the finishing touches on her apple pies for tomorrow's Harvest Lunch. The whole house was wreathed in the delicious scent of apple and cinnamon, combined with crisply baked shortcrust pastry.

Dee regarded them, all neatly lined up on her table and she smiled with satisfaction. *Yes, they've turned out very well.*

She put the kettle on for a final cup of camomile tea before bedtime. Cat wound around her legs and purred but headed straight out of the door the moment Dee bent down to stroke her. Accustomed to her rejection, Dee straightened and focused on tea-making. She was a little tired after all the events of the day so she decided to use a teabag rather than bother with a teapot. As the tea brewed she made a determined effort not to replay in her head her terror as she'd put her foot on the brake and nothing had happened.

Pushing away the memory of her racing pulse and the sound of her heartbeat thrashing in her ears, as in slow motion she careered out of control, instead, she focused on tomorrow's Harvest Lunch.

I'm looking forward to seeing everyone. I haven't seen Jo for an age and always enjoy her company. Of course, she's one of the busiest people I know, so getting dates in the diary for a meet-up is always difficult. Speaking of which, I must check which day we're going to Warthing Woods to do the bird recording. It's always interesting going to the hide with her and bird-spotting – she's a positive ornithological encyclopaedia.

Dee had schooled herself not to think about that unpleasant visit to the hide at Warthing Woods when she had spotted a clown corpse rather than a nightingale.

I do hope Jo is the next Lord-Lieutenant, she would be excellent at it, although of course, I don't really know Jim Stuart. Tomorrow will be a good opportunity for me to get to know him and congratulate him on his appointment as school governor and maybe just give the tiniest hint about the library.

Judging the tea to be the perfect colour, she added a drop of cool water from the filter jug and took her mug of camomile to enjoy at the kitchen table.

Sitting she savoured a sip; it was both warming and calming. She smiled.

Yes, Jo would be an excellent Lord-Lieutenant. I adore dear old Sebastian but I'm afraid he's a bit too much of an old buffer to suit the role. While I think of it, I need to drop off that blackberry jam.

Unbidden she had a flashback of her panic, the fast-approaching hedge and ditch, the terror and then the jarring halt. She took a large gulp of tea and three deep breaths.

Yes, Jo would be better suited to the role than dear old Sebastian or Christopher for that matter. I do hope Vivian won't make things awkward at the Michaelmas Ball if Christopher doesn't get it.

She took another sip. The camomile was doing its job and she yawned.

I need to get a new dress for the ball – what fun! And speaking of fun, Emily and Tristan make a delightful couple. I'm so glad Sophie suggested the Stilton for Tristan — he did appreciate it. Emily is just right for him but I'm afraid she won't be to Vivian's taste.

Finishing her tea she washed up her mug and with another yawn headed up to bed for a good night's sleep.

Dee's new neighbour, Winston Charter-Fox, was also thinking about the Michaelmas Ball and the upcoming change in Lord-Lieutenant. He took out his beloved copy of *The Life of Lenin* from the packing case and, having checked it for damage, put it on the bookshelf.

Comrade Smith will be outraged when I tell her.

He had a fleeting recollection of a recent coupling with Comrade Smith in her bedsit in Putney but, as ever, revolution took precedence over romance.

I will give Comrade Hugh in Leytonstone a full account – Michaelmas balls! Lord-Lieutenants! Something must be done!

His mental planning for mounting an insurgence in Little Warthing was interrupted by an insistent meowing at the window.

That wretched cat again! It must belong to one of the neighbours.

Of course, he was right, the feline was none other than Dee's large white Cat. The very luxuriance of Cat's fur coat offended Winston's sense of restraint. He swore and made violent gestures to shoo the animal away.

Cat, for her part, decided that she liked this new neighbour.

Not far away, sleep was totally eluding Vivian Plover.

She had gone back to bed immediately after the shock of seeing Dee FitzMorris alive. The sight of her had flooded Vivian with a myriad of overwhelming emotions that she could not identify. Many years ago she had blocked the word 'failure' from her vocabulary and conscious mind. It had been a label that had haunted her childhood, first used by her mother when she had failed to secure a rosette at the Pony Club Gymkhana.

'What defeats me,' her mother had declared at the next Sunday lunch with family and friends, 'is how the child could have failed to get a clear round in the show jumping. Why that pony practically jumps itself – when Venetia rode it they won everything and she was two years younger than Vivian. I'm afraid we just have to accept that Vivian is, always has been and always will be a total failure.'

Everyone, family and guests alike, had laughed. Vivian thought that the loudest laughs had come from her father and sister.

I can't let it happen! I can't live out a life of mediocrity! Christopher will be the next Lord-Lieutenant and I will do whatever I need to, to make it happen!

When Christopher brought up some soup for her on a tray and clumsily spilled it on the duvet cover, Vivian whispered, 'Just go away.'

Defeated, he withdrew. His feet, clad only in his thick socks, were silent as they stepped on the stairs and Vivian had shut her eyes and thought of how smart he would look in his Lord-Lieutenant uniform, and thought too of herself meeting the monarch.

Josh Parks pulled into McDonald's and ordered fries. It was a ritual he always performed after spending an evening with his parents and Granny and Grandpa Parks. After a feast of red rice cakes, bulgogi beef, and a million different side dishes, not to mention the fermented cabbage, and kimchi, Josh was always ready for some fries.

It didn't help that he was without fail the designated driver so he always had to watch, stone-cold sober as his parents and grandparents got steadily merrier on soju.

The girl in front of him was a grubby Goth. Josh looked at her and thought, *She's not nearly as stylish as Amelia. Much as I like the whole black lace-corset thing, I thought she looked cute when we went on that bike ride in the Isle of Blom, without all her gear on, just dressed normally and without all that makeup. Just natural, like.*

Chapter 5

She'd look good as a Goth but vicars don't tend to be Goths. Shame as they are already halfway there with their flowing black robes and the dog collar, thought Dee absently as she helped the team put the finishing touches on the tables for the Harvest Lunch.

The Vicar Virginia Howard came up to her; she was young, perhaps twenty-eight or nine and her mouse-coloured hair had a strong natural curl that refused to be tamed, no matter what she did to it. She thought of herself as lanky but Dee would have described her as willowy. Dee was right, she would look good as a Goth; the makeup would bring out her rather washed-out eyes and pale complexion, and a laced-up corset would do more for her figure than the shapeless black sweaters she tended to wear.

'Do you think everything looks alright?' she asked nervously, scanning the room. There were mini-pumpkins and sheaves of wheat decorating every table, along with orange and yellow paper napkins. Her voice was rather pronounced with shades of the old-fashioned. Dee always thought of it as being very '1930s Mitford sisters' and therefore good for delivering sermons from the pulpit.

'It all looks lovely,' reassured Dee.

'You don't think people will think the pumpkins are too … well, too American?'

Dee patted her arm. 'Really, you don't need to worry. Now, do you have your opening speech ready?'

Virginia nodded. 'And you'll introduce me to the Lord-Lieutenant and his wife when they arrive?'

'Of course. Don't worry, Oliver and Justine Robertson are sweethearts; you'll like them.'

Virginia gave an apprehensive glance around the hall and nodded. The hall itself was a recent addition to the village and the result of a lot of arguments and fundraising. It was spacious and fit for purpose with its modern facilities.

'I just so want it to go well; it's my first big do as a proper vicar.'

There was a crash and the sound of breaking crockery from the kitchen. Virginia muttered something she would never have said from the pulpit and hurried off.

Sebastian Rivers strolled up to Dee. He looked very distinguished with his aristocratic nose and height but she couldn't help noticing that his old tweed suit smelt of mothballs and that there was a darn on the left elbow. She wondered if he was going to ask about the blackberry jam she'd promised him but he had other concerns.

'Dee, would you mind coming and having a look? The vicar asked me to shove some sheaves of wheat in the milk churns and to put some pumpkins around the base. What's with the pumpkins? Does she think we're Americans? Even the wheat sheaves are a bit of a stretch – harvest was a couple of months ago and wherever they've been stored has a mouse problem; they've definitely been nibbled.'

He looked so downcast that Dee gave him an extra-generous smile before going to take a look. At the entrance, she was pleased to find that the sun was shining which was a good start. Anyone coming to the Harvest Lunch would be welcomed by three glorious beech trees in all their autumn splendour. The trees were situated just to the front of the hall and their maintenance had been part of the conditions for the hall's planning permission being granted. She regarded the sad wheat that was thrust haphazardly into the churns, and the pumpkins Sebastian had dumped on the steps.

'I'll just tweak this,' she said cheerfully as she knelt down on the step. Somehow she managed to transform the chaos into passable arrangements.

'They look nice – very autumnal and inviting,' commented Sophie as she walked up to them carrying a large cardboard box. She had her blonde hair tied back in a ponytail and was in her jeans, but without her apron on. 'I'm not stopping; Sundays are one of our busiest days and I left David with a shop full of customers.'

'Here, let me take that,' said Sebastian gallantly taking the cardboard box from her. Inside were neatly packaged small oblongs of cheese for the Harvest Lunch.

'You're so wonderfully generous,' beamed Dee.

'Well, we like to do our bit and it's for a good cause.'

Dee nodded. 'Yes the local food bank is always in need of funds but I can't remember what the international charity is this year. Do you know?'

Sophie shook her head. 'No, but it's bound to be something worthy. You'll have to listen to the vicar's opening speech; she'll mention it there. Anyway, must dash. Sebastian, you see that little package in the brown paper bag?'

Sebastian, with his arms full of the cardboard box, looked down and nodded.

'That's a little bit of some new Stilton we've got in, I think you'll like it.'

Sebastian coloured; his discomfort was painful to watch. Both Sophie and Dee guessed he was thinking about the expense.

Lightly Sophie added, 'It was an offcut – too small to sell and it's far too excellent to waste. I know you'll appreciate it.'

In order to further cover up the awkward moment, Dee commented, 'I gave Tristan some when he came to lunch and he went into raptures about it. Did you know that blue cheese is simply wonderful for your gut bacteria?'

She added the last note conversationally but instantly wished she hadn't as Sebastian looked horrified. *Oh dear, I hope I haven't put Sebastian off Stilton for life! I must try and remember that not everyone finds gut bacteria as fascinating as I do.*

Sophia laughed and turned to go, saying, 'Don't forget to listen out for what the international charity is this year and be sure to tell me when you are next in the shop.'

As it happened, Dee was far too busy helping in the kitchen during the opening speeches, so she never did find out where the money was going apart from the local food bank. In fact, she was kept so busy that she only had a chance to catch up with her friends at the very end when everyone was milling around with coffee cups in hand.

The first people she came across were Justine and Oliver Robertson.

Oliver hailed her, 'Dee, perhaps we can catch up properly now? You just had time earlier to introduce us to your delightful vicar then you were called away to your duties.'

Oliver always reminded Dee of a jovial Friar Tuck as he was round, good-natured and his hair had balled to a perfect tonsure, though he had a diagonal scar through his right eyebrow and cheek. He liked to joke that it was a duelling wound from a sabre fight defending his good lady wife's honour. It did look like the sort of scar a sword would leave, but in fact, it was from a car crash.

Dee wondered how he could have managed to have such a distinguished army career. *After all his looks are so far removed from what one imagines a soldier to be.*

Justine was speaking; she was equally round and invariably laughing. 'I was just telling Vivian that I can't wait for Oliver to step down from being Lord-Lieutenant.'

'No more hats!' laughed Dee.

'Absolutely! I plan on spending all day every day in my oldest gardening trousers and sweater and what's more, I will never wear a pair of smart shoes again. For me, it will be Wellington boots all the way.'

Oliver's roar of laughter echoed around the hall.

Vivian, standing stiffly beside them gave a tight smile. *Stupid woman! Ridiculous! I've been collecting hats for years in preparation for this.*

'We will miss you; you've been an excellent Lord-Lieutenant – you have done such a lot to make people feel valued,' said Dee.

'*Noblesse oblige,*' announced Vivian piously. 'It is so important to give back to those less fortunate than oneself.'

Dee caught an amused look exchanged between Oliver and

Justine and she knew that it was taking all their self-control not to erupt into gales at laughter at Vivian's sanctimonious air.

Jo Roper saved the situation by coming in at that moment. She was brisk, neat and efficient, from her short bob to her crease-free trouser suit.

Even her greeting was short and to the point. 'Hi, all!'

Vivian winced. *How can such a vulgar woman even be considered for the honourable role of Lord-Lieutenant?*

Dee and the Robertsons were evidently delighted to see her and warm greetings were exchanged.

When the general chat had been exhausted Dee enquired, 'Jo, I wanted to catch you. Are you still alright for our bird count at Warthing Woods next week?'

'Wouldn't miss it! Bird watching is about the only thing I get to do to relax.'

Justine smiled. 'I can imagine, what with running your family hotel chain, all your charity work and not to mention having three teenage sons at home, I shouldn't think you get a minute to yourself.'

Jo beamed. 'Don't get me wrong, I love each and every minute of my life, it's just somehow I seem to struggle to find balance.'

Oliver smiled and ruefully said, 'Don't we all?'

Jo seemed to lose focus for a moment and went a little pink.

Concerned, Dee asked, 'Are you alright, dear?'

Jo regained her normal self and explained, 'Oh I'm fine, it's just the bloody menopause.'

Vivian went rigid. *No! Surely not! That settles it! It is my patriotic duty – my noblesse oblige – to see to it that that woman* never *becomes Lord-Lieutenant!*

'Poor you!' sympathised Justine. 'It's hell when you are going through it, but heaven on the other side. Isn't that right, Dee?'

I couldn't agree more. I'll make you some soya cake that can help with the symptoms and is quite tasty.'

Oliver, feeling he couldn't contribute much to this conversation, drifted away.

'What worries me,' Jo said, 'is that my mother went

through early menopause too and now she suffers terribly from osteoporosis.'

'I have some wonderful calcium tablets for that – excellent stuff from America. I'll give you a spare bottle to try. You can't start taking them too early,' stated Vivian.

Dee, Jo and Justine stared at her in surprise.

Eventually, Jo stammered out a hesitant, 'Vivian, that's very kind of you.'

'Not at all,' said Vivian truthfully.

I knew that potassium cyanide I picked up the last time we were in the States would come in handy. America is so refreshingly lax about what you can buy and it will only take me a moment or two to decant some crystals into one of those little calcium capsules.

Vivian smiled a warm, happy smile and Jo smiled back.

'Dee!' called Robert from nearby.

'Do excuse me, I think Robert wants me for something,' said Dee as she headed over to where he was looking fresh and fragrant.

He was standing next to an equally well-groomed Jim Stuart.

What a joy to see two chaps who take pride in their appearance. I get so tired of those jeans that show more of a man's behind than I wish to see. As she got closer to the pair she was struck by a new notion. *They both take a different approach to tailoring; Robert is all Saville Row and Lobbs' shoes whereas Jim is more European – his clothes have a softer, edgier cut and floatier fabric. My guess would be that his suit is from Florence – those shoes are unmistakably Italian.*

'Dee FitzMorris, allow me to introduce Jim Stuart.'

Dee shook him by the hand. 'I've been wanting to meet you.'

'So I gathered – I had the pleasure of having supper with your daughter Zara last night and I gather that the school library needs a little update.'

All in all, Dee found the Harvest Lunch very satisfactory. Her only regret was that she hadn't managed to have a word with Paul over his and Robert's upcoming anniversary. Paul, with his upright military stance and shiny shoes, had joined her, Robert and Jim just as Jim had been talking about a wonderful walking and wine-tasting holiday he had had in the Piedmont region of Italy. He enthused about the beautiful hills and the multifaceted wines, especially Barolo. Dee had hoped to move the conversation on to anniversary trips, but somehow the moment had passed and the next time she saw Paul he was earnestly talking about military matters with Oliver.

Still, he must be very dense, she mused. *Robert is throwing him filthy looks and he must have mentioned how thoughtful some partners are ten times in Paul's hearing. No wonder Jim seemed confused as he was talking about the lighting system he had put in the garden.*

Sebastian, Christopher and Vivian were among the last to leave. Christopher and Sebastian were well matched, both tall and slightly dated; but whereas Sebastian was dilapidated and somehow dusty, Christopher had Vivian to keep him on tip-top, shining form. She saw to it that every item of clothing was new, pressed and in mint condition. Christopher regularly visited the barbershop – his wife made the appointments – and she personally checked that he was properly shaven and his nails trim.

Vivian was looking tired but held herself in an upright pose.

Dee joined them just as Christopher was saying, 'Yes, terrible shame about old Jackson.'

'I don't think you need to sympathise with him; the man stole from his clients' pension funds,' said Vivian tartly.

Tentatively Sebastian suggested, 'Perhaps he intended to pay it back.'

There was a gleam in Vivian's eye and all hint of tiredness vanished as she pinned Sebastian with a laser eye and quietly said, 'Oh but he did pay it back, every last penny, but embezzlement is still embezzlement. You of all people should know that, being in the same line of business.'

Sebastian paled.

'Are you feeling alright?' asked Dee.

'Yes, yes but got to go – can't leave the dogs too long.'

'But Sebastian, what about your blackberry jam?' called Dee

but Sebastian had already stumbled out of the door.

Jim Stuart had enjoyed the Harvest Lunch.

What would Mum have thought about me hobnobbing with all the toffs and talking about fine wines?

As he drove down his magnificent drive to his even more impressive house he said out loud, 'No doubt about it, Mum! Your Little Jimmy has done alright by himself. I'd have made you proud!'

Unbidden, a tear trickled down his cheek and he batted it away. Ridiculous, he was a grown man and he'd been fourteen when she'd died and here he was still sobbing for his loss.

'You'd have a laugh though, Mum! I can hear you now! "*What you want with that swanky swimming pool, Jimmy Boy, when you won't go near water – not since you fell in the canal?*" Well, Mum, I'm going to learn to swim like a fish and what's more, I'm going to be the next Lord-Lieutenant! Just you wait and see!'

Chapter 6

Dee woke up the next morning with Sebastian Rivers on her mind.

He's not quite been himself for months now and then for him to leave abruptly like that after the Harvest Lunch ... Something is definitely off.

She tried to ring him the previous evening but couldn't get through.

As soon as I've done my Taekwondo and had my breakfast I'll cycle over to Sebastian's with a pot of blackberry jam.

A couple of hours later she was zipping down the familiar lanes en route to her old friend's home. *This must be a little foretaste of heaven,* she thought as the breeze caressed her face and her body relished the exercise.

It was a glorious autumn morning, the sun was shining in a blue sky, birds were singing and the hedgerows were burnished and spotted red with bright berries. Golden leaves drifted down like gentle confetti and with every breath Dee took she inhaled the rich heady scent of autumn.

A jar of rich purple jam nestled in her bicycle's wicker basket, cushioned from the bumps and jolts by a tawny cashmere scarf. She had started her journey wearing the scarf along with her jeans and a soft, camel-coloured V-neck but the morning was warm and that, combined with her physical exertions, soon led to her shedding it.

She turned in at a half-hidden and very overgrown gateway and bumped down Sebastian's much-pitted driveway.

All these potholes must play havoc with his car's suspension but it would cost a fortune to resurface it.

In front of the house, there were more weeds than gravel and the lawns were in desperate need of a cut. The majestic Georgian house was perfectly proportioned, a small architectural gem in sandstone, but the window frames were peeling and the front door was faded.

Dee got off her bicycle and started wheeling it around the back to the kitchen door; in all her many visits to Sebastian's she couldn't ever recall using any other door but the back one.

As she approached the rear entrance she knew something was wrong. For a start, the door itself was shut – normally Sebastian left it open, as he said he liked to let the outside in. Then Dee could hear the Labradors scratching on the door wanting to be let out. Ordinarily, they were either comatose in some comfy spot or firmly at Sebastian's side. Habitually mute, they were even whining.

She called, 'Cooee!' as she pushed her way in through the door careful not to let any of the dogs out. There was no response except the exuberant and cumbersome wagging of the dogs' tails. Once inside, having performed the necessary patting of doggy flanks, she called again. Still no reply.

The kitchen was empty of Sebastian but full of mess. There was the normal debris of an untidy person's daily living; a number of chipped and stained mugs were on the side, a congealed plate of scrambled eggs and ketchup and a pan sat in the sink. Their solidity suggested they were from the night before rather than breakfast. Seemingly unused but grubby tea towels littered chairs, the dresser and even the filthy floor, and a warm teapot was on the kitchen table along with some papers, a pen and two envelopes.

Oh, dear! I do wish poor old Sebastian could afford to get some help. I'd happily put on some rubber gloves and give everything a scrub but I would hate to offend him.

'Sebastian, are you there? I've bought some blackberry jam.'

Jake must be out too; he's probably at some tutorial or lecture with Amelia, learning all about narcissism. But Sebastian can't really be out as in away, he might have forgotten to lock the door but these old dears are definitely agitated. She patted the dog nearest to her as it clumsily bumped against her leg. *Usually, they settle down and have a kip if their master has jobs to do. Besides* which his ancient car is in the drive, though of course, it could have broken down again.

It was then that one of the black dogs scooped up a crumpled piece of paper that had been lying on the floor by the chair leg and obligingly offered it to Dee in its slobber-covered mouth.

'Thank you,' said Dee.

Her first thought was, *I wonder if I can bin this or should I put it on the side? Either way, I need to wash my hands.*

She looked at the A4 sheet; it was a mass of folds and creases. Presumably the original sender had folded it neatly into an envelope and then when Sebastian had finished with it, he had screwed it up ready for the bin. It took a few moments for Dee to register what she was looking at. On one side were neatly cut-out letters from a glossy page; they were stuck to the page to form a message, with the precision worthy of any Agatha Christie TV adaptation.

It read: REMEMBER WHAT HAPPENED TO JACKSON.

Jackson? Why is that name familiar? Oh yes, it was in the local paper and then there was some talk about it at the Harvest Lunch. He's just been done for embezzling his clients' pensions.

Dee swallowed. She felt slightly sick and her heart was beating fast.

Oh, no! Sebastian wouldn't have, would he? Surely he wouldn't have helped himself to his clients' funds however desperate for money he was? And if he had done anything so foolish, surely he would face the music rather than ...

She leant over the kitchen table and snatched up the nearest envelope. In her haste she knocked Sebastian's ancient black and gold fountain pen; it rolled to the edge of the table and clattered onto the flagstones. Dee stared at the beige envelope. Written in black ink in Sebastian's sloping hand was 'Jake'.

Dee grabbed the other envelope up and just as she feared this one said, 'For the attention of the Coroner'.

Clarity seized her mind as adrenaline flooded her body. *Hopefully, I'm not too late – the teapot is still warm. Where and how would Sebastian choose to kill himself? He wouldn't want Jake to find the body so he won't be in the house.*

She stood still, frantically trying to think. One of the Labradors put a wet nose on the back of her hand.

'Not now old boy,' she muttered and then she thought again.

Rushing to the back door she flung it open and the three Labradors burst through it and began to run as if their lives depended on it.

But it's not their lives that depend upon their speed, it's Sebastian's, thought Dee as she ran after them.

They hared down the overgrown garden path, past the neglected kitchen garden and through the side gate that led to the deserted home farm. Rushing by the old pigsty and a rusting tractor, they disappeared through the open barn door.

Panting, Dee was immeasurably relieved to hear Sebastian's surprised words, 'I say, how did you chaps get out?'

Bursting through the barn door Dee took in Sebastian. He was wearing his tweed suit with his old school tie and was standing by a step ladder under a rope formed into a noose which was suspended from a high beam.

Tears streamed down Dee's cheeks as she flung her arms around him and sobbed, 'Oh, Sebastian.'

She felt him stiffen, hesitate and then hug her back. The dogs were all milling around them, keen for reassurance.

'Steady on, old girl,' was all that Sebastian said, but Dee could hear he was crying too.

A little while later as they sat in the kitchen waiting for his solicitor to arrive, Sebastian explained. In front of him was a large mug of strong PG Tips with extra sugar while Dee had used one of her emergency camomile teabags that she always kept about her.

'You see, I thought everything was going to be alright. After all, I had managed to sell that old Landseer painting – frightful thing, so macabre – and I'd paid back all the money.'

'But why did you take it in the first place?' asked Dee gently.

'I needed cash in a hurry, emergency roof repairs and the bank won't lend me another penny. And then Jake needed an iPad for uni.' Wide-eyed he stared at Dee. 'Oh my God … Jake?'

Dee leaned over and patted his hand. Soothingly she said, 'Don't worry about Jake, we'll look after him. I managed to get hold of Amelia and she's bringing him home.'

Sebastian nodded and a tear trickled down his cheek. 'Anyway, I thought everything was okay but then these letters started coming.'

'Like that one?' asked Dee pointing to the cut-out letters on the crumpled sheets.

Sebastian nodded again. 'The first one said, 'Don't think you've got away with it.' I just assumed it was some crank – as a magistrate you sometimes get threats, it goes with the territory – but the next one was more specific and mentioned pension funds and embezzlement. Then yesterday I heard that Jackson, who had done exactly the same thing as I'd done and had also paid back the money, was still being sent to prison.' He paused, took a mouthful of tea and collected himself. 'Well, that shook me. Then, this morning I found this in the letterbox.' He gestured towards the crumpled missive. 'It was the final straw. I couldn't see any way out.'

When Vivian was told the news by a very distressed Christopher, she just said flatly, 'Oh! Really?'

Chapter 7

For the next few days, Warthing was reeling from the revelations about Sebastian Rivers.

Sophie was finding it particularly challenging, as she explained to her son David in a rare quiet moment in the deli.

'It's all anyone seems to want to talk about,' she hissed as two customers left the shop. Her fine features were marred by her pinching her lips together in frustration. She was tapping her fingers on the countertop in a vain attempt to release some of her pent-up anger.

'Those two were annoying me so much that I went and spilt oil on my white shirt when I was trying to portion out some olives for them.' She glanced in disgust at the shiny patch that stood out on her otherwise spotless blouse. It had missed the smart navy apron by a mile. She put her hand to her blonde ponytail.

'They've never even met Sebastian and yet they were very free with their opinions. The fat one with the unfortunate teeth had the gall to say she hopes they throw the book at him.'

David paused in his arrangement of fresh local honey on a shelf; it was as golden as the summer sun. Placidly he tried to soothe her. 'Like you said, they don't know him.'

'I think some of the comments from locals can be worse,' exploded Sophie as she went over to the table where different varieties of apples, in every size and shade of red, were attractively displayed in wicker baskets. She started rearranging them roughly.

Fearing the produce might be ruined by bruising, David said, 'Here let me do that. Why don't you fill up the anchovies?'

A smell of brine pervaded the shop as Sophie set about her task. 'Take Vivian, for example. I almost lost my temper with her when she popped in earlier to pick up her oyster order.'

'Why? What did she say?'

'It wasn't so much what she said, it was the infuriating way she looked so bloody smug when some other customer mentioned Sebastian, saying how he'd never be Lord-Lieutenant now.'

Sophie's agitated ladling resulted in her slopping some anchovies onto the floor. She swore softly and went to fetch some kitchen paper and a mop. As she cleared everything up she continued to offload onto her docile son.

'That horrid Winston Charter-Fox came in and after he'd complained about our prices he—'

She paused to tackle an anchovy she had missed and David took advantage of the break.

'Winston Charter-Fox? I don't think I know him?'

'Odious man – he has just moved into Mrs May's old bungalow and I must say I pity Dee having him for a neighbour. When he'd finished grousing about paying a fair price for good food he went on to describe dear old Sebastian as '*a relic of the bloated aristocracy that had oppressed the workers for centuries*' and said that they are all thieves by nature, stealing from those less fortunate than themselves.'

The doorbell tinkled, warning Sophie and David that they had a new customer.

Sophie looked up and was immensely relieved to see it was Dee.

Dee smiled and greeted them both but it was easy to see she was feeling the strain; her smile was stiff and she looked tired. 'Hello, both of you. How are you doing?'

'We're fine but what about you?' Sophie asked gently as she tilted her head to one side.

'I'm alright, thanks, just so concerned about Sebastian. He so hates being shut inside; I can't imagine how he's coping with being locked up. And then there's Jake; it must be so overwhelming for him. Anyway, I was just sitting brooding at home so I thought I'd pop in here and get something delicious for lunch – as a little pick-me-up.'

'Very sensible,' said Sophie, 'and it looks like Robert had the same idea. Here he is now.'

He was wearing a neat pair of toffee-coloured cords with a sharp crease down the front and a maroon sweater under a smart trench coat.

Sophie smiled at him. 'Are you looking for something for lunch?'

'Supper actually. We're having some friends over this evening.' Robert sighed. 'They're military colleagues of Paul's so it will be a late night – port until after one am. Paul is in charge of the main but I have to get all the other bits.'

'I'm sure we can help with that. Do you have a list? And I can recommend some Stilton we've got in to go with the port.'

He handed over a list, meticulously written in blue ink and a cursive hand. Sophie scanned it, nodding her head as she ran down each item.

He turned to Dee. 'Any news about Sebastian? Gossip is rife; almost everyone is talking about it. I keep on glowering at people who say mean things about Sebastian, which isn't at all the thing when they're customers.'

'Afraid not, but David will know more about Jake. He's taking it in turns with Amelia and Francesco to stay over at the Hall. I would have liked to have Jake to stay with me but understandably he didn't want to put the dogs in kennels.'

Robert nodded. 'Sebastian would hate the thought of them away from their creature comforts. So how is Jake doing?'

David stopped polishing the apples with a tea towel, shrugged and wrinkled his forehead, 'Well … you know.'

They did know or at least could guess. A young, unfledged adult who finds out his only parent is guilty of embezzlement, has tried to kill himself and will be spending time in prison, not to mention that the only home he has ever known will need to be sold, won't be in the best shape.

'He greatly appreciates the way everyone is pitching in to help him – like the food rota that Dee and Mum have set up – but of course, he doesn't have much of an appetite.'

The bell tingled as Virginia bustled in. She was looking even more windswept and dishevelled than normal, her open mac exposing her baggy navy sweater, unattractive spongy-soled shoes and her elasticated nylon trousers.

Dee was very fond of her but … *I wonder if she thinks that dressing as if she is an unloved octogenarian in a care home makes her holy? I wonder if I could organise a charity makeover for her? She'd never agree to spending any time or money on herself normally but if it's for a good cause …*

'Hello,' she announced in her cut-glass accent. 'I was passing and saw you all through the window. I knew you'd want to know the latest on Sebastian. I've just seen him.'

'I thought he wasn't allowed visitors when on remand?' queried Dee.

Virginia nodded. 'He's not but I got in as a Prison Chaplain.'

'How is he?' Concern was written all over Dee's face.

'Not good, I'm afraid, but his solicitor seems to think he'll be able to get him out on bail soon. The only thing is, I don't think he should be left alone and it's really too much responsibility for Jake.'

Dee spoke up, 'Don't worry about that, I'm in touch with Sebastian's younger sister and she's ready to drop everything and move in with him and Jake when needed.'

'Well that's a relief,' sighed Virginia before looking at her watch and shrieking, 'Must fly! I'm late for the seniors' bingo in the village hall.'

She clattered out, inadvertently slapping the shop door in her haste.

'I ought to be going too,' said Robert. 'I have a meeting with Jim Stuart.'

'At his house? I thought it was finished and the bees' knees?' queried Sophie.

Robert prided himself on discretion and was normally extremely careful not to say anything to anyone about clients. *I must be more rattled than I realise.* He didn't probe as to whether he was discombobulated by the revelations about Sebastian or his concerns about Paul. 'Oh, just a social call.'

'Have fun tonight!' called Dee. 'I know that you'll be in for a treat with whatever Paul prepares; he's such a good cook.'

Robert smiled a little sadly. 'Paul is always good at anything he does.'

Driving through the autumn drizzle to Jim Stuart's house gave Robert time to collect his thoughts.

I told Jim when we were doing the guest bedrooms that they would look soulless unless we included some objets d'art and one or two books that had actually been read rather than pristine leather-bound classics. Robert turned off classic FM – he wasn't in the mood for Debussy. *I suppose he had to see it for himself to realise I was right. Still, it will be a fun side-project. I have an enamel snuff box and a Georgian travel box which would go well in the main guest room. As for the twin room perhaps something a little more feminine? A Victorian fan? Or a silver-backed brush and comb set? Both will need books but any excuse to go around second-hand bookshops is fine by me.*

He was overtaken by a white van travelling far too fast in these wet conditions, but he was too absorbed in his own thoughts to find it more than vaguely annoying. His mind was still on book collecting.

Paul used to love spending time combing through musty old books, searching for treasures. In a flash, thirty years rolled back and he could smell the distinctive scent of a chaotic second-hand book shop in London, where books stood haphazardly on shelves and tables and even on the many crooked stairways on the shop's three storeys. It had been one of their favourite haunts, close to a café that did an excellent Sunday morning brunch. It had been there that Robert had found Paul an early history of the Napoleonic Wars.

He still has it in his study – he loves it but I doubt he remembers where he got it from.

Looking for a distraction he put Classic FM back on. Vivaldi's *Four Seasons* was playing. *You know where you are with Vivaldi, whereas you need to be feeling emotionally secure to enjoy the enigmatic beauty of Debussy.*

An enigma, a mystery, difficult to understand – even after thirty years Paul is still in so many ways an enigma to me.

Dee is right. Tonight he'll prepare something sophisticated and delectable. Our guests will be charmed and amused and go home saying, 'What a lovely couple.'

As he slowed to turn off the main road and down the side road to Jim's, a tractor pulled out in front of him but he didn't mind; he wanted time to think.

Perhaps I want too much – perhaps some ambiguity in a relationship is good. What is it that I actually want?

Vivaldi had moved from the lightness of spring to the richness of summer.

Have I ever, in thirty years, felt certain of what Paul's feelings are for me?

Through the drizzle of an English autumn, he saw the shocking azure of the Mediterranean in the summer sun. The first trip they had ever made together to the Amalfi Coast. *Can it really be thirty years ago? Yes, then there was no ambiguity about the way Paul looked at me.* Robert smiled. *I was his ... everything.*

The country lane wound sharply through rolling countryside, dark ploughed fields on one side and stubble on the other. He gave his mind over to the heat of that summer; there seemed to be lemon groves everywhere they went, vivid yellow fruit against the brilliant blue of the sky.

We must have walked miles, exploring vineyards and villages.

He could see Paul exactly as he had been then, his eyes as piercing as the Mediterranean itself, his straight nose, his smooth, muscled torso glistening as he swam in the waves. He could see himself and smiled ruefully at how thick his strawberry blond hair had been then.

He couldn't remember fish ever tasting so good; he could almost taste the sea as he recalled savouring anchovies under vine-shaded canopies. *What were those antipasti called? Oh yes, Alici Di Cetara – Anchovies of Cetara. And the wine? A rosé – no, I can't remember its name but then that area has so many native grape varieties dating back to Roman times that it would take a genius to recall them all. Paul would know, though.*

He reached the gate to Jim Stuart's home.

Why do I always feel like Elizabeth Bennet approaching Pemberley when I come down this drive? Jim's like Paul; he can remember every wine he's ever sipped. Strange that there's no partner – male or female – perhaps he prefers wine. He's attractive, well-groomed and engaging, but somehow he's so self-contained – he doesn't really give off any sexual vibes. There's no evidence of friendships in the house, there were no requests for a guest room to be set up for visits from nieces or nephews, and the only photo he has framed in his bedroom is one of his mother; it looks like it was taken in the late seventies. Odd the way he's had me do out the changing room by the pool but he says he can't swim – not that he doesn't swim, but that he can't swim. I wonder why he wanted such an elaborate pool if he's not going to use it. It must have cost a fortune to install and the running costs will be astronomical.

As he reached the front of the house, Jim was there to meet him.

One mercy about this appointment is that Jim Stuart likes to focus on his own affairs so at least I won't need to deflect negative comments about Sebastian.

Christopher looked with pride at the basket overflowing with fresh produce; he thought the Savoy cabbage looked especially magnificent. He could hardly wait to show Vivian. And there she was writing her to-do list at the kitchen table. Eagerly he walked in, holding the basket in front of him, the array of vegetables on full display. She didn't look up.

He paused, still looking hopefully at her in much the same way Bramble was looking at him.

'I say, old girl, just look at this – all from our own veg plot.'

'Not now, I'm busy – some of us have things to do.'

She glanced up, then, but her eyes didn't light up in wonder at the veg; they narrowed as she glimpsed the floor and the muddy trail. Her shoulders stiffened and Bramble slunk behind the protection of Christopher's legs. In a quiet voice full of menace she demanded, 'How many times must I tell you not to wear your Wellington boots in the kitchen?'

Sheepishly, Christopher looked at his feet and out of embarrassment shuffled them, which dislodged more earth.

Vivian sighed.

'I'll be off then,' he murmured, his shoulders slumped and his hands hanging slackly by his sides.

'Before you go, I need to run through some dates with you.'

Christopher brightened. 'Have you worked out when we could get away for a little holiday, just the two of us?'

'Certainly not, we have far too much to do before the Michaelmas Ball. I just wanted to tell you not to book any of your suppers with your golfing people or trips to London with your old army chums as they're bound to clash with what I've got planned.'

'Don't worry, I've nothing in the diary, but I did think I'd pop in on old Sebastian when he's out on bail.'

Vivian looked at him coldly and curled her lips. 'Don't be ridiculous!'

'Uh? Look, I say, Vivian, you can't drop a fellow just because he's down.'

Vivian didn't appear to hear him, she was busy jotting notes. Absently she said, 'One good thing about Sebastian being found out is that he's no longer in the running for Lord-Lieutenant.'

'I should think that's the least of his concerns. Poor chap will have to—'

Vivian cut him off. 'If you're so keen to see people you can make more of an effort to be charming when I get the Parkinsons round.'

'The Parkinsons?'

'Yes, you know those friends of Victoria's parents. They were at Oxford with the PM. Now if they put in a good word for us about you becoming Lord-Lieutenant and then Victoria's parents are back from their cruise soon and are bound to have a word too, what with Victoria and Tristan being so close. It will all help.'

Sebastian frowned. 'What about Emily?'

'Oh, I don't think that will last long. By the way, Victoria is staying this weekend – there's some problem with the plumbing. Tristan and that girl will be here too.'

Christopher's eyes widened. 'What? Emily and Tristan visiting again so soon?'

'I specifically invited them.'

'You did?'

'I'm preparing a little surprise for that girl. Now will you kindly leave so that I can get on without all these interruptions?'

Christopher and Bramble turned to go back outside but Vivian called him back. 'For goodness sake, take that with you!' She gestured towards the basket, abundant with Christopher's vegetables. 'You really are hopeless, the carrots have dropped soil all over the table.'

As Christopher sadly picked up his bounty, Vivian wrote down on her to-do list: *pick up oysters*.

Nicholas Corman sat back in his chair. His desk was a model of order, with no piles of files or messy Post-it notes, just one neat aloe vera plant and a forensic report. He tuned out the normal police station noises of phones ringing and sirens starting, and focused on the report.

Disappointed, he put it down. No luck – no fingerprints or DNA. He didn't like what was going on in Little Warthing: first Dee's brake line, now this.

It's more than just blackmail, there was no demand for money, it was an incitement to suicide which makes it attempted murder. So that's two attempted murders connected to one village in the space of just a few days. I dread to think what's going to happen next.

Chapter 8

'What the hell do you think you are playing at?' shrieked Emily as she fought a semi-naked Tristan off.

A flood of thoughts coursed through her sleep-befuddled mind:

Where has my protective wall of pillows gone? I know I put them in place down the middle of the bed last night.

Where is the T-shirt he normally sleeps in?

And when did he get so ... well, so manly?

The last time I was squashed up against his bare chest was the first week at uni at a Freshers' water volleyball match and then he was distinctly weedy and not at all ...

She made a desperate bid to get out of the bed and away from a disturbingly buff Tristan but he held her tight and urgently whispered, 'Shut up and snuggle!'

'What?' she shrieked, again totally outraged.

Then she heard it, rapping at the bedroom door, and realised it was the sound that had first disrupted her sleep before she felt Tristan's arms about her.

Vivian's voice came through the closed bedroom door. 'Everything alright? I've brought you a tray with coffee and croissants.'

'Does she normally do this?' queried Emily, while worrying that she hadn't had a chance to clean her teeth and that Tristan's face was awfully close to hers.

'Not often.' His tousled black hair was falling over his face, half-covering his bemused blue eyes. 'In fact, I don't think she's ever done it before.'

Emily gave him a quizzical look. 'So why now?'

He shrugged. 'I told you, she's warming to you.'

Emily pulled a face as Tristan drew her closer to him and called, 'Come in.'

Somehow a smiling Vivian carrying a breakfast tray gave Emily the creeps. The tweed, the perm and the fixed red lipstick were all familiar, but the smile? And breakfast in bed? Emily shivered and actually did snuggle up closer to Tristan.

'Wow, thanks, Vivian. You're a gem, isn't she, Emily?' Tristan sounded overly jolly.

Emily nodded.

'My pleasure and I have a little treat for you for lunch, so no nipping off to Dee's.'

Vivian's smile was really freaking Emily out, but Tristan was thrilled. 'What?'

'It's a surprise! Something I got especially for Emily.'

'That's so kind of you, isn't it, Emily?'

Tristan squeezed her tight and she managed to squeak out, 'Yes.'

For Emily, this weekend was proving to be one confusing scene after another.

Have I misjudged Vivian in the same way I've misjudged Victoria? I can't remember ever feeling so bewildered. I don't seem to be able to find any certainty. A few weeks ago all my interactions with other people were simple and straightforward but now ...

Perhaps if I run through the events of the weekend in chronological order I'll be able to untangle my thoughts. That's it – I'm an intelligent, rational woman. All I need to do is to take an analytical look at my emotions.

So this weekend we arrived in Little Warthing ... but that's odd, I started feeling perplexed before we even got here ... When was I first aware of being befuddled?

She considered for a moment and then there it was, that lightbulb moment.

It was when Tristan picked me up after work to drive me down here. To start off he was his normal offhand self and took my bag, asking if I'd put bricks in it as it weighed a ton. It was then that he noticed ... me. *He stopped speaking and just looked – well to be more accurate he stared.*

Emily smiled as she recalled his expression before he stammered, 'You look ... okay!'

So he had noticed! Well, there was quite a bit to observe: the new haircut, which the hairdresser assured me framed my face to perfection and showcased my natural curl, the eyelash tint – even I was surprised by how long my lashes are, the brow shape – apparently now my eyes do – what's the expression – 'pop', and of course the lipstick!

Not to mention the jeans which cost more than I thought possible, but boy do they hug my hips – in a good way! Then there's this cropped cardigan – she stroked her own arm – *so soft that it cries out to be caressed. It may be a dramatic change from my norm but I'm glad I got it in bold red rather than boring green.*

So confusion point one – he noticed my new kit, but why should that put me out? If I hadn't wanted to stand out why did I go to so much trouble?

Confusion point two is easy – Friday night Star Wars. Watching Star Wars is pretty inevitable whenever we both get together, so no confusion there, but was it really necessary for us to cuddle up on the sofa like that? His concern that Victoria or Vivian might walk in on us was just about plausible. She considered that whole scenario. *I suppose my real confusion is that I didn't object – in fact, it felt really nice, sort of cosy and safe but then I was really tired after a long week at work and that drive from London with all the traffic had been exhausting.*

For a moment she indulged in recalling the warmth of his body next to hers as she'd drifted off to sleep with the dramatic Star Wars music as a backdrop, then mentally she gave herself a shake and moved on to confusion point three – Victoria.

She looked so tired and vulnerable when she came into the kitchen on Saturday afternoon. Naturally, I'd got up the moment I heard her come in as my main hope had been to avoid spending any time with her and her condescension, but one glance at her slumped shoulders and slightly smudged mascara had me asking,

'*Rough day?*'

She'd nodded and said, 'Hellish! Work this week has been a nightmare and now the renovations have hit an issue with the plumbing and they're not sure if they'll have it finished by the time Mummy and Daddy come back.'

Of course, I sympathised and what could I say but, 'I'm sorry! Let me make you a cuppa.'

And so Emily had found herself in the unlikely position of having a tête-à-tête with Victoria Pheasant. As they sat at the table, teacups in hand Victoria had given her a sad smile. 'You really are very sweet; I can see why Tristan is smitten.'

Emily had felt herself go warm and had glanced away.

'There's no need to be coy; you only have to see the way he looks at you to know he's head over heels in love with you.'

Emily had had a sudden flashback to the feel of Tristan holding her in bed that morning and she knew she was no longer blushing pink but crimson.

'I've always had a bit of a thing for Tristan,' continued Victoria. 'After all, we've got so much in common: tennis, loving the opera, knowing all the same people. Everyone says we're made for each other.'

Emily winced and tried to cover her confusion by sipping her tea but Victoria reached out and grasped her fingers.

Compelling Emily to look into her large blue eyes she said, 'If anyone was going to steal my Tristan's heart, I'm glad it was someone as adorable as you.'

Emily was flooded with thoughts.

You can tell she's American! Why can't we just talk about the weather?

While she tried to extricate her hand she run through Victoria's words.

My Tristan? Bloody cheek! She doesn't know I'm only a fake fiancée!

Then came the remorse.

She's right! They are made for each other, they do have so much in common, she would be a perfect partner for Tristan. She

would love all the same events he loves, go to all those interminable
operas, partner him in the mixed doubles tournaments and Vivian
would be ecstatic. Perhaps I should tell her the truth? After all, it
seems pretty mean to break her heart for no reason.

Finally, she managed to pull her hand away from Victoria's
tenacious grip but not before she'd caught the look of utter
helplessness in the girl's eyes.

'Victoria, there's something I should tell you.'

'Yes?' smiled Victoria.

Emily swallowed. 'It's about Tristan and me—'

'What about you and me?' asked Tristan as he walked into
the room.

'Aww, I was just telling Emily how you make the sweetest
couple,' drawled Victoria, all trace of tiredness and vulnerability
gone. She was sitting up straighter and as Emily noted, *the pout*
is back.

Tristan smirked and ruffled the top of Emily's head in a way
that was both highly affectionate and really annoying.

'Well, in that case, why doesn't the finest southern belle I
know join us at the Flying Pheasant?'

'Charmed, I'm sure.' She gave Tristan a dazzling smile and
with a swish of her slim hips left the room, archly explaining, 'I'll
just go and freshen up. I must look a positive fright.'

When she'd gone there seemed to be an awkward vacuum in
the room. Tristan stood in a kind of limbo, unsure whether to sit
down or stay standing. For her part Emily was keen not to look at
him, finding his intense gaze unsettling.

To fill the void, she stood up and carried the dirty cups over
to the dishwasher. To get to it she had to walk right past Tristan
and found his long-limbed presence unnerving. She could sense
he was watching her, really observing her, not just an idle glance.

By way of distraction, while carefully not looking up from
the dishwasher, Emily said, 'You really must try to be kind to
Victoria.'

His voice rang with surprise as he uttered a startled, 'Uh?'

She turned to him – he looked perplexed. Tristan, with his

ruffled hair, fair skin and those mesmerising blue eyes was safe to face only when his confidence was pricked with doubt – like now.

'Now I'm getting to know her better she's not nearly as … assured as I first thought.'

He raised one eyebrow in surprise. 'She isn't?'

'No, she's actually quite vulnerable.'

'Victoria? Vulnerable?'

'Yes and you should make more of an effort to be kind to her; she really is very fond of you.'

'Okay, if it will make you happy, I will be extra nice to her.'

Emily hadn't thought through what his making more of an effort to be kind to Victoria would look like in reality or how it would make her feel – it was only later on in the evening that she found out.

The three of them had walked through the dark and drizzle to The Flying Pheasant where they'd been welcomed by a roaring fire and Alex.

'Thank goodness you've come,' said Alex. 'I was wanting someone to have a drink with – the dog and I have been hovering by the fire and repelling all comers in the hope that you'd pop down and we'd have the cosiest corner.'

Alex was right – between her electric wheelchair and the large black Labrador, there was very little room for the punters to get to the sofa, which had the prime location by the inviting fire.

Drinks were organised, cider all around, and then they went to sit. Emily held back to let Victoria go first but Tristan pulled her so that she ended up sitting extremely close to him on the sofa. When Victoria sat down next to her, he moved even nearer to Emily, and she could feel his warmth against her side.

Alex glanced at her. 'Hey Emily, love the hair and that red looks amazing on you.'

Emily wasn't sure what she felt about Tristan's expression at the compliment.

Is that smug pride?

'Where's Francesco?' asked Victoria, neatly changing the subject.

'He's with Jake but it will be the last night as Sebastian is getting out on bail and his sister is coming to stay,' Alex explained gloomily then she added, 'Have any of you met Dee's new neighbour? Just moved into Mrs May's old bungalow?'

They all shook their heads and Alex grinned. 'You haven't missed much. He's a scruffy chap called Winston Charter-Fox. He came in here for a pint and was very vocal about his opinion on Sebastian or as he put it '*the bloated aristocracy*'. He then gave us his unvarnished opinion on the role of Lord-Lieutenant – seems that if he had his way all the candidates would be joining Sebastian behind bars. When he started talking about how we should abolish the monarchy, I thought Dad was going to bar him from the pub before he'd even finished his first pint.'

Victoria cut across the general laughter. She hadn't even tried to hide her boredom as Alex spoke and now she was on her feet and leaning over Emily to pull on Tristan's arm. 'Come and play snooker with me!'

'I'm fine here,' stated Tristan, making no effort to move from his spot on the sofa.

Emily dug him in the ribs with her elbow and hissed, 'Go on! Be a gentleman!'

Reluctantly he got up and went to the snooker table.

Emily noticed that his demeanour quickly changed; Victoria seemed to be needing a great deal of guidance.

Surely she knows how to play snooker or why did she ask him for a game? Is it really necessary for him to put his arms around her to demonstrate how to hold the cue? What's with her girlish giggles? And how dare Tristan enjoy it all! Doesn't he realise he has a fake fiancée? And what's more, she's sitting right here!

Emily's fingers tightened around her glass, she could feel that she was clenching her teeth as her jaw ached.

Alex's shrewd eyes went from Emily to the snooker table. 'I wouldn't put up with that if I was you.'

Caught off guard, Emily quickly got a grip of herself. She shrugged and, attempting to make her voice sound light, said, 'Oh, they're just old friends.'

Alex didn't say anything but raised one eyebrow.

Emily glanced again at the snooker table, where Victoria was batting her long lashes at Tristan and imploring him to show her that shot again.

'Victoria is really, er, much sweeter, um, than you'd think.'

Alex still didn't say anything.

'It's raining hard now,' said Emily to fill the ensuing silence between her and Alex as well as to block out the sound of Tristan and Victoria's laughter.

Eventually, Victoria's phone rang. With pouting lips she drawled to Tristan, 'It's Mummy – she'll be wanting to hear the latest about the house. It's bound to be a long call so don't worry about me, just go home when you're ready.'

Sure enough, when Emily and Tristan were ready to leave she was still on the phone.

'Come on!' said Tristan, taking Emily's hand and pulling her to her feet.

She glanced over to where Victoria was talking animatedly and loudly into her mobile. 'Yes Mummy, of course, I told the plumber he was an idiot!'

'If you're sure? Bye, Alex, see you next time we're down.'

Alex buzzed her wheelchair to one side. 'Great – you should try and make it for the All Hallows' Eve party. It sounds cheesy but it's usually fun, bobbing for apples and whatnot.'

'A Halloween party?'

'Without the witches, less Halloween, more All Souls' Day,' said Tristan reaching for his umbrella. 'It's another local custom. Bye, Alex, say hi to Francesco for me.'

And that was it, they were out of the warmth of the Flying Pheasant and into the pouring rain. Large puddles were forming on the pavement and water gushed down the side of the road and into the guttering. A car went past, windscreen wipers on and lights blazing. As it overtook them it sent up a spray of water and Tristan instinctively pulled her towards him.

'Here, stay close or you'll be drenched by the time we get home.' His voice was deep and husky and he kept his arm wrapped tightly around her long until after the car had gone. They'd laughed as they splashed through the puddles; their feet were wet but their hearts were full of childish glee.

In fact, he kept holding her all the way to his godparents' back door. Then as he stood in the little overhang of the kitchen door in the glow of the outside lamp he stopped laughing and with his arm still embracing her looked down at her.

Suddenly she didn't feel like laughing either, there was a stillness between them with just the drumming of the rain on the umbrella. Emily noticed that the pupils of his eyes were enormous as he looked at her intensely then, very slowly he released her and with the greatest care raised his hand to her face.

Emily wasn't sure if she was still breathing. Her heart was beating fast as he stroked a wet curl from her cheek. His touch was light, caressing and gentle, and as he leant in towards her she closed her eyes and tilted her face.

The romantic moment was shattered by a familiar Southern drawl.

'Oh, there you are! Quick, open the door! I'm soaked through!' Victoria's voice was strident and loud. They sprung apart and neither spoke for the rest of the evening.

And now here I am! Eating croissants with him in bed!

She took another bite of croissant, showering the duvet with crumbs.

She had to be honest: *I think running through the events of the weekend has only made me more confused. Anyway, at least lunch will be fun – I wonder what the surprise treat can be?*

Lunch, when it did come, was anything but fun.

Vivian had refused all help preparing it and when Emily surveyed the formal dining room, all laid out with an array of fine glasses and silver cutlery, she realised that this wasn't going to be a relaxed meal.

Tristan nudged her and whispered. 'Bit different from lunch at Dee's.'

Emily swallowed and nodded.

'Do sit down. No need to stand on ceremony,' said Vivian. She was smiling, her lips marked out by a seasonal burgundy lipstick that matched a fleck in her tweed skirt.

Emily sat down, dismayed at the choice of knives and forks before her.

There was a pop and Christopher came in carrying an open bottle of champagne.

'Gosh, champagne, what a treat! Was this the surprise you mentioned, Vivian?' asked Emily.

Vivian was quite jovial; there was real warmth in the smile she gave Emily. 'No, but it will go well with the surprise that I've prepared especially for you, and today I feel like celebrating.'

Christopher poured them each a golden glass.

'I love how pretty the bubbles look,' said Emily admiring her elegant champagne flute.

Vivian beamed, 'Let's toast.' She raised her glass. 'To happiness and success.'

They toasted.

'Now for the surprise,' beamed Vivian as she disappeared into the kitchen.

'Can I help?' asked Emily.

'No!' called Vivian from the kitchen. 'This is your special treat.'

Perhaps this is going to be an enjoyable meal after all, thought Emily, taking another sip of champagne and enjoying its light taste.

Vivian returned, the smile still firmly on her face. She carried a tray in her hands; on it were four neat plates. Each plate contained five beautiful oysters in their coarse grey shells, accompanied by half a lemon wrapped in muslin on the side.

Triumphantly she put the first plate down in front of Emily.

'Voila!'

Emily swallowed, feeling hot. She looked up into Vivian's happy expectant face and stammered. 'I'm sorry Vivian, it really is kind of you to go to so much trouble but I can't eat oysters.'

'What?' Vivian's face and body were frozen into immobility but her voice and eyes were ablaze with fury.

'I'm allergic to them.'

'But you have to have them – I've gone to a lot of bother, not to mention the expense.'

'I'm sorry, but I really can't.'

Vivian glowered at her and Emily wasn't sure what to do.

Christopher came to her rescue with a jovial, 'No problem, I'll eat Emily's.'

'No you bloody well won't!' screamed Vivian, storming out of the room with the tray of oysters and slamming the door behind her.

There was an embarrassing silence broken only by the sound of Vivian crashing around the kitchen.

Awkwardly Christopher tried to lighten the mood. 'Did I mention that I think we've got a mole? Something seems to have dug a hole in the lawn, dandiest thing, first noticed it at the beginning of the week then last night, it looked like the blighter had been at it again in just the same place.'

Chapter 9

This is just what I need, thought Jo as she drove towards Warthing Woods. *Getting out into nature always de-stresses me and Dee is delightful company. I could really do with a bit of birdwatching after the last few weeks – work is always stressful but with that outbreak of norovirus among the hotel staff ...* She shuddered at the memory.

Her mind wandered over to family matters. *Then that call from Michael's house master – what was the boy thinking, getting caught drinking on school grounds? I wonder if it's typical middle-child syndrome or is it that I just don't give him enough time, what with work and all my charity commitments? If only David wasn't away so much, but then as an international corporate lawyer he does get paid well, and having decided to privately educate the boys we need the money.*

She slowed her pace as she caught up with a slow-moving tractor. *Perhaps I shouldn't even think of becoming Lord-Lieutenant – how will I manage all the extra work without dropping any of my existing balls?*

The tractor turned off the road and she was able to speed up. *The thing is I can see what a lot of good I could do in the role. And I really am best qualified. I mean dear old Sebastian may be out of the running now but he wouldn't exactly have been able to bring anything fresh to the role. The same goes for Christopher, but then I think it's really more Vivian who wants the glory.*

She slowed down to let a car pull out in front of her. *Vivian's an odd one, she was so put out when I had to confess I kept forgetting to take the calcium tablets she gave me; she gave me quite a lecture on the horrors of osteoporosis and only stopped banging on about the pills when I mentioned that Dee and I are doing a bird count in Warthing Woods today. I didn't know she had an interest in ornithology.*

Carefully Jo overtook a bicycle, the rider's fluorescent jacket bright in the autumn light. *Jim Stuart would be bound to bring some innovations to the Lord-Lieutenant role but I can't help thinking he doesn't have the same connections in the local area that I do. He's only been here a relatively short time and to make the most of the position you do need to have your ear to the ground. After all, that's the whole point of the office – to inform the sovereign what's going on in each area.*

She drew up at one of the many parking areas which had a path that led into the woods. Even at this distance, the trees of the woods looked magnificent clothed in their autumn glory. She wound down her window to breathe in the crisp air and admire the colours.

It's good to get out and forget everything for a bit. She reached over to her passenger seat and her trusty old field bag – a childhood gift from her father for carrying notebooks and other sundries when birdwatching. She smiled at the memory of him and all the fun they'd had together. Although now she made her notes on her phone, she always took it with her for sentimental reasons, besides which it was just the right size to carry a warming flask of hot chocolate.

As she lifted the bag she saw a small political flyer. On the front, scowling, was an ill-kempt man and emblazoned on the bottom was the caption, 'Vote Winston Charter-Fox for council and get oppressed workers heard'.

The man had thrust it into her hand when she'd been at the Town Hall then given her a diatribe about the inequities of the role of Lord-Lieutenant. As far as Jo could gather, if she accepted the role she was personally squashing the underprivileged.

Stupid man, the whole point of the role is to make sure that those people who may be marginalised are heard.

She screwed up the bit of paper, took her bag and got out of the car, just as Dee drove up and parked behind her.

'Glorious morning,' declared Dee.

The walk along the path to the woods was enlivened by Dee spotting two winter visitors, a fieldfare and a redwing. The elegant, thrush-like recent arrivals brought smiles to both Dee and Jo as they took the time to observe them, and then it was into the woods.

They were heading to the hide, deep in the heart of the forest and the scene of many happy hours of birdwatching for Dee, and also one unhappy encounter when Dee had spotted a clown corpse rather than a robin.

Field and hedgerow gave way to woodland, on a rowan tree, enjoying the red-berry bounty was another visitor – a waxwing. Jo saw it first and silently gestured to Dee. With its grey-pink feathers, eye-catching crest and black mask, the bird was certainly striking. They took the time to enjoy observing it before continuing their walk.

They plunged into the wood proper, the wet paths squelching beneath their wellies.

As she soaked in the richness of the forest Jo thought, *It's easy to see why the Japanese advocate 'forest bathing' for mental and physical health.*

Over the sound of the babbling brook, she caught the sweet song of a blackbird and then the melodic robin who was interrupted by the harsh caws of some rooks. She breathed in the rich earthy scent of fungi and rotting leaves and relished in the sepia colours with all their hues of russet and amber.

As they stepped into the forest her eye was caught by a perfect spider's web, its strands mapped out by sparkling dewdrops as it hung against a blackberry bush. She sighed and murmured to Dee, 'I think autumn has to be my favourite season. It's so much less flamboyant than summer.'

Dee smiled. 'I think that every autumn, it's such a celebration of fruitfulness, then Christmas comes and I think that's my favourite season, and I do the same at the first spring flowers and naturally when the garden is at its height in June, summer is my absolute best-loved time of year.'

They both laughed softly and went into the small wooden hide.

It had that indoor wood-shed smell, somehow a few curled brown leaves had blown in and skittered around the floor in the breeze from the open door. Dee pulled the door shut; it was only later when she was recalling events for the police that she realised that there had been a click, an innocuous sound at the time but which later proved to be a padlock clicking tight.

They were just settling themselves in the folding garden chairs that were conveniently placed in front of the viewing hatch.

Jo reached for her bag. 'Can I tempt you to some hot chocolate?'

'How lovely,' began Dee, getting out her notebook but she paused, arrested as a pungent chemical odour assailed her nostrils.

A glance over to Jo confirmed that she could smell it too; her eyes were wide with concern.

'What the heck?' Jo's words were engulfed by a sudden whoosh and flames appeared, dancing in front of the viewing hatch.

In an instant, the calm safe hide was transformed into an inferno of heat and noise. Acrid smoke filled the cabin, burning their eyes and suffocating their lungs. With their hearts pounding and tears from fear and smoke streaming down their cheeks, they both lunged to the door.

Dee reached it first, imagining the cool fresh air beyond but hope vanished and was replaced by terror as she realised it was locked shut.

'Let me!' rasped Jo, pushing Dee to one side. She put her shoulder to the door and rammed it with all her body weight and strength, but neither the lock nor the hinges gave way.

The heat was intense and the sound of the menacing crackling assailed them from all sides. A gush of wind fanned the flames visible through the hatch licking up into the air, burning deep red and purple.

The shed's walls seemed to be closing in. All Jo could think was, *It's a burning coffin.*

She stared at the flames, petrified, while Dee grabbed her hand and through wracking coughs, shouted, 'Our only hope is to go through the hatch!'

'I'll never fit!' screamed Jo who was seized by asthmatic coughs, doubling her over and rendering her unable to move.

Dee propelled her towards the opening.

Thoughts tumbled through Jo's mind.

Dee will never have the strength to lift me, I have to try – the boys – what will happen to the boys if I die? I must live!

With that thought coursing through her veins she heaved herself up to the opening. She heard Dee murmur, 'Well done!' and felt her let go, presumably safe in the knowledge that she could get herself through the hatch.

But I can't, I can't *– I'm wedged!*

Something, it felt like a broken spike of the frame, was pinning her into the hell of flames and pain.

She could smell her hair burning and inexplicably, the memory of singeing her fringe on a Bunsen burner at school popped into her mind. She opened her mouth to scream but no sound came, just searing agony as flames wrapped around her.

The next bit came in jolts as she swam in and out of consciousness.

Dee implored God to help as she pulled at Jo's arms.

The thud of hitting the ground.

Dee rolled her over and over in the cold dew heavy grass, putting out clinging flames that wrapped around her body.

And the relief as she spat out a lump of mud.

I'm alive!

Christopher came into the kitchen rubbing his chin and with his brow furrowed. As always, Bramble followed in his shadow, mirroring his body language.

Seeing Vivian sitting at the kitchen table, with a bone china cup and saucer in front of her and a pen in hand as she tackled the Times crossword puzzle, he coughed. 'The strangest thing just happened.'

Vivian didn't look up.

He stared at her regarding the paper and repeated himself.

'The strangest thing just happened. I went to the shed to get some more petrol for the mower – last cut of the season, meant to do it at the weekend, but it was too wet. Should be okay, no frost forecast for the next few days.'

He paused. Vivian's eyes widened, she smiled and bent forward to scribble down the answer to five across.

'As I was saying the strangest thing just happened, I went to get more petrol for the mower and ...' he took an intake of breath for dramatic emphasis, '... and the can was empty.'

Vivian carried on looking at the paper.

After a moment Christopher and Bramble shuffled out to go to the petrol station.

Chapter 10

Nicholas Corman was tending one of his office's bonsai trees with a pair of secateurs flown in from Japan. He trimmed a leaf and meditatively inhaled calmly. Outside drunks shouted, and sirens wailed but here all was serene.

He envisaged his mind as a smooth pond with his thoughts as mere ripples. There were minor niggles, such as Winston Charter-Fox.

I'm not quite sure why he says Marks and Spencer's is the high street representation of the world's financial inequalities. He admired his work and reached for his water spray, another work of art flown in from Japan. *I suppose it is a bit pricey but they do make exceptionally good sandwiches.*

Whatever the case, it's not appropriate that he stands with a placard outside the main entrance and heckles shoppers.

He let his mind flow from the inconsequential to the paramount: Dee FitzMorris and Jo Roper.

Thank goodness Dee escaped with minor burns – painful but not serious. Jo is another matter – I'll ask Josh to get the latest from intensive care. Shame the fire investigation unit could come up with little more than confirming that it was arson.

From the corridor, a clear voice rang out. 'Don't be ridiculous, Josh! Of course, he'll see me!'

Nicholas looked beseechingly at the ceiling. *Here we go again.*

Zara burst in, her green eyes flashing with a brilliance that left him breathless. Her porcelain skin was flushed, her lips were slightly parted, she was breathing heavily and all this emotional intensity was wrapped in a copper-coloured wool dress that looked so soft, he longed to caress it.

She glowered at him and he put down his bonsai watering can.

'So!' she demanded.

'Ms FitzMorris, if you are here in connection with the unfortunate incident involving Dee FitzMorris I am unable to give out any information about an ongoing investigation.'

He couldn't help noticing that her rather shapely chest was heaving with fury.

'Nicholas Corman! Don't you Ms FitzMorris me! Fine, if you are going to be like that, you leave Amelia and me no alternative but to investigate this matter ourselves.'

'Zara, I really must insist—'

He got no opportunity to insist on anything as she left as quickly as she had arrived.

Nicholas hadn't got very far returning his mind to a still pond rather than a tornado-ravaged ocean, when Zara stuck her head around the door.

'Don't forget we're leading a ballroom dancing class in Little Warthing's village hall at six o'clock on Saturday. The Michaelmas Ball will be a total shambles if people don't get at least one practice in. Don't be late!'

And that was it, she was gone again and this time for good as he could hear the sound of her high heels diminishing.

He picked up his secateurs again, inhaled and visualised that elusive tranquil pond but it was no use – all he could focus on was Zara.

I can't remember agreeing to help her with a dance class.

Many miles away in London, Tristan was struggling with his own female-friend bewilderment. In a desperate hope to find clarity of mind, he swapped his work suit and tie for his trainers and was soon jogging down damp pavements in the orange glow of streetlights.

I don't know what's wrong with me! My concentration has always been phenomenal, so what happened today? How could I have so totally lost focus in the partners' meeting this afternoon?

He rounded a corner and paused for the pedestrian light to change so he could cross a busy four lanes of traffic. *Bit unnecessary for the chairman to enquire when I was going to wipe that inane grin off my face and grace them with my presence!*

The memory sent a spurt of adrenaline through his body and he speeded up so that for a few blocks he was running abreast with a red double-decker filled with grey and weary-looking commuters. He skirted around a young couple walking frustratingly slowly, totally wrapped up in themselves. Their careless happiness forced him to both slow down and reflect. *The problem isn't really that I keep having lapses in concentration, it's that my mind will keep going back to one thing – or rather to one person.*

Emily Laddan.

Even recalling her name made him smile so broadly that an attractive girl he was passing mistook it for one directed at her and returned it. For the first time in his life, he looked away from a pretty girl and had no interest in her inviting glance. The realisation made him laugh out loud as he skirted a park. He gave up his futile attempts to try and think about anything else and conjured up an image of Emily.

When did she get so – well, so gorgeous? How could I have spent so much time with her and never realised how darn sexy she is? Those eyes! And her lips! And that figure! How could she have been hiding all those curves under her baggy sweatshirt? He swallowed and slowed to a walk as he registered that he had a major problem.

What now?

Perhaps it was just as well Victoria interrupted our kiss. That kiss could have been the biggest mistake of my life. Emily has been a mate for years and with my track record on dating if I did make a move on her we might not even last the few weeks between now and the Michaelmas Ball.

The thought made him sad, deeply depressed but he quickly brightened. *Still, we've got the dance class in Little Warthing this Saturday so I can hold her in my arms while maintaining the friend zone.* And with that happy thought he jogged home.

While Tristan had been so caught up in his reflections on Emily he hadn't given Dee's recent injuries more than a brief horrified thought, other friends had been more concerned.

Dee had been surprised when answering a knock on her front door to be confronted by Sebastian Rivers. He was pale and gaunt, his normal healthy outdoor colour had blanched to an unhealthy grey. He tended towards looking moth-eaten and unkempt but today he gave an impression of destitution. It was the first time in all the decades that Dee had known him that his conventionally clean-shaven face spotted a distinct five o'clock shadow.

As Dee opened the door, Sebastian glanced furtively from side to side, scanning the street, hoping no one would see him. The second he saw her he murmured, 'Do you mind if I come straight in?'

Once inside and away from unfriendly eyes, he relaxed enough to say, 'How are you?' and to thrust a battered bunch of Michaelmas daisies at her. They were wrapped in newspaper and water dripped from the end onto the floor.

Graciously Dee accepted the gift. 'Thank you. How lovely to see you; can I make you a cup of tea?'

'No thanks, I've got my sister circling in the car. I'm not stopping, I just had to see how you were getting on. Burns are the very devil, I've heard.'

'Actually, I got away very lightly,' smiled Dee. 'It's far from glamorous but thanks to that forest management scheme to have cattle grazing in the wood, I fell out of the fire and straight into a cowpat. It meant that when I was pulling at poor Jo my hands were coated in the stuff. I just need to wear these muslin gloves for a while to protect them. Jo's the one who is in a bad way; her burns are far worse but the real problem is the smoke inhalation coupled with her asthma. We couldn't break down the door and by the time we got out she'd been breathing in smoke for quite a while.'

Sebastian nodded. 'Those old Nissan huts were built to last – if it had been one of those modern affairs from B&Q you would have taken the door off its hinges with ease. Don't suppose the police have any idea who started the fire?'

She shook her head. 'No, and I'm afraid I wasn't much help. I didn't see or hear anything; the first I knew we were engulfed in flames.' Her voice choked up at the memory and she hastily changed the subject. 'But how are you, Sebastian?'

He was silent and looked away from Dee and at the floor.

'Sorry, silly question.'

Still not looking at her and with his voice barely above a whisper he said, 'The house will have to go; it's a shame after all these generations. My father will be turning in his grave. I feel as if I've let down the long line of Rivers and as for Jake ...'

His voice trailed away. Dee felt helpless in the face of his unhappiness. With the hand that wasn't holding the dripping Michaelmas daisies, she patted his arm; it was a small gesture but it seemed to inject a bit of strength into him.

'Afterwards,' he swallowed and took a breath to regain his composure, 'when I've served my sentence, Jake and I will move far away – somewhere no one knows us. Hopefully, there'll be enough money left from selling everything to buy a small cottage somewhere.'

Dee threw caution and the damp daisies to the wind and embraced him. 'Sebastian, you mustn't do that. All your friends are here and we'll all support you in any way we can.'

When Sebastian was able to speak his voice was choked up. 'That's generous of you Dee but you see I'm too ashamed to face anyone.' His face crumpled and he looked as if he was about to cry. 'Must be getting along – my sister will be waiting outside, probably double-parked. By the way, she sends you her love.'

After he was gone Dee felt so dejected she had to get out of the house.

What I need is a change of scene and a breath of fresh air; a walk around the village will be just the ticket.

Pulling on her trench coat and determined to be happy she headed out of the door. Almost immediately her hopes were dashed.

Initially, she was pleased when she saw that her new neighbour was in his front yard.

Oh good, I've been wanting to welcome him. If only I'd done some baking, it's so much friendlier to greet a newcomer with an offering of cupcakes.

With determination, Dee approached Winston Charter-Fox while brushing away the unwelcome thought that this new neighbour looked as drab and grey as her old neighbour, Mrs May, and in fact as ashen and uninspiring as the bungalow itself.

'Mr Charter-Fox? I'm Dee FitzMorris, I live in the next-door cottage. I'm so sorry I haven't been able to introduce myself before.'

Neither her smile nor her proffered hand was reciprocated.

He scowled. ' Your ruddy cat has made itself known to me though – you should keep it under control. And I've heard about you, you're another one of these Lord-Lieutenant groupies.'

Dee wasn't sure how one remained gracious in these circumstances.

'I'm not quite sure what you mean, Mr Charter-Fox,' she replied, her eyes steadily regarding him but her smile a shade dimmed.

He explained, 'One of those sycophants who toady up to the high-ups and attend wastefully extravagant things like the Michaelmas Ball.'

'Well, yes, I will be going, but I don't quite see—'

'I can't see the point of any of you!'

'Any of us?'

'Royals and royalists – and the worst of the lot is Kate.'

Dee took a sharp intake of breath. She could forgive a lot of things and forget even more but really, to criticise the beloved Catherine, Duchess of Cambridge, that was going too far. She feared that she would never be friends with Winston Charter-Fox.

With the same serene dignity she had so often admired in Kate herself, she smiled and said brightly, 'Well I mustn't hold you up. No doubt I'll see you around.'

As Dee resumed her walk to the high street she was bothered by an unwelcome thought. *If I have to run the gauntlet of a grey and grumpy Winston Charter-Fox every time I nip out for a pint of milk it'll soon get a little wearing.*

Fortunately, at that moment Blossom Bim Bam and Joseph Popov rounded the corner, both in full costume and makeup. Blossom's dazzling pink fit-and-flare dress was matched by an equally brilliant smile. Popov's comic oversized boots and red nose were enough to bring joy to even the most downcast heart.

'Dee!' called Blossom with affection. 'How are you? We've been so worried about you.'

'Oh, I'm fine but thanks for asking. I can see you are on your way to a party.'

'Just coming back actually,' said Popov. He gave Blossom a loving glance and added, 'Kiddies' parties are so much more fun now we do them together.'

As Dee walked on she thought happily of the romance of two professional actuaries finding love in a shared passion for clowning. *What's more, two grumpy old neighbours are of little consequence when one has the honour of sharing a village with two genuine clowns.*

She reached the high street. It was as attractive as ever with its honey-coloured buildings tumbling down the steep hill. Dee preferred it in its autumn serenity than when it was packed with high-season tourists.

I think I'll do a bit of window shopping, she mused. It wasn't that she wanted anything tangible but rather she felt in need of distraction. She debated walking straight up the hill and starting with Robert's interiors shop. Her bedroom makeover had taken rather a back seat with everything else going on. Perhaps now was the time to focus on fabrics and cushions. The idea appealed to her and having a little gentle chat with Robert who would be fragrant and charming only added to the scheme's charm.

But she only got as far as Sophie and Son's deli when she nearly bumped into Vivian, who was hurrying out of the shop with a shopping basket in hand. She did not look quite her usual self, but Dee could not pin down exactly in what way. Perhaps her hair was not as immaculately set as normal or was it that her lipstick was smudged and a different shade to her nail polish?

Her manner was more agitated and less Iron Lady than normal. Dee didn't even get a chance to say, 'Hello Vivian,' before she was assailed with, 'She's not dead then?'

Dee blinked, took a step back as Vivian was using her superior height to lean over her and stammered, 'Sorry?'

'Jo Roper – she's not actually dead?'

'No.'

'But she's seriously ill in hospital?'

Dee nodded.

'So she won't be running for the role of Lord-Lieutenant?'

'Vivian, are you alright?'

'Of course, I am!' she snapped and strode off down the hill muttering to herself and leaving Dee totally bewildered.

Failure is not an option, mumbled Vivian under her breath as she sped down the hill to the sanctuary of her kitchen table. She needed time to think. It had been a shock when she'd just been choosing a nice bit of cheddar for lunch to hear from Sophie that Jo *was* still alive. The last she'd heard she'd been rushed by ambulance to hospital and was in intensive care. *Why didn't the bloody woman take the calcium tablets I gave her? Doesn't she care about her bone density?* She felt personally aggrieved. *The cyanide would have been so neat, clean and effective but no, that wretched woman couldn't even remember to take a simple tablet. Bloody incompetent! How could she ever fulfil the duties of a Lord-Lieutenant?*

The vicar walked past, late for taking a lunchtime assembly at the village school, but Vivian was too wrapped up in her mind to even notice the cheery hello.

Oh no, she couldn't be bothered swallowing a pill so I had to go trampling through the wood lugging that fuel and then she didn't even have the decency to die.

Admittedly, not that Vivian herself was prepared to admit to anything, as she trudged through the woods she had been filled with a certain amount of glee. The poetic nature of what was about to happen appealed to her. She had chuckled as she kept repeating to herself the saying, *two birds with one stone*. She had been confident that one little act of arson was going to take care of both Dee FitzMorris and Jo Roper. The anticipation of success had fuelled her drug of choice, that surge of power that kept her terror at bay.

Failure is not an option! And I haven't failed! she told herself determinedly and out loud which startled a passing young mum with a toddler. The thought calmed her a little.

No, I have succeeded. Sebastian might be out on bail but he'll never be Lord-Lieutenant. That Roper woman is going to be wired up to a hospital bed for a bit rather than gracing the Sovereign with her services. Even Dee, judging by the bandages on her hands, won't be doing Taekwondo for a while.

She smiled.

So actually I've achieved quite a lot. Now I just need to deal with Jim Stuart – I wonder where his weakness lies.

As she reached home, Christopher and Bramble were in the drive. As ever, the very sight of her beloved husband annoyed her, largely because he wasn't his older, more dashing, brother.

'I say, old girl, I've had the chappie for the marquee for the ball here measuring up on the lawn.' He eyed his wife and without much hope said, 'Going to make a terrible mess of the lawn. Don't suppose you'd think about having it somewhere else?'

Vivian eyed him with contempt and said coldly, 'Don't be ridiculous.'

As she walked towards the kitchen door Christopher said, 'Another thing, old girl.'

She didn't bother to stop or turn round so Christopher carried on talking to her back.

'While the marquee chap was measuring up on the lawn, that scruffy new neighbour of Dee's was sort of loitering around. He seemed to be staring at where the marquee was going. When I went to tell him to clear off he actually asked if that was where we were going to have the ridiculous – no, that's not the word he used – *fiasco*, yes that's what he said. *Is that where you're going to have the fiasco of announcing the next pawn-in-service oppression?* What do you think he meant? Can't quite see what oppression has to do with the Michaelmas Ball. Anyway then the blighter gave me an earful about it being a free country and he could stand and look at whatever he wanted. What do you make of that?'

'Not now, Christopher – I've got one of my headaches coming on.'

Chapter 11

Vicar Virginia looked perplexed as Nicholas and Zara walked into the new village hall. Her wild curls bounced in agitation as she watched Dee with Amelia, who was looking like a glittering Goth, with sparkles catching the light from both her eyeshadow and her tutu. Virginia suffered a rare moment of envy as she wondered what it would be like to have the confidence to wear a tight black leather corset provocatively laced up rather than a shapeless navy sweatshirt. What she wouldn't give to have those glorious curls rather than her unmanageable frizz! But Virginia was not able to indulge in this sartorial desire for long as the young and rather attractive police officer she believed was called Josh arrived, then the dashing Robert in a natty waistcoat and his husband Paul, to be followed shortly by the village newcomer Jim Stuart, whose newly-built house she was longing to visit.

Virginia regarded them all and stammered, 'Oh dear, I appear to be in the wrong place. You don't look like you are here for the over-eighties Bible study and craft workshop – we're doing fisherman Paul meeting Jesus on the Lake of Galilee and making these rather jolly boats out of origami.'

She brandished a shiny pink paper boat.

Dee gave her a sympathetic smile. 'I think you are meant to be at the vicarage. We're having a practice run for the Michaelmas Ball.'

Virginia paled. 'Goodness, they'll be locked out and wondering where I am.'

'Don't worry, it's a mild evening and our over-eighties are always up for a bit of adventure,' comforted Dee.

Virginia was not so easily reassured and, seizing her bag, boat still in hand, she made a dash for the door, calling over her shoulder, 'Have fun and I hope to see you all at the All Hallows' Eve party.'

As she bolted out she nearly collided with Emily who was tight-lipped with anger and Tristan who was saying apologetically, 'It was a joke!'

'Not a very funny one,' snapped back Emily. She was going to say something else but she realised that all eyes were on her, obviously curious to know just what the non-funny joke was that had stirred her normally mild persona into fury. Instead, she murmured, 'Sorry we're late.'

Nicholas took up his position near one end of the airy hall and coughed to gain everyone's attention before beginning his well-prepared introduction. 'As many of you know, the Viennese Waltz is one of the oldest ballroom dances. It is rich in history.'

Zara regarded Nicholas, in all his suave elegance, straight nose, even straighter crease down the front of his trousers and shiny dance shoes and thought, *Bless him, but he's being pedantic to the point of boredom.*

With an elegant flick of her narrow wrist, she turned on the music and Strauss' Emperor waltz filled the room. Years of training at his mother's dance studio snapped Nicolas into action and he stood erect, stomach in, shoulders back. Did Zara imagine it or was there even a Prussian clicking of his heels together as he bowed to her? Then the rest was a whirl of graceful sophistication as he spun her around the room. She allowed herself to rest and be guided by him as he took the lead in a masterful fashion. Zara was an ardent believer in women's rights but there were times like now when she'd happily ditch her copy of Spare Rib.

Nicholas, for his part, was finally getting to feel the softness of Zara's fine wool dress; it may have been a different colour from the one she'd worn in his office but it was, to his mind, quite delightful. A final *fleckerl* and they were done. They came to a halt to the applause of the assembled group.

Tristan's eyes had been fixed on Emily rather than the dancing duo. Hopefully, he'd thought the tightness around her mouth had softened and her taut brow relaxed. *She's so darn pretty; how could*

I have been so crass as to say that anal glands were more her thing than Viennese Waltzes? Still, I thought she'd laugh rather than get in a huff.

Tentatively he reached out his hand and tried to put it in hers. Angrily, she snatched it away without looking at him.

She might not have been looking at him but she was thinking of him. *How stupid am I? I've been dreaming of this evening, thinking it would be like something out of Anna Karenina where he'd take me in his arms and hold me while heavenly music played, but all he thinks of me is bloody anal glands! I bet he doesn't think of Victoria Pheasant like that! Bet he sees her in a stunning ball gown smelling of bloody roses.*

Zara smiled graciously and said, 'So if the gentlemen could follow Nicholas and the ladies follow me.'

Paul, tall and commanding and used to being in charge due to his impressive military career, automatically took a step towards Nicholas' happy band of brothers, but Robert put a restraining hand on his forearm.

'I think not. For one evening, at least, you are going to follow my lead.'

Reluctantly, Paul went over to where Dee, Emily and Amelia were standing. The phrase Nancy Boy came to mind, he couldn't fathom why Robert had been so sensitive recently. Quite unnecessary and very unlike him.

Zara gave him a warm welcoming smile before grimacing as her eyes alighted on Amelia's footwear.

'Darling, you might have ditched the boots for one evening.'

Amelia gave her mother a broad smile and held one heavy black, laced jack-boot out in front of her. 'I gave them a polish in honour of the occasion.'

'Very nice, dear!' Zara muttered. 'Now, Emily, have you ever done anything like this before?'

Emily shook her head.

'Don't worry you'll soon pick it up, especially as Tristan is quite experienced.'

Emily threw Tristan a mutinous look. *I bet he bloody is,*

probably attended dance classes with Victoria as a teenager.

Tristan caught the look and naively felt encouraged. *At least she's looking at me. Thank goodness Victoria and I took all those dance classes as teenagers; I'm bound to be able to impress Emily with my reverse turns.*

In Nicholas' group, only Josh looked distinctly uncomfortable; ballroom dancing was not really his sort of thing. Nicholas gave him an encouraging smile but Josh was too nervous to return it. Nicholas wondered what sort of pressure Amelia must have exerted on him to get him here but he did not dwell on it for long as he was still slightly baffled as to how Zara had roped *him* into this evening.

Jim Stuart stood at ease next to Robert. It occurred to Nicholas that they looked good together, both of a similar height and slim build, whereas Paul was both taller and broader than Robert. Always a man who was partial to a bit of tailoring, Nicholas cast his eye over Robert and Jim's attire. They were both immaculately turned out. Although he didn't know Jim, judging by the Italian flare of his trousers he would have taken him to be a more flamboyant dresser but this evening Robert was looking especially dashing in his waistcoat and open shirt.

Nicholas cleared his throat. 'We'll begin with the box step in its simplest form, starting with the left foot, to a count of one, two, three – forward, side, close.'

Robert, who had done this before, followed with ease, as did Tristan. As for Jim, he might be a novice but he was evidently a natural and moved with an innate grace. Then there was Josh – Nicholas regarded his clumsy steps as he tripped over his own trainers and he could but sigh.

After they had practised both without and then with music they paired off. Emily looked less than thrilled at Tristan's eager approach and held him literally at arms' length but even this enthralled him. As she lightly placed her left hand on his shoulder he felt a jolt of electricity run through him. Her steps were light and graceful; fascinated, he wondered what else he didn't know about her.

Courteously, Robert addressed Paul while wishing he didn't find his undone top button and broad shoulders so attractive. If he didn't fancy him so much, then perhaps his indifference wouldn't hurt in the way it did. Jim Stuart chivalrously strode up to Dee, executed a bow and with a smile asked, 'May I have the pleasure of this dance?'

'Delighted,' said Dee and held out her gloved hands.

Jim hesitated and Dee smiled. 'Sorry, doctor's orders, but my hands aren't too bad; just don't squeeze them.'

'Wouldn't dream of it.' He grinned and gently took hold of her.

Josh walked up to Amelia and attempted to mimic Jim's gallant act but Nicholas intervened. 'Not so fast, I think it might be an idea if you start off with Zara and I'll look after Amelia.'

Nicholas gave Amelia's footwear a wary glance and then the music began.

To begin with, Jim was so absorbed in muttering, 'one, two, three, one, two, three' that there was no conversation between Dee and him, then as he relaxed into it he suddenly smiled and confided, 'My old mum used to love this sort of dancing; she was always one for a tea dance. I don't think I've danced since I was a nipper and I waltzed around our front room with her. We had a scratched record of Strauss waltzes.'

'What about your dad? Did he like dancing too?'

Jim shrugged and executed a perfectly balanced reverse-turn. 'Wouldn't know, I never met him, but my mum did alright by me.'

'She sounds like a wonderful lady.'

'She was that, died much too young. I was still a kid.'

'Oh! I'm sorry.'

'You remind me of her.' He looked thoughtful as he avoided colliding with Josh who had finally been allowed to dance with Amelia. 'Although of course she was taller than you and more rounded, and she was a bottle-blonde and not a redhead.'

Dee smiled to herself. *So basically the only thing I have in common with his mum is that I'm older than him.* She glanced around the room and was pleased to see that Emily actually seemed to be enjoying dancing with Tristan. *She must have thawed out somewhere between the Blue Danube and the Emperor Waltz.* She couldn't recall having ever seen him looking so attentively at any woman before.

The thought that the troubled teenager was maturing into a stable adult made her happy. Josh and Amelia seemed to be treading on each other's toes and everyone else's, too, but they were laughing so perhaps it didn't matter. She wasn't surprised to see Paul and Robert gliding serenely. *They're the sort of people who do everything well – but I do wish Robert looked happier.*

Jim broke into her musings. 'I always did want to learn how to waltz properly.'

'And now you've done it and extremely well if I might say so.'

'Thank you.'

Zara and Nicholas waltzed past, as usual, there was something sublime about the two of them when they danced together, something other-worldly.

'Now there's just one other thing I want to learn how to do properly.'

Dee thought, *Just one? I have dozens!* But what she said was, 'What's that?'

'I want to learn to swim. I've got a great big indoor swimming pool and I'm frightened to go in it.'

For the first time, he faltered on a step. They paused and on the next suitable bar began again.

'How come?' Dee asked gently.

'I nearly drowned in a filthy London canal when I was a kid.' He swallowed and stammered out, 'I still get nightmares. I don't know why I'm telling you all this – I've never told anyone before.'

Calmly Dee stated, 'It's because I remind you of your mum. She'd be very proud of your determination to overcome such a horrible trauma.' She looked up at him and he smiled through watery eyes. 'Tell you what, why don't I pop in every morning and we can just have a splash around? You'll be swimming in next to no time, probably by the time we have the Michaelmas Ball.'

'I couldn't. It would be too much of an imposition.'

Dee laughed. 'Are you kidding? When else am I going to have the opportunity to have a daily dip with a good-looking guy in his own indoor pool?'

Jim began to laugh too and spun her joyously around the room.

Chapter 12

Dee got into bed that night still humming. *Strauss' waltzes are definitely life-enhancing.* Happily, she relived Jim laughing and spinning her around the room.

He's a nice lad.

She snuggled her duvet around her and relished in the feel of her comfy bed and soft pillow.

It will be fun getting to know Jim better and I reckon he'll be swimming in next to no time.

I like the way he's throwing himself into local life. She smiled to herself. *He seemed confident that he would be able to enter a credible carved pumpkin at the All Hallows' Eve party. With his enthusiasm for life, he'll be a good school governor; I must pin him down about books for the library. I can see that he'd bring energy and a new way of doing things to the role of Lord-Lieutenant.*

The thought of the upcoming announcement of the next Lord-Lieutenant brought Jo to mind. Unhappily Dee rolled over onto her side and pulled the covers more tightly around her. *It's so awful to think of Jo all alone in her hospital bed, struggling to breathe with her smoke-filled lungs and on morphine for the burns.*

Dee blinked in the gentle night-time light; a full moon filtered through her curtains a restful silver light.

So much has changed since last year's All Hallows' Eve party. Jo brought her husband and all three boys to it. Boys of that age are so full of life. She chuckled as she recalled all the water that had to be mopped up after the Roper clan had finished bobbing for apples. Her happiness was short-lived. *But this year there won't be any Ropers at the party, nor will Sebastian be there to judge the cookie competition or as he'd say, 'biscuit competition'.* She sighed, willing herself to think happy thoughts so that she could drift off to sleep.

Emily and Tristan – that's a happy thought. It was as romantic as watching something out of Anna Karenina, but then, of course, they should have been playing something by Tchaikovsky not Strauss – the waltz from Swan Lake perhaps. And with the image playing in her mind of Emily, looking fresh and young, smiling up at Tristan as they danced around the village hall, Dee fell asleep.

Meanwhile, Zara drifted into slumber recalling delightful clouds of music, while Nicholas lay in his bed unable to get the sensual memory of moving with Zara in perfect harmony out of his mind. He had wanted to mentally run through recent events. He knew there had to be a link between Dee's brake failure, the fire and potentially Sebastian's poison-pen letters, but he couldn't work it out.

Jim was asleep, as the saying goes, as soon as his head hit the pillow. He felt happy and could hardly wait for Dee's help with swimming. For once he slept through the night without choking memories of acrid canal water intruding into his rest.

Robert was still awake when Paul's breathing had slowed to a restful slumber. He wished things were different but still the sound of him close by and the weight of his arm on his hip was comforting.

Tristan lay looking up in the darkness at the ceiling, his every thought was of Emily, who was physically in the same bed but somehow totally out of reach. Eventually, he did fall asleep and dreamt that he was dressed as a dashing Imperial Russian officer in a magnificent St Petersburg golden ballroom and at the centre of it all was Emily, dazzling in a ball gown.

Vicar Virginia said her prayers and with her cosy winceyette onesie on, popped into bed and felt for her hot water bottle. Happily, she recalled how successful the evening had been. Surely the Good Lord wouldn't mind that the over-eighties obviously enjoyed the paper-folding more than the Bible study – if Virginia was totally honest with herself, so did she. Village life was certainly busy, in a minute it would be the All Hallow's Eve party. She would try and invite that newcomer, Winston Charter-Fox to it. They hadn't got off to a good start, she didn't quite know why – she'd just invited him to a service and he'd told her she was a tool for oppression – still, he might enjoy bobbing for apples, she thought happily as she fell asleep.

The only person who sleep totally eluded was Vivian and it wasn't just Christopher's loud snores that kept her awake.

Somehow through a fog of remembered taunts by her family and schoolmates, she told herself:

I can't fail; Christopher has to be the next Lord-Lieutenant, and then everyone will see that I am a person of importance. I've taken care of Sebastian and Jo – Emily and Dee can wait a bit – it's just Jim Stuart that I need to neutralise.

Chapter 13

Who does he think he is, Mr Darcy? thought Vivian, her tight lips thinning as she clenched her jaw. She gripped the steering wheel tightly as she negotiated Jim Stuart's opulent drive. Finally, she rounded a corner and there it was, a magnificent Georgian reproduction of a mansion.

Vulgar.

In the normal course of events, Vivian would not be making house calls to someone like Jim Stuart.

But needs must! How else am I going to get a handle on him? She sneered, *It's not as if we have any mutual friends. How someone like Jim Stuart can even be in the running for the role of Lord-Lieutenant is beyond me! The world has gone mad! But I am here to make sure that that travesty doesn't happen.*

She smiled at a novel thought – *I'm rather like a modern Robin Hood – in reverse.*

Humming '*I vow to thee, my country*' she parked her car and with distaste, she realised that the small, shiny car which was already in the drive belonged to Dee.

What's that woman doing here? She's always where she shouldn't be – she'll have to go!

In her sensible low-heeled court shoes she crunched on the gravel up to the imposing front door. In her hand, she clutched a flimsy white piece of paper with a bright orange pumpkin on it. It was the vicar's idea of a jolly invitation to the All Hallow's Eve party. In Vivian's world, invitations were stiff and engraved, but then in Vivian's world, one didn't have All Hallow's Eve parties.

Her plan was to knock on the door and with all the charm of her hundreds of years of breeding, use the invitation as an excuse to gain entry into Jim's home. She felt confident that he was bound to offer her coffee and that she could use the ensuing conversation to find out some nugget of information that she could use to subtly bump him off. She guessed that the invitation was a flimsy excuse as the over-excitable vicar was bound to have already invited him, but it would serve her purpose.

Upon reaching the door she was surprised to find it slightly ajar. *The man has no notion of security!* When she had arrived at the turning to Jim's drive she had been taken aback that the electric gates were open and as she surveyed the front of the house she couldn't see any security cameras. With her limited thinking, it did not occur to her that they might be hidden.

Silly man! He's simply asking to be murdered! She pushed the door open and stepped into what she considered to be an unnecessarily lavish hall. She was relieved that her entry wasn't heralded by a volley of dog barks. *Good, no canine alarm system – if he had a dog, the frightful man would be bound to have some appalling yappy thing probably called Butch.*

She whispered, 'Jim – it's Vivian.'

This satisfied her sense of manners; plotting homicide could not mar her standards. She tiptoed over to where she could hear voices.

Off the hall was what Vivian could see at a glance was a needlessly sumptuous kitchen. *Far too much white marble and who ever heard of having a chandelier in a kitchen?* She shuddered and silently moved closer to find out what was being talked about. Since childhood, she had known that eavesdropping rather than diamonds was a girl's best friend.

Dee and Jim were talking with a warmth and happiness that made Vivian stiffen in annoyance.

Dee was sitting at a table, wearing some sort of inappropriately contemporary camel-coloured outfit and when she spoke her voice had her habitual irritating lightness. 'You've certainly earned that coffee.'

Jim was busy at the kitchen island with a cafetière and mugs. As the rich smell of freshly-ground coffee reached Vivian, she registered that Jim was wearing a rich burgundy cashmere sweater and that his hair was wet.

Come to think of it, why is Dee's hair wet? I mean I know the woman is eccentric but surely even she wouldn't go out with her bob dripping?

'I can't thank you enough, Dee, for taking the time to get me swimming,' said Jim as he carried a tray over to Dee's table.

'No need to thank me – I really enjoy our time together. Your mother would be so proud of you. At this rate, you'll be swimming like a fish by the time of the Michaelmas Ball.'

Triumphantly Vivian thought, *So that's it! Jim Stuart can't swim and conveniently the man has a pool. This will be fun! I haven't used drowning for a while.*

She allowed herself a moment of indulgence as she recalled the happiness she'd felt as a child when she'd drowned her sister Venetia's puppy and the pleasure of Venetia's subsequent tears.

Carefree and full of glee, she walked into the kitchen. She found Dee and Jim's startled looks satisfying.

'Hello, sorry am I interrupting? The door was open and I did call out.'

Jim rose to his feet, while Dee conquered her surprise enough to smile and say, 'Not at all – Jim was kind enough to let me pop over and take a dip in his pool.'

Liar! Liar! I knew it! You, Dee FitzMorris, might like to pretend that butter wouldn't melt but you're a sneaky little liar! I heard you! Jim Stuart doesn't swim and you are here teaching him. Very sensible – after all it's a dangerous thing to have a pool and not be able to swim. Who knows what might happen?

Vivian smiled.

Jim was caught somewhere between surprise and scepticism but thanks to the last hour he had spent in Dee's company, he was full of bonhomie so he gave her a half-smile in return. This was all the encouragement Vivian needed. 'You have a pool? How ...' she struggled for the word; in her mind, she was thinking 'naff' but for the purpose of a successful murder, she said, '... nice. I would love to see it.'

Jim blinked.

Hastily Vivian added, 'Christopher and I are thinking of installing one.'

He blinked again.

Guilelessly Dee widened her eyes. 'Gosh! You do surprise me, I wouldn't have thought it was Christopher's thing at all. He finds putting a marquee up on his lawn stressful enough. I can't imagine him sacrificing it totally for a swimming pool.'

Vivian smiled at Dee but her eyes were narrow with rage.

Jim drew his brows together in puzzlement and with his head tilted to one side he enquired, 'So you came here to look at my pool?'

Vivian let out a high brittle laugh. 'Hardly. I didn't even know you had one until a few moments ago. I came to drop off this.'

She held out the white paper invitation with its orange pumpkin on.

Jim took it and with a glance said, 'Thank you. The vicar has already given me one.'

With a tight, rigid smile in place, Vivian said, 'What a busy little bee our vicar is.'

Dee cheerfully agreed. 'She's a total delight.' Then she caught a glimpse of her watch and with a gasp stood up. 'Sorry Jim, I'll have to leave the rest of my tea. I'm helping with reading at the village school in half an hour. Don't worry about seeing me out, you just carry on with showing Vivian your lovely swimming pool.'

After Dee left, Jim reluctantly led the way along a corridor to the giant conservatory that served as his indoor pool. The room echoed with their steps and Vivian detected a smell – not chlorine, but something high-tech and salty. The pool was vast and its size was further magnified by the way the water was reflected by blue tiles. The room itself was surprisingly bare with just a couple of forlorn chairs to one side but even Vivian had to acknowledge that views of the landscaped garden through the panoramic glass were impressive.

At the far end was a stylish if rather ornate pagoda.

Vivian nodded in its direction. 'Changing room?'

If Jim was surprised that she hadn't commented on anything else he didn't show it, he just nodded and then with a note of pride added, 'And sauna.'

Yuck! How unhygienic! All those sweaty bodies.

She gave him another of her tight-lipped smiles. This was not her natural habitat; she was visibly perspiring in her tweed and twin set. With an enthusiasm she clearly didn't feel she gushed, 'How exotic.'

He was finding her hard to read. The East End fighter in him was tense but he told himself he was being ridiculous. One just had to look at her sensible shoes and pearls to know she was harmless.

Vivian was scanning the room and for some reason, Jim felt compelled to say, 'It's a bit bleak at the moment but Robert is going to change that.'

With her eyes still darting around the cavernous conservatory, she muttered absentmindedly, 'Robert, yes, Robert with his little interior business.' With a quickness that startled him, Vivian flashed him a direct look and said, 'Surely you have a broom?'

'What?'

'A long-handled broom – for cleaning the pool.' *And for holding people underwater.*

'Yes, it's over there,' he stammered.

'Oh yes, I see it now. I don't see any security cameras in here.'

'What?'

'Christopher and I are thinking about upping our security. You can't be too careful – there are a lot of odd people about.'

'There certainly are,' he said. 'Now, Vivian, I really must see you out. I have a conference call in twenty minutes.'

Graciously Vivian allowed herself to be shown the door, satisfied with her morning's work.

Back in Little Warthing, Robert was pondering what he could do with all that glorious space around Jim's indoor pool.

I may as well focus on work as Paul seems to be engrossed by the news on his phone. Silly me thinking that as he had an eleven o'clock meeting in the area it was an ideal chance for us to spend

*a bit of time together – I'm sure I read somewhere that brunch had
been voted the most romantic meal of the day.*

He looked at the small round table, stylishly set with a lavish
breakfast on chic white plates. This table for two in the bay window
of the kitchen had been the first interior design decision he had
made regarding their home. He could still recall his pleasure when
the estate agent had first shown them this room with its dated
kitchen; the old units could easily be replaced but for Robert,
the room's selling point was this bay window overlooking the
back garden. Upon seeing it, he had instantly envisaged a round
table for two where he and Paul could enjoy leisurely weekend
breakfasts or candlelit suppers together.

And in the early years, there had been so many intimate meals
together, much as he had imagined. They had sat at the table,
laughing, eating and sometimes simply looking at each other.
They would both find any excuse to brush against each other;
the simple act of passing the toast would be laden with erotic
undertones. Their conversation had been different then, too – they
had actually spoken to each other and listened, but perhaps what
Robert missed most was how Paul had noticed and praised any
little act of kindness.

Now when Robert said, 'I got you your favourite marmalade
with champagne from Fortnum's,' Paul didn't look up from his
phone but he did make a grunt of acknowledgement.

With care, Robert placed his silver tea strainer over his fine
porcelain cup and poured himself some delightfully fragrant tea
from his pot. The tea was another recent purchase from Fortnum's.

All in all, it had been an excellent brunch as far as the food
was concerned: dry cured bacon from the local butcher's that had
smelt heavenly from the moment it hit the frying pan, free-range
eggs with yolks as yellow as the summer sun, and seeded bread
still warm from the oven and well worth the early trip to Sophie's
deli.

Yes, the food had been perfect the only thing lacking was …

'I wonder who will win this year's All Hallow's Eve pumpkin-
carving competition?'

Again a grunt from Paul.

'Jim has asked me to do his pool area; it's going to be an interesting project. It's an amazing space and I haven't done anything like it before.'

Not even a grunt this time.

'Speaking of which I'd better get going. I've done some 3-D images for him on my laptop and I want to run them past him to get a feel for what sort of look he wants.'

Deliberately leaving his plate and steaming tea on the table, Robert rose and started to walk away. He had reached the door before Paul looked up.

'Where are you going? You haven't finished your tea.'

Robert paused on the threshold and regarded his husband; he was still breathtakingly beautiful with those dazzling blue eyes, straight nose and perfect jawline but now Robert wasn't sure if that was enough. With a sigh and a sad smile, he said, 'You haven't been listening to a word I've said.'

Paul folded his arms on his chest and subconsciously tucked up his top lip. When he spoke his voice was slightly raised. 'Of course I have, you said you'd bought me my favourite marmalade.'

Chapter 14

For Jim, the time he spent in his pool was rapidly becoming the highlight of his day. He found it hard to believe that he actually enjoyed the cool water caressing his skin. There was no longer a tightening in his chest or the panicked beating of his heart as he approached the pool. He always started his swim gently, from the shallow end where there was a Hollywood-style staircase descending into the water. Each step was of an easy depth and space so walking down them was a pleasure. The way the staircase narrowed at the top and splayed out at the bottom appealed to his sense of beauty.

Today he entered the pool with such confidence that the water soon reached the bottom of his Bermuda-style swimming trunks. These trunks were a gift from Dee and were pale blue, dotted with pink flamingos and made him smile every time he looked at them.

Dee's late today – that's unlike her.

He walked until the water was up to his waist. He stood upright and let his hands make little figures of eight in the water by his legs.

Good thing Robert is going to do something about this room; it's so empty and bleak. It would be great to get some more chairs and a couple of tables. Some plants, too – perhaps a big palm or two.

He lowered himself down into the water, his feet still firmly on the bottom, and allowed the water to wash over his shoulders.

He could hear Dee's voice in his head. 'Breathe in, breathe out. Imagine you're on a tropical beach and relax.'

He tilted his face towards the ceiling and smiled. By gently moving his hands, he allowed the water to support him as he slowly lifted his feet off the bottom. He found it easier to totally relax by shutting his eyes.

As he floated peacefully a wave of joy spread through him. He laughed and proclaimed out loud, 'Just look at your Jimmy, Mum!'

When it happened it was sudden, forceful and violent.

He felt something solid strike his face and his feet struggled to find the pool's floor. Water flooded his nose and mouth. His eyes widened and the salty water burned them. Thrashing all his limbs he tried to get away from whatever it was that was holding him down. He struggled to turn his head away but he was just pushed further down and away from the life-giving air.

His initial surprise was soon overtaken with disbelief, then with blood rushing hot in his veins, skin tingling, heart racing and limbs stiffening, he was back again in that filthy canal – an overwhelmed kid battling for his life. His mind screamed, '*No!*'

Then he was consumed by anger and with renewed force he flexed his arms and legs. His hands were tight fists fighting for survival; he clenched his jaw with determination.

But it was no use, still the hard, solid object pushed him down.

His chest was being crushed. That line from Stevie Smith came to his mind, 'Not waving, but drowning.'

There was a drumming sound in his ears and a strange taste in his mouth then his body went weak and he could no longer make his limbs move.

Sorry, Mum.

And that was it. Blackness.

Dee met Vivian on the doorstep. It was another bright, crisp morning.

'Hello, Vivian,' smiled Dee. Her green eyes sparkled and her skin glowed, which for some reason grated on Vivian, as did the fresh crisp bob which glowed a subtle silver-saffron shade. *Does that woman live in the hairdressers? And I bet her glowing complexion owes more to a facial than her recent bicycle ride.*

Vivian, wearing her classic coat and trademark tweed skirt and sensible shoes, surveyed Dee's jeans, trainers and gilet with distaste. With a polite smile, she waved an envelope in front of Dee's nose and casually stated, 'I came to drop this off, it's an invitation to the Michaelmas Ball.'

Dee raised her eyebrows. 'I'm sure Jim said he'd already accepted; he even partnered with me at a dance practice.' Seeing Vivian's narrowed eyes, she hastily added, 'How kind of you.'

Coldly Vivian said. 'I've rung the doorbell but I got no response. I think Jim must be out.'

'Let me try the door. He's expecting me but I'm late as my car had a flat tyre and I had to cycle.'

Dee slung her small sports bag onto her shoulder and put a hand on the large brass door handle.

She was just about to turn it when Robert's shiny car scrunched up on the gravel. Pausing only to reach for his iPad, Robert leapt out, 'Hello, are we all here to see Jim?'

Dee gave him a welcoming smile that lit up her face with laughter lines. 'Yes, but Vivian says he's not answering the doorbell so I suspect he's in the pool. He's expecting me, so I'm sure it will be alright if we let ourselves in.'

She led the way, calling loudly to give Jim warning of their arrival.

As they neared the end of the passageway and there was still no answering call from Jim, Dee began to feel uneasy. The hairs on the back of her neck started to rise and she strained her ears to catch the slightest sound but apart from the singing of a robin in the garden, all was silent. She didn't like it, it was too quiet, the house felt empty. Something was wrong.

It was she who spotted him first, a pale body slumped and inert on the steps he so admired. With a shriek, she started to run toward him but Robert was faster and he reached Jim first. Without a thought to his brown suede brogues he plunged into the water and wrestled the dead weight onto the side, flipping him onto his stomach and into the recovery position. She knelt beside Jim, the spilt water soaking through her trousers and wetting her knees. Consciously breathing slowly and deeply to remain calm, she felt for a pulse in Jim's neck.

'I think I can feel something – he's freezing cold.'

Robert had already grabbed a nearby towel and was rubbing Jim's body with it.

'Can you roll him onto his back? I need to do CPR.' Dee spoke with authority while frantically thinking, *I hope I can remember what to do.* 'Vivian, ring for an ambulance.'

But Vivian didn't move. She stood stiff and immobile, her lips thin beneath her dark lipstick, her eyes cold. Dee glanced at her sensing she wasn't moving. *Poor thing – she's in shock.* It didn't occur to her that far from Vivian being in shock she was outraged. *How dare that dreadful little woman tell me what to do!*

Robert, having got Jim onto his back, said, 'I'll do it!' He reached into his pocket for his mobile.

Dee ran through her mind what she needed to do – *two quick breaths to the airway and thirty compressions.*

With two fingers under Jim's chin, she tilted his head back and pinched his nose between her finger and thumb. She shot two breaths of air into his mouth then drew a line across his armpit to the centre of Jim's chest and placed the heel of her left hand down on it. Swiftly, with her other hand on top, she did thirty compressions while singing the lyrics to Nelly the Elephant in her head. She seemed to remember from her last life-saving refresher course the lyrics recommended had changed to Staying Alive but now was not the moment for her to stray from Nelly.

Under the pressure of the compression, Jim started to vomit up the pool water. With difficulty, Dee manoeuvred him onto his side to clear his airway; that done she went straight back to another head tilt and two breaths.

She wasn't sure how many rounds she did but she was relieved when Robert said, 'They're on their way – let me take over.'

Dee sat back as Robert set to work. She felt consumed by utter exhaustion so it was a moment or two before she noticed that Vivian was still standing statue-like with a fixed expression on her face. It was the lack of emotion that startled Dee.

'Are you alright, Vivian?'

The words brought her out of her trance-like state. She

glanced at Dee and snapped back, 'Of course, I am!'

Jim was coughing, spluttering and struggling to sit up. He was still in fight mode and his limbs thrashed about with the same violence that he had used when being held under the water and fighting for his life. Robert laughed with relief and tears streamed down his face as he held Jim tightly to his chest and murmured soothingly, 'You're alright, you're safe now, Jimmy.'

As he spoke, he gently rocked backwards and forwards, lightly patting Jim's shoulder and allowing the warmth from his body to seep into Jim's body.

Slowly Jim stopped struggling and allowed himself to be held.

Chapter 15

For Nicholas Corman, the attempted drowning of Jim Stuart raised many more questions and no answers. He stared at the witness statements on his desk. They were from Jim, Dee, Robert and Vivian and contained nothing helpful; the same could be said for the forensic report and all the medical report did was confirm that the bruises on Jim's head and body were consistent with him being held underwater by the pool's long-handled broom. There was no revelation in that; Dee had even pointed the brush out when he and Josh had arrived at the crime scene.

The attacks on Sebastian, Jo and now Jim suggest there is a link with the upcoming new appointment of the Lord-Lieutenant. Nicholas drummed his fingers on his desk. *But then what has Dee got to do with it? She isn't running for Lord-Lieutenant.*

He stood up and wandered over to the filing cabinet where he kept a small water spray for his office plants. *I don't want to cause unnecessary concern but I need to warn Christopher Plover to be careful – as a candidate for the office, he must be in danger.*

He noticed that the spray was empty as was his special bottle of liquid fertiliser; he would need to get some more. Thoughts of going shopping brought to mind the recent incident outside M&S.

Perhaps I should question that scruffy Winston Charter-Fox. Clever of Josh to turn up that old newspaper report of a nineteen-year-old Charter-Fox chaining himself to the railings outside Buckingham Palace.

He recalled the grainy black-and-white photo of a long-haired angry Winston shouting as the police used hefty chain cutters to remove him. *He's anti-monarchy as well as being anti-M&S, but that hardly makes him a would-be murderer. Still, it's worth asking him a few questions; after all from what I've heard he has been very vocal about his contempt for the office of Lord-Lieutenant.*

Reaching for his wallet and car keys, he headed out of the door in pursuit of fertiliser.

A change of scenery will help me think better; at the moment my mind feels like a stagnant pond. I skipped my lunch break so I do have a bit of time. It would be helpful to have someone other than Josh to bounce ideas off. Someone more mature, someone sophisticated, someone who knew socially all the people involved, someone with glorious red hair, green eyes and a piercing wit.

He sighed, got into his car and drove to an excellent nearby garden centre.

He parked and walked through the automatic double doors and was immediately struck by the comforting smell of earth and plants. He was totally unaware of the admiring glances cast his way by various lady shoppers. He was oblivious as to what a striking figure he was, with his shoulders held back and his confident stride. The cleft in his chin, grey eyes and distinguished silvering at his temples only added to his good looks while his light cologne marked him out as a gentleman of style.

He knew exactly where he was going and walked past a couple of yummy mummies with buggies as well as a member of staff in a navy sweatshirt and brown apron. He ignored the lifestyle section with its overpriced clothes and furniture, then he bypassed the man playing ambient music on a baby grand piano.

The houseplant area was artistically presented. It was reminiscent of a jungle, with trailing plants suspended from beams and other plants arranged in pyramids on round trestle tables. There were light and airy horse ferns, not to mention every flowering plant imaginable with perhaps the greatest emphasis on orchids. Here, there was a faint sound of rustling leaves and a bird that must have flown in by mistake was competing with the piano for melody. The scent of greenery drifted towards him via a fine water mist. Natural daylight flooded in from generous skylights, making the room bright and airy.

Nicholas was just heading towards the shelf where he knew they kept his favourite fertiliser when he caught a glimpse of Zara through the trailing ferns. He stopped walking and stared. He took in her saffron curls, her jade eyes, and her confident dancer's stance. Her chin was tilted a little, exposing her porcelain neck. She looked serene and thoughtful as she compared two different orchids. It seemed to Nicholas that all this foliage had somehow lulled her normal aura of high energy into something approaching tranquillity.

He had never pictured her in this setting; a darkened salsa bar – yes, a bordello in Argentina – yes, but never a flower shop. The bordello was a bit of a flight of fancy, but it was understandable as they had performed a rather stirring tango in a dance competition at the Manx Villa Marina that summer.

Nicholas looked some more and decided that this verdant setting suited her. She was wearing a bottle-green military coat which emphasised her fair skin.

Perhaps the coat is a shade warm in here – she looks a little flushed.

He swallowed and walked over to her.

She glanced at him and smiled.

It is extremely warm just here; they must turn the heating up for the potted plants, thought Nicholas as he smiled back.

'Ah! Nicholas, you are just the person I need,' she purred.

'I am?' he stammered and swallowed again.

'Yes.' She looked up at him through her long lashes. 'I need your help.'

'You do?'

She nodded and he noticed the way the light caught her saffron strands.

'I'm trying to pick an orchid for my mother – a little pick-me-up from all the nasty business at Jim's, but I can't decide which one.'

She held up a large one with ruffle-edged white petals with a brash purple centre. 'This one is too blousy but this one is …' She picked up a standard plain white orchid.

'Too ordinary,' supplied Nicholas.

Pensively he surveyed the many orchids on display, then he

smiled and selected a perfect specimen with delicate small yellow flowers. And in a line reminiscent of Goldilocks and the Three Bears he announced, 'Whereas this one is just right.'

He presented it to her with a flourish and was rewarded with a warm smile.

Before his cautious, rational mind had time to intervene, he heard himself ask, 'Do you have time for a coffee?'

'Another excellent suggestion.' She beamed and, tucking her hand in the crook of his arm, she directed him to the restaurant.

Like the rest of the garden centre, the eating area was beautifully designed and laid out. Sturdy wooden chairs were placed around neat tables, each decorated with a plant in an antique terracotta pot. Fairy lights twinkled in the rafters. Nicholas had always considered fairy lights to be rather twee but now, as he pulled a chair out for Zara to sit, the lighting struck him as enchanting, perhaps even romantic.

He bought a mint tea for her and a coffee for himself. She chose a chocolate cupcake that Nicholas initially thought looked far too rich but then he noticed that she had picked up two cake forks, so obviously intended for them to share it. Suddenly that cupcake seemed most appetising.

'Won't coffee keep you awake tonight?' she enquired.

'I'll be up anyway; there seems to be a lot happening around Little Warthing at the moment.'

She brushed a stray curl away from her eyes and regarded him steadily. 'Yes, what do you make of it all?' she asked.

He looked at her sparkling eyes and her slightly parted lips and suddenly the last thing he wanted to talk about was grubby little crimes in Little Warthing.

Hastily he said, 'Let's not talk about that. Tell me, where would you most like to travel to?'

He wanted to add, 'with me' but his courage failed him.

Chapter 16

Robert arrived at the art gallery on time. The train ride into London had been easy, he'd found a taxi immediately and traffic had been light.

Jim was waiting for him outside, wearing a sleek cashmere coat and a silk scarf. Robert liked the way his eyes creased with warmth when he saw him.

'Hello and welcome,' was Jim's greeting as he clapped Robert on the shoulder. 'We'll just get rid of our coats then we can join Dee inside.'

Robert was confused. 'Sorry, am I late?'

'Not at all. Dee and I came up together and were early.'

The art gallery was one Robert had read about in the glossy sections of the Sunday papers as was the artist whose works they were about to view. He had read articles about the young woman that were peppered with adjectives like 'visionary' and 'skilled'. She favoured sculptures that were contemporary but with a nod to Renaissance realism.

It soon became apparent that far from only reading about this exclusive gallery in the papers, Jim was a frequent visitor. The young woman taking coats greeted him by name and he in turn, asked after her little boy.

He led Robert through a spacious entrance with a single intriguing sculpture on a plinth. Here, they were greeted by the artist herself – again Jim knew her personally and he introduced Robert to her and made some charming comment about how her sculpture in the lobby had filled him with anticipation.

The gallery itself was surprisingly large, given its central London location. The ceilings were high and the artworks were few, so there was a feeling of space. A slight citrus scent hung in the air and Robert couldn't decide whether it came from the room or Jim's cologne. There were three rooms linked by open doorways and a smattering of well-dressed patrons in each room, admiring the works and discussing them in low voices with their crisp glasses of champagne in hand.

In the first room, he spotted Dee. She seemed very much in her element, taking her time to walk around a tall and willowy work. She was wearing a beautifully-cut tuxedo trouser suit in caramel with a pop of colour supplied by a statement necklace in a shade of coral that complemented her auburn colouring.

This was Robert's idea of a perfect evening: culture to feed his soul, friends to warm his heart and an aesthetically pleasing setting. He smiled and relaxed, willing to enjoy every moment.

Jim's 'thank you for rescuing me from a watery grave' package did not stop at the gallery; when their appetite for the visual arts was satiated, he whisked them to an equally elegant restaurant. Again there were high ceilings and the clientele spoke in low voices while wearing understated tailoring.

Robert was not surprised that Jim was well-known here nor that the maître d' took great pleasure in talking him through the wine list. They started with Bollinger, with the promise of a Barolo to come. He enjoyed every element of the meal, from the thick linen tablecloth and the weight of the crystal glasses to the exquisite subtlety of the food, but what he found most pleasurable was Jim's animated enthusiasm as he talked about wine, vineyards and walking holidays combining the two.

It was towards the end of the evening when they had all opted for a mint tea to finish off the meal, that the attempted drowning came up.

In the first silence of the evening, Jim looked up from staring at the steaming green tisane in the cup in front of him. Quietly he confessed, 'Strangely, after what has happened, I seem to be spending less time wondering who could have done it and more time reflecting on my life.'

'Your life?' prompted Robert.

Jim directed his gaze openly into Robert's eyes and with a

wry smile explained, 'There's nothing like almost losing your life to make you evaluate how one spends one's time.'

Robert smiled and almost reached out to touch Jim's hand. 'I know what you mean. I've been questioning my life choices a lot recently. Perhaps it's our age – after all, we've got less time in front of us than behind us, so we need to make every moment count.'

Dee who was far too busy enjoying her life to ever question how she was spending it, asked, 'So, any conclusions?'

Jim shook his head. 'Not really, but I'm contemplating taking a year's sabbatical to tour the world's vineyards and simply live. I've always been pushing for the next deal, the next step and looking for new opportunities. As for the role of Lord-Lieutenant – I'm not even sure I want it.'

There was a silence around the table then Dee cheerfully chipped in. 'If you're travelling the world we need to get you swimming again.'

Jim was caught between fear, amusement and longing. 'Okay!' he said with a degree of hesitation.

'Count me in; we'll make it a party,' announced Robert with a grin.

'A spa day is such a wonderful idea! Zara, you are both a genius and very generous.'

Dee could not have been happier. Here she was wrapped in a fluffy white robe having been massaged with fragrant oils and generally made to feel like a goddess by a bevy of charming young women in crisp uniforms and impeccable makeup. Her muscles were relaxed, she took easy breaths and thought about how lucky she was to have Zara and Amelia in her life to share idyllic days like this.

'Yeah, Mum, it's wicked,' confirmed Amelia who, in a towel robe and without makeup, looked very young and pretty and not at all Goth-like. Her red curls were wrapped up in a white towel turban and she looked the picture of ease as she lay back on the beige steamer bed with a glass of lemon water at her side.

Zara smiled. Her eyes were shut with a slice of cooling cucumber on each one. 'I do love it here. They've got everything just right from soothing lighting to the professionalism of the masseuses. This relaxation room has to be the best bit – I could stay here forever. I rather like the soft background sounds of birdsong and gently running water.'

Dee found the sound of the gently running water made her want to go to the loo but she didn't want to spoil the moment by mentioning it. Instead, with a lightness in her chest and a delicious warmth spreading through her body, she focused on a feeling of satisfaction and mentally congratulated herself on a job well done. *Zara and Amelia are both wonderful and I'm so proud to be their mother and grandmother.*

She sighed and shut her eyes allowing herself to simply doze.

'So what are both of your thoughts?' asked Amelia, breaking the calm silence.

'On what?' asked Dee.

'All the stuff going on in Little Warthing – Sebastian's blackmail letter, Granny's brakes, the fire at the woods and now the attempt to drown Jim Stuart. We've got more drama going on than an episode of EastEnders.'

There was a very mild note of asperity in Zara's voice when she replied, 'Darling, I specifically wanted us all to come here so we could forget about all that nastiness and think about nice things instead.'

'Well, since we're all together we may as well just do a little brainstorming,' said Dee hopefully.

Zara sighed. 'Alright, I can see I'm outnumbered.' Then with haste and enthusiasm that totally belied her previous statement, she eagerly asked, 'Are you sure you didn't hear or see anything which might help when you arrived at Jim's house?'

'No, it was like I said; I was late and when I went to my car the tyre was totally flat, with a nail sticking in it. Goodness knows where I picked it up.'

'Well, that sounds deeply suspicious to me,' said Amelia. 'After all, if you hadn't had a puncture you would have been there at your normal time and no dastardly deed could have been committed. Who knew what time you and Jim usually have a swim?'

Zara, from beneath her cucumbers, said, 'That won't wash. Granny has been going every morning at nine; you know what villages are like, they will have all been talking about it.'

Amelia nodded thoughtfully, 'That's true, when I was in the Flying Pheasant the other day, Alex and Marcelo were teasing me that my Granny had a toy boy and that the sports bag she takes every day is just a ruse.'

Dee spluttered, spilling some of her lemon water. 'What? Surely not? But how do they know I've been going to Jim's? I could be going anywhere.'

Still serene from under her cooling cucumbers, Zara added, 'That's from the postman – I gather he drops the post at Jim's at about the time you normally arrive there and then he comes on to the village.'

'Well, really!' said Dee indignantly.

Amelia was still in interrogation mode. 'So we'll need to leave the question of the nail in the tyre for now. Granny, what exactly happened when you arrived at the house?'

'Vivian was there trying to get in. I mean she was on the doorstep, knocking. She had an invitation for Jim for the Michaelmas Ball.'

Zara interjected. 'She is rather overexcited about the ball.'

Amelia was determined to keep things on track. 'Then what?'

'Not a lot. Robert arrived and I suggested we went inside.'

'And you noticed nothing unusual?'

'Nothing until we saw Jim slumped on the steps of the pool. There was some water on the poolside, but not as much as I would have expected from the fight he must have put up. Oh, and the long-handled broom was lying out. Sorry, I really can't tell you any more. It's like the fire; I really can't see any use in trying to work out who is doing this.'

'Oh Granny, I really would have expected you to be more observant. I don't know where we go from here.' Amelia sounded despondent as she snuggled down into her comfy chair with a sigh.

'Sorry, dear. I have been through it all over and over again in my mind but really there's nothing. I must say I was pleased Robert was with me; I'm not sure I would have been strong enough to haul Jim out of the water by myself.'

'What about Vivian?' asked Zara who was still looking the picture of relaxed repose, lying swathed in her fluffy robe.

'The poor lady went into a total daze and wasn't really good for anything. Once I'd got over the initial shock of Jim's predicament, I was quite worried about her.'

Amelia smiled. 'You do surprise me, she always strikes me as being frightfully efficient. She's exactly the sort of bossy woman I imagine running the home front during the war and being in her element telling everyone what to do.'

Dee smiled back at her. 'Yes, I do know what you mean but I think the sight of Jim looking like he'd drowned triggered something in her and she just sort of froze.'

Zara removed the cucumbers and sat up a little on her tilted recliner. 'Oh, I know what that's all about. Christopher once mentioned how he would like to put a water feature in the garden, you know an ornamental pond or some such, but Vivian wouldn't hear of it.'

'Why?' asked Dee.

'Some sort of childhood trauma involving her sister's puppy that drowned. She's fine with swimming in the sea and swimming pools and the like, but she has a thing about water otherwise.'

Dee nodded. 'That explains a lot. The poor thing really was in a bad way. Apart from the way in which she just stopped functioning, she went so white and her eyes were sort of glazed.'

Amelia had lost interest in Vivian and announced, 'With the blackmail letters to Sebastian, the fire with Jo and now this with Jim, whoever is doing this must be motivated by the race for the Lord-Lieutenant.'

'Darling,' Dee deployed her gentle voice, always useful when hoping to disagree without provoking conflict. 'You are assuming it's only one person, but blackmail, arson and attempted drowning are all very different crimes. Also, why involve me? I have nothing to do with the office of Lord-Lieutenant.'

Amelia replied calmly, 'I know Little Warthing is an unusual village but I really think it's highly unlikely there would be two criminal nutters operating there at the same time. And as for you, Granny, let's face it, as far as murderers are concerned you are as attractive as picnics are to ants.'

Zara nodded. 'You know she's right – I don't know why but you are a total murder magnet; it's one of your least attractive qualities.'

'I'm not sure how to respond to that,' said Dee placidly as she selected a couple of chilled cucumber slices from a saucer on the side table and relaxed back in her chair with one on each eye. 'I'm not sure you're right, Amelia, about the motivation being linked to the role of Lord-Lieutenant. I mean, does anyone really care that much about it?'

'Wow, Mum, you should have been at a lecture I had last week all about the psychological effect of status or lack of it – it's literally mind-blowing. And as for no one caring, just get Granny's new neighbour, Winston Charter-Fox, onto the subject – it really is a case of "light the blue touch paper and stand back".'

Zara frowned. 'What, that scruffy old chap who always looks as if he could do with a shave and an iron? Surely, he doesn't want to be Lord-Lieutenant? I wouldn't have thought it would be his sort of thing at all.'

Both Amelia and Dee started to laugh. In Dee's case, she laughed so hard the cucumbers slid off her face. When she had stopped giggling enough to speak she explained, 'No dear, he doesn't want to be Lord-Lieutenant, he wants the role abolished along with the monarchy, but the idea of him in all the regalia is priceless.'

She started laughing again and both Zara and Amelia joined her. Their laughter was infectious and soon they were laughing not so much at the vision of Winston Charter-Fox being driven to crime in his drive to become Lord-Lieutenant, but by the sight and sound of the others giggling away.

After a few moments, Dee regained enough equilibrium to inject a note of seriousness into the conversation. 'If you are right and there is a link to the office of Lord-Lieutenant, the candidates are thin on the ground now. Sebastian is out—'

'Jake thinks it's all for the best, he's quite excited about that old pile being sold. They plan to get a flat in London and both think that cottage in Little Warthing you found them, Mum, is ideal.'

'I thought the Aga in the kitchen would be ideal for the dogs,' smiled Zara, indulging in a bit of professional pride.

'Yes, it's excellent that the Labradors are happy, but as I was saying, Sebastian is out and Jo told me when I visited her in hospital yesterday that she isn't sure if she will be up to it, and Jim is talking about heading off for an extended tour of European vineyards, so that only leaves—'

'Christopher!' supplied Zara.

'Perhaps, he's behind it all?' suggested Amelia.

Thoughtfully, Dee shook her head. 'No, I don't think he really wants it, certainly not enough to want to harm anyone. He's such a gentle soul and I think he would be quite happy left alone with his vegetable garden.'

Zara sat up straight and alert. 'But Vivian desperately wants him to be Lord-Lieutenant – she is already busy buying hats.'

With a giggle, Amelia finished her suggestion. 'So perhaps Vivian is behind all this.'

They all looked at each other and then began to laugh totally uncontrollably.

After laughing until their stomachs ached and tears run down their faces they began to calm down, only to be set off again by Zara saying, 'I didn't think anything could be funnier than the idea of Winston Charter-Fox being Lord-Lieutenant, but Vivian as a villain beats it into a cocked hat.' She started laughing once more. 'Can you imagine her plotting mayhem in her sensible shoes and tweed skirt?'

Zara lost her words in her own laughter.

Giggling away Amelia added, 'Lipstick in place with her

perm pristine and rigid.'

Wiping away a tear, Zara attempted a serious note, 'I wonder what the correct etiquette for blackmail is?'

Amelia quipped back, 'Always cut out the letters from a suitable source such as *Country Life?*'

Zara nodded and added, 'Imagine Vivian carrying petrol along all those muddy paths in Warthing Woods – she'd have to swap her sensible shoes for wellies!'

After another bout of communal giggles Dee said, 'Joking aside, I will have a word with Christopher. I'm sure Nicholas will have already spoken to him but if there is a maniac about with a thing about Lord-Lieutenants, he needs to be careful.'

Vivian and Christopher were blithely unaware that they were being talked about. Vivian was in an ebullient mood which made Christopher and consequently Bramble, happy. Christopher was pleased that the warning from the policeman chappy had not dampened Vivian's happy anticipation of the evening.

She's made of stern stuff, thought Christopher proudly. *It takes more than knowing her husband might be in danger from an anti-establishment madman to put her off preparing for a dinner party. The old girl is in her element organising this sort of thing. She would be excellent in the role of wife to the Lord-Lieutenant.*

He mused as he watched her directing Mrs Jenkins' replacement. Mrs Jenkins, with her big thighs and excellent cleaning skills, had been substituted for two young girls who chewed gum and rolled their eyes whenever Vivian reprimanded them. Christopher was surprised that she put up with them, but when he'd asked she'd muttered something about her preferring them because they didn't snoop into things that didn't concern them.

The silver candelabra had been polished, the best china brought out and a sumptuous meal was about to be delivered by an exclusive caterer. Not only was the caterer sensational at cooking but she was also discreet, which was necessary as Christopher knew that Vivian would lie and say she'd cooked it all herself.

'So lovely that Victoria's parents are back and were free this evening,' announced Vivian gleefully as she placed the floral centrepiece down on the table that was already groaning with silver and crystal. She stood back with her head on one side and admired it. Even Christopher could tell that the florist had done an excellent job. He pushed to the back of his mind the uncomfortable knowledge that in the same way Vivian would shamelessly take credit for the food she would also suggest that the flowers were her doing; when the guests would compliment the lavish arrangement Vivian would modestly blush and say something about flower arranging being one of her little pleasures.

'It will be so interesting to hear about their cruise,' continued Vivian while actually thinking that she would be sure to press them about speaking to the PM about Christopher's suitability for the role of Lord-Lieutenant.

The guests were expected at seven-thirty and Vivian was confident that the house looked its best. She took a moment to check her own reflection in the mirror in her bedroom and she was well-satisfied both with her reflection and with where she was in her campaign.

She was wearing a bottle-green velvet dress which softened her bony thinness and her hair was bouffant and stiff from a visit to the hairdresser.

I am at my prime; certainly, my intellect is at its height. I wouldn't be surprised if on some level my subconscious hadn't arranged it so Jim Stuart didn't actually die but got enough of a fright that he's reconsidering his life and whether he wants to be Lord-Lieutenant. After all, his death would have had the police swarming like flies, whereas this way I achieve my objective but with less fuss.

She cocked her head thoughtfully to one side.

Not that I need to worry about the police – idiots, the lot of them. Take that imbecile of a policeman, Nicolas Corman – he was totally clueless when he sat in my drawing room this morning. He looked so concerned as he wittered on about Christopher having to be careful as there was just a chance that someone was conspiring against the candidates for the role of Lord-Lieutenant. The fool of a man – I only had to look and squeeze out a trickle of a tear and he was totally taken in; he was positively oozing sympathy.

She gave a snort of derision.

'What was that dear?' asked Christopher, sticking his head in the door.

'Nothing,' replied Vivian, a faint smile curling her dark-red lacquered lips.

'My mistake, thought I heard you say something.' He regarded her for a moment, 'You do look … nice.'

Vivian winced at the use of such a common little adjective but smiled graciously and surveying Christopher's shiny shoes and velvet smoking jacket said, 'You look very acceptable yourself.'

His heart soared and he was as happy as Bramble was when she received a pat on the head.

Christopher greatly enjoyed the evening, especially the oysters.

At three o'clock in the morning, the calm of Little Warthing was abruptly disrupted by the deafening sound of an ambulance siren.

Chapter 17

'Christopher would want us to carry on,' said Vivian, looking into the far distance.

She was rather enjoying the role she had decided to play; she felt noble with a pleasing hint of humility. Her chin was held high, her shoulders back; she knew she was invincible.

'Oh, that is so good of you, I do admire your fortitude,' exclaimed the wide-eyed vicar.

Fortitude? Yes, that's right – I am a woman of fortitude. Take the Persian rug in the bedroom for example, it will never be the same again; why Christopher had to vomit all over it is beyond me but that's so typical of him. He never has any consideration. Yes, the Persian rug may be ruined but I am facing its damage with fortitude. I haven't even mentioned it.

It was taking all of Vivian's iron will not to let her air of bravery in the face of adversity morph into smugness.

Fortitude and genius – yes, those are my key characteristics. She suppressed a smile.

Just enough rotten oyster – a mere hint – and Christopher is ill but not dead. That idiot of a policeman might say it's probably food poisoning, but I know he suspects foul play. So there we have it: Christopher and I cannot possibly be thought of as in any way to blame for all these attacks as we too are victims.

Bramble was rubbing up against the vicar's leg, desperate for a bit of love. Vivian hadn't fully taken into account that in Christopher's absence she would be Bramble's sole caregiver, but Tristan would be down soon and he would look after the dog, so, for now, she could focus on being brave, resolute and generally admirable.

Vivian had been about to modestly add, 'It's nothing,' but the vicar was speaking again. 'We couldn't really have cancelled the All Hallow's Eve party as all the invitations have gone out and besides, I understand that Christopher is much better.'

Vivian pressed her lips together in a tight smile. *You stupid little woman; you have no idea, but then how could you?*

She had felt annoyed when the vicar had knocked at the kitchen door. *Why does no one use the front door? Don't they know the back door is for trade? I blame Christopher – he will encourage this overfamiliarity with the neighbours.*

Now there was another knock on the kitchen door and, as if this gangly vicar wasn't enough, it was the ghastly FitzMorris woman.

'Dee, how lovely to see you.'

Dee was wrapped up against the cold in a cosy navy Puffa jacket with a coordinating beanie hat and gloves. Vivian found it vaguely annoying that for Dee, that morning's winter wind hadn't produced a pink nose and chapped lips as it had on the vicar. If anything, the inclement weather only made Dee glow with good health. *Odious woman!*

'Good morning.' Dee sounded as bright as she looked. 'Vicar, you are probably here on the same errand I am.'

Vicar Virginia smiled and felt relieved that Dee had arrived. Being alone with Vivian was somehow unnerving. 'Pumpkins?'

'Exactly!' beamed Dee. 'I just popped in to see Christopher in hospital and I must say he is a wonderful man. I mean, he has obviously had an awful time, but his only thought was to make sure that his pumpkins made it to the All Hallow's Eve party.'

Vivian clenched her jaw and Bramble hid behind Dee's legs. *Bloody man! Why does everything have to be about him? And how dare he grow pumpkins on the sly for the All Hallows' Eve party when he knows I want to discourage it? That's not at all the sort of thing we want going on in the village. I don't know how many times I've told him that I only volunteer to help out for appearances and because for some reason the old Lord-Lieutenant and his wife seem to think it's fun.*

Both women were eyeing her with concern but it was Dee

who spoke. 'Vivian, do you need to sit down? You've gone a bit pale. Tell you what, we'll help ourselves to the pumpkins – Christopher told me they're in the greenhouse – and then we'll leave you in peace.'

They were relieved to be out of the warm kitchen and in the late autumn cold. They headed towards Christopher's domain. What he liked to refer to as his 'vegetable patch' was actually a small walled garden that had been a kitchen garden for the house since it was built. It was on the other side of the lawn and beautifully laid out in a way that would have brought joy to Mr McGregor and Benjamin Bunny's hearts. Christopher kept his garden to the same standard of excellence that Vivian kept the house; the gravel paths were raked, every bed turned over and matured and the fruit trees against the south wall were a lesson in espalier.

The greenhouse at its centre was the sort favoured by King Charles and featured at Chelsea – a monument to practicality and beauty in glass. Warmth and the pungent scent of damp earth and plants greeted them as they went inside on their pumpkin quest. It was easy to spot the area set aside for pumpkins; the enormous curly leaves and inquisitive tendrils spilled out from one corner. On the nearby bench was an array of golden beauties that Christopher had already harvested in preparation for the All Hallow's Eve party.

Virginia, with some difficulty, picked up the largest one and grinning at Dee said, 'You can easily see why Cinderella's fairy godmother made one of these into a carriage.'

Dee laughed and picked up another one. 'I think we'll need to borrow Christopher's wheelbarrow or we'll never manage to get all these to the new village hall.'

'Oh, rather!' agreed Virginia.

Moments later as they were loading the pumpkins into the clean and well-oiled wheelbarrow Virginia tentatively asked, 'Dee?'

'Mmm?' said Dee, while admiring a particularly fine specimen.

'I say …'

Dee looked up. She liked the way Virginia used expressions straight out of the 1930s; they went with the rounded vowels. She looked at the young woman's wild frizzy hair, shiny nose and shapeless coat and wondered why the look didn't match the voice. She had a quick vision of Virginia with her hair cut in a shiny flapper bob under a tight-fitting cloche hat and wearing a stylish fur-trimmed coat. She glanced at the squidgy-soled lace-ups that Virginia habitually wore on her feet and immediately replaced them with a pair of kitten heels.

'Dee?' persisted Virginia.

Dee refocussed. 'Yes, dear?'

Virginia's pale smooth forehead was creased and her thick unkempt eyebrows were drawn together. 'As you know, this is my first year in Little Warthing, and I was just wondering if it was always so …' She trailed off, at a loss for the right adjective.

'Friendly?' suggested Dee, looking up hopefully at the much taller woman.

Virginia shook her head. 'No, so full of crime.'

'Oh,' said Dee, rapidly calculating that it was probably better not to mention all those clown murders that plagued the village a few months earlier. *Nothing can be served by alarming the poor girl. After all, this is her first parish and I would hate to worry her.*

'What do you mean?' hedged Dee.

Virginia picked up the handles of the wheelbarrow and winced at the cold. Dee made a mental note to give her gloves for Christmas.

'Well, first there was all that unpleasantness with Sebastian and those vicious blackmail letters, then that horrific arson attack on you and Jo at Warthing Woods, then Jim nearly drowned and now this with Christopher.'

'But they think Christopher just had food poisoning. Oysters can be dodgy, so there's nothing sinister in that,' said Dee hastily, while holding open a gate for Virginia to wheel the barrow through.

'So you think it's all just coincidence? I'm not allowed to believe in luck – good or bad – but common sense suggests that all these happenings would make Little Warthing the unluckiest village in the Cotswolds.'

'Um,' said Dee again desperate not to let slip that the vicar had forgotten to include her brake line being cut.

By now they were on the pavement outside the Plovers' home and walking steadily towards the village hall.

'I'm beginning to wonder if there is some madman living in this village. He would have to be a very angry troubled soul to want to harm so many people.'

They rounded a corner and collided with Winston Charter-Fox. His grey mac was flapping in the wind and his lifeless complexion looked even more pallid with the cold weather. Dee couldn't help thinking she'd seen more colour on a cadaver in the morgue.

The two women exchanged slightly worried meaningful looks before Dee recovered her innate good manners.

Smiling she spoke rather too quickly. 'Mr Charter-Fox – it's getting cold, isn't it?'

He scowled. 'What do you expect? It's nearly winter.'

'Quite. Aren't these beauties?' Dee indicated the mass of voluptuous orange pumpkins; her jaw was beginning to ache in her effort to remain bright and friendly. 'We're just taking them down to the village hall for the All Hallow's Eve party. Are you sure you won't change your mind and come?'

'It's going to be frightfully jolly – apple-bobbing, pumpkin-carving and there's always lots of delicious food,' agreed Virginia.

Winston Charter-Fox looked at her with narrow eyes. 'I don't hold with events that sanction puffed-up symbols of inequality. I hear that the Lord-Lieutenant judged the last cookie competition.'

'Well, yes, he did, but the evening isn't really so much about sanctioning puffed-up symbols of inequality it's more about playing silly games and eating a lot,' Virginia said, but without much conviction.

Dee came to her aid. 'Tell you what, Mr Charter-Fox, let me buy you a ticket to welcome you to the village – at least you won't have to cook yourself supper that night.'

Winston hesitated, calculating the weight of his principles

against the chance of a free meal and the saving in electricity if he accepted. Eventually, he said, 'What time?'

The first thing Emily noticed as Tristan turned the car into Little Warthing was how much evidence there was that autumn was turning to winter. Clusters of red-berried shrubs shone in front of sandstone cottages and Virginia creepers now blazed ruby where before they'd been golden. The numerous tall and stately beech trees boasted canopies of rusty leaves that were now translucent rather than impenetrable, but the most telling sign of winter was that it was a lot colder.

Emily snuggled in her cosy sweater and remarked, 'I'm surprised Vivian was happy to have us down for the weekend with Christopher still in hospital.'

Tristan shrugged, 'She said something about how we must do our bit to support the village by attending the All Hallows' Eve party and that the show must go on whatever Christopher was doing. Besides, I think she's finding Bramble a bit much.'

Traffic out of London had been bad so they were late reaching the Plovers' home; Victoria was already in her room getting ready for the party and Vivian was out at the village hall helping with setting everything up.

'I'll just go and change,' said Emily nervously as she firmly shut Tristan out of his room.

Her costume wasn't what she would ideally have chosen – it was rather too overtly suggestive and seductive for her tastes but it was all the man in the shop had left.

Still, thank goodness Victoria rang to warn me to bring a costume – typical Tristan not to mention that everyone in the village dresses up. I would have felt like a right twit in my jeans and sweater with everyone else looking like ghosts and goblins. I wonder what Vivian has gone as – somehow I can't imagine her in fancy dress, although she would make an excellent witch.

She quickly reprimanded herself for such an uncharitable thought and regarded her reflection in the mirror. She was surprised by how much the outfit had cost, given that there wasn't a lot of it. It was little more than a black body stocking; it skimmed over every curve in her body but somehow was cut in a way that emphasised her boobs.

Oh, help! Well, there's nothing I can do about it now so I may as well go the whole hog.

She placed the Alice band with two triangular cats' ears into her blonde curls, then took her black eyeliner and carefully drew cats' whiskers splaying out along her cheeks and added a convincing black dot on the end of her nose.

'What's taking so long?' called Tristan. 'Victoria and I are waiting.'

'Just coming!' Emily replied giving herself a final glance in the full-length mirror.

'We'll be in the kitchen and for goodness sake hurry up; we're already late.'

As Emily took the stairs two at a time she vaguely wondered what Victoria would be dressed as. *Something flamboyantly fabulous no doubt. Tristan is probably just putting a couple of fake tattoos on his face, as he hasn't changed.*

She paused outside the kitchen door and steadied herself with a deep breath, then another, as she thought of her reflection in the mirror and realised that Tristan was about to see her – more or less all of her – as the costume left very little to the imagination.

Deciding she needed to cover her embarrassment by making a grand entrance, she threw open the door and sang out, 'Ta-da!'

Both Tristan and Victoria stood in their jeans and sweaters, staring at her. Tristan, with a total lack of subtlety, scanned her from top to toe; there was a notable pause when he reached her chest area. His eyes were wide and his mouth dropped open.

'You're not in …' Emily began but her voice trailed away and her eyes went from Tristan to Victoria.

Victoria with her perfectly casually-styled hair, her expensive sweater and her beautiful face was smirking, no, not smirking, she was trying to hold in the gales of laughter that were threatening to explode. Her eyes were shining with delight.

Emily looked back at Tristan and to her horror she saw that

his lips were curling into a smile. Her shoulders drooped; never had she wished more to be anywhere else than where she was.

Her eyes filled with tears and her voice cracked as she quietly mumbled, 'It's not a fancy dress party, is it?'

At this Victoria could contain herself no longer and with laughter filling her reply said, 'Hardly!'

Emily turned to run. She ignored Tristan calling her name and Victoria's drawl insisting, 'It's a joke, can't you take a joke?'

As she threw herself, sobbing, onto Tristan's bed, her mind was in too much turmoil to work out why she was so upset. She only knew she had to get out of there and fast.

Downstairs Tristan was laughing, more out of a hot embarrassment at the effect of seeing Emily looking so curvaceous and sexy than out of a sense of fun.

Victoria took his mirth as confirmation that she really had been rather clever and witty, so she was surprised by the look in his eyes as he turned to her and said, 'You didn't tell her it was fancy dress, did you?'

'Yes!' said Victoria, still laughing.

'Why?' Tristan's voice was cold.

This was not at all how Victoria had imagined things playing out; she'd visualised a return to their old pre-Emily comradeship as they shared this prank.

'It's a joke! Can't she take a joke?' she snapped, narrowing her eyes and staring at him intensely.

He wasn't laughing now; there wasn't even a hint of a smile. She started tapping her foot and fiddled with her chunky gold bracelet.

'God, talk about being oversensitive! Can't she even take a little fun?'

Tristan was already walking away. He was at as much of a loss to decipher his feelings as Emily was; beyond being aware of his own heartbeat and longing to hold her in his arms he was unsure as to what was going on between them.

The bedroom door was locked, which didn't surprise him, but did somehow annoy him.

'Emily?' His voice was soft and tentative as was the gentle knock on the door that accompanied it.

There was no reply but he could hear her moving around the room.

'Emily, please let me in.'

Still no reply.

'She didn't mean it nastily. It was just a joke.'

There was still no reply, but there was a crash as something was thrown on the floor, so obviously that wasn't the right thing to say.

He knocked again and this time when he spoke there was an unmistakable pleading note in his voice. 'Please let me in. I thought you look sensational.'

There was the sound of the lock turning in the door and Tristan felt a surge of relief but when the door opened he could see that there was nothing to be relieved about.

Emily was back in her jeans, her eyes were red and she had only half-managed to wipe off her whiskers. She had her coat on and her suitcase was packed and in her hand.

He stepped forward, desperate to embrace her and make everything right, but the look she threw him froze him to the spot.

Her voice had a cold edge he'd never heard before. 'I've called a taxi. I'm going home. I don't belong here and I never will.'

The village hall was almost ready for the party. Christopher's pumpkins took pride of place; displayed near the entrance, they set the scene.

Virginia was flitting around nervously. In her hand was her list of when things were going to happen and what she needed to check.

She was muttering under her breath, 'So, seven o'clock greet arrivals, seven-thirty parade of the kiddies in fancy dress. I have emphasised that this is a church festival, not a Halloween party, so no *dark* costumes, but what am I going to do if any of the little dears turn up as witches?'

Dee overheard her as she was walking past and said, 'Don't worry, I think all children that are likely to come already go to Sunday school and you have made it quite clear what is expected.'

She didn't add that she had mentioned it there to the point of boredom, nor did she share that when she had been helping little Johnnie Watterson with his reading at the village school last Wednesday, he had asked why the vicar was always talking about witches.

Virginia looked at Dee with relief and then rather wistfully added, 'Do you think next year we ought to open the dressing up to adults? I've always rather fancied myself as someone out of a Jane Austin novel or one of Lavinia Lovelace's historical romances – you know, all flowing muslin.'

Dee glossed over the fact that she adored Lavinia Lovelace too and had actually met the author in person and just said, 'Excellent idea and you would look stunning.'

Virginia blushed but quickly moved on. 'And you think the tables against the far wall will be alright for the carved pumpkins?'

Dee nodded. 'They'll look very striking there, especially when they're lit.'

'And the cookies will go on the round table in the middle.' She glanced at it. 'Oh good, the tablecloth is already on it and that arrangement is suitably tall and seasonal.'

Again Dee nodded. 'Those Chinese lanterns look great – really, Virginia, everything is ready and there's nothing for you to worry about.'

But Virginia's forehead was still puckered in concern. 'I'm not very happy about you having to do the apple-bobbing in the storeroom – you'll be so cut off from all the fun.'

Dee laughed. 'We'll be having plenty of fun ourselves and it really is the only place we could put the bobbing for apples – there is always such a lot of water spilled and although that's half the fun, it does mean that if we set it up in the main hall someone would be bound to slip, even with all the towels I've put round the bowl.'

Virginia shuddered. 'I've never been very keen on apple-bobbing, not since I saw David Suchet as Poirot in Agatha Christie's *Halloween Party*. That poor girl drowning while bobbing for apples gave me nightmares.'

At that moment Vivian walked past wearing an oversized plastic apron decorated with autumn fruits and carrying a tray of drinks. 'I'll put these on the table by the door so people can help themselves as they arrive.'

Virginia gushed, 'Vivian, you are a star. I understand you've got quite a houseful this weekend.'

Vivian smiled; she was still feeling rather noble about soldiering on with Christopher in hospital and now she could look modest about hosting several guests. 'It's wonderful that the young people are so keen to spend time with me. Tristan and Victoria will be along soon.' She just managed to stop herself from saying 'with that girl'; at the last moment she managed to change it to 'and dear little Emily.'

Meanwhile back at Vivian's home, 'that girl' was preparing to make a hasty exit.

Tristan's eyes were overbright, almost feverish, he knew he was trembling, his mouth was dry and he kept folding and unfolding his arms in front of him. In his mind, he just kept thinking, *I must stop her.* He wasn't so much worried about her going back to London; what he couldn't bear the thought of was her walking out of his life.

'Can we talk about this?' His voice choked. He took a half-step so that his body blocked her way.

Emily's lips were pressed together, her jaw set and there was determination in her eyes. When she spoke her voice was steady and low-pitched. 'There is nothing to talk about. Get out of my way.'

'Look, Emily, I need to tell you that I—'

He was cut off abruptly by Victoria who was very pale and had tears in her eyes. Emily stiffened and with a flicker of annoyance noticed Victoria's face. *How come when I cry my mascara snakes down my face and I get total panda-eye but with ruddy Victoria*

Pheasant the tears just give her eyes an extra sparkle?

Victoria pushed past Tristan and threw her arms around Emily. Emily registered cashmere and expensive scent. Victoria was easily a head taller than her so she found herself squashed against Victoria's bosom.

'Emily, darling, please forgive me!' Victoria cried in an impassioned voice. She released Emily enough to be able to gaze down into her face. 'You will forgive me, won't you? I'm so very, *very* sorry. I feel just terrible!'

'Er … well,' stammered Emily, who was finding it difficult to breathe with the froth of cashmere and the Chanel scent.

'You will? I knew you would – you are just the sweetest little thing!' exclaimed Victoria rapturously as she pressed the reluctant Emily once more to her chest. Emily let go of the suitcase and her arms hung limply by her side. Tristan observed the relinquishing of the suitcase and took a deep relieved breath. Victoria looked over Emily's head and beamed at Tristan. 'Now we can all be friends again.'

Paul was a reluctant partygoer.

'For goodness sake, hurry up!' called Robert from the foot of the stairs.

'Coming!' muttered Paul as he checked his reflection in the mirror.

He'd originally put on a tie, but Robert had said he looked too formal. No, not *too formal* – what he'd actually said was *too old and fuddy-duddy*.

Whatever it was he'd called him, Robert had insisted that he went back up to their room to change.

Paul couldn't see anything in the mirror to suggest either old or fuddy-duddy. He still had a good crop of hair, though admittedly now there was silver than blond, but that just made him look more distinguished. His eyes were still a striking blue, his jawline was firm. He pulled his stomach in and went downstairs.

He didn't really like these village dos – one never knew what was going to happen; give him the order of a formal dinner anytime.

And then Robert knew everyone in the village and Paul didn't; he wrongly assumed that was because Robert worked in the village.

'I'm really looking forward to this evening,' commented Robert as they headed towards the Village Hall.

'I just hope there aren't too many noisy children,' replied Paul under his breath, but Robert heard him.

'The children are half the fun. You really are turning into an old grump!'

Robert had spoken lightly but Paul didn't like it and they walked on in silence until they reached the hall.

They were barely over the threshold and Paul's worse nightmares were confirmed when he saw a troop of small children dominating the room. A Native American, a spaceman and an octopus ran past in one direction while some sort of a meeting of small princesses was going on near the door. In Paul's opinion, both groups were unnecessarily loud. He didn't say anything to Robert as he didn't fancy being accused of being a grump again.

I really don't know what's got into Robert lately, he's so ...

He had just shrugged off his coat when Robert eagerly announced, 'There's Justine and Oliver talking to Jim. Let's join them.'

Paul liked both Justine and Oliver so was pleased but when he and Robert approached them there was something about the warmth with which Jim and Robert shook hands that he didn't quite like.

'Nice shirt and sweater,' smiled Jim.

Robert laughed and explained to the group. 'I told Jim that I loved the way he dresses and he was kind enough to give me the name of the Florence-based company where he buys most of his togs from. These are part of their latest collection.'

Paul hadn't noticed it before but Robert was wearing a new shirt and cashmere sweater in a soft lilac colour; it looked different from what he normally wore.

Jim went on. 'Justine was just telling me that you and she are judging this year's carved-pumpkin competition.'

Oliver added, 'You should have seen the dove of peace complete with an olive branch that Robert carved the year before last. I was judging and it was an easy winner.' He glanced at the table that was laden with pumpkins, their candles all flickering away. 'But looking at the competitors this year, I really don't envy you two having to choose a winner.'

Paul was not enjoying this conversation. He'd forgotten that Robert was judging tonight – *could that be why he was being so unreasonable about us being late?* Actually, he wasn't aware that Robert had ever won a pumpkin-carving competition, nor did he have any recollection of a dove of peace, with or without an olive branch, so he was pleased when Dee came up and said, 'Hello everyone, can I possibly borrow Paul? I need a bit of muscle.'

They all looked at her with interest and she explained with a sheepish grin, 'Zara and I set up the bobbing-for-apples bowl in the middle of the storeroom floor and filled it with water. We put the apples in and the towels all around it and then we felt like right idiots when we realised that it was blocking the door and the shelves – if we leave it where it is no one can access the supplies, like crisps and juice. It's far too heavy for us to shift as it's more a cast-iron sink than a bowl.'

'Delighted to be of service,' beamed Paul.

As he followed her to the storeroom she continued, 'I'm afraid the bowl will have to be hard against the back wall – it's not ideal as whoever is bobbing for apples will have to have their back to the door.'

'I shouldn't think that matters,' said Paul absently.

'You're probably right,' agreed Dee. She regarded him and noticed his expression; his brows were drawn together, making the crease between his eyes deeper, his lips were pressed together and he was clenching his jaw. 'Anything up? You look a bit – preoccupied.'

'Do I?'

'Well, actually you look worried.'

Paul looked into Dee's warm, gently smiling face and was reminded of his mother. He'd known Dee for years and trusted her and right now he felt he needed some support. With a cough to clear his throat, he said, 'Things seem to be a bit off between Robert and me.'

'Sorry to hear that – every relationship goes through its ups and downs.'

Her neutral statement gave him courage. 'Actually, I feel a bit at a loss, he's being so critical and biting my head off at every little thing.'

Innocently Dee said, 'Perhaps he's feeling a little taken for granted; it's so easy to let any long-term relationship go stale.' Then, as if the thought had only just struck her rather than it was something she'd been wanting to bring up to Paul for weeks, she said, 'You have a significant anniversary coming up. Why don't you plan something special to celebrate it?'

Paul was surprised. 'Anniversary? What anniversary?'

Dee was beginning to lose patience. 'Honestly Paul, I'm not surprised Robert's a bit fed up with you. It's the thirtieth anniversary of the two of you getting together.'

Paul's mouth drooped into a sulky pout, so she softened her argument. 'There's always a danger we take those closest to us for granted, so that's why it's lovely when there are deliberate acts of affection. For example, the other day Zara treated Amelia and me to a spa day.'

Paul's eyebrows raised in alarm. 'What? You think I should take Robert to a spa for our anniversary?' Sitting around in a fluffy white robe and having strange women massage him was even less his idea of fun than village parties.

'No.' She laughed at Paul's look of horror at the idea of a spa. 'I was thinking of a trip away to the Amalfi Coast.'

'The Amalfi Coast?' said Paul wistfully. 'I've always wanted to go there.'

She stopped in her tracks and swung around to face him. He had a vague sensation that he was about to be savaged by a small but very angry Chihuahua. She glanced up and down the passage; there were numerous people milling around, gents nipping to the loo, ladies bustling in and out of the kitchen, and a small octopus who seemed to be tormenting an even smaller astronaut.

'I need a serious word with you, but not here, there are too many people. If we go in the storeroom and shut the door, it's virtually soundproof,' hissed Dee as she pushed him through the nearby door.

Paul nearly tripped over the vast vat of water that dominated the floor space. It had half a dozen rosy apples floating in it and it was surrounded by lots of colourful towels. The small room was made even smaller by the metal shelves all neatly stacked with supplies ranging from crates of soft drinks and boxes containing packets of crisps, to loo rolls and cleaning products.

Dee almost slammed the door shut. She faced him with her hands on her hips and her eyes blazing. 'Paul, do you actually want to be with Robert?'

He was too taken aback by the question to do more than stammer defensively, 'What sort of a ridiculous question is that?'

'Well, if I was Robert, I would be seriously questioning whether I wanted to be with you!'

Paul stared at her open-mouthed; it had never occurred to him that any living soul could ever feel less than honoured by his presence.

Could Dee be going senile?

She was well into her stride now. 'You have been to the Amalfi Coast.'

'I have?'

'Yes, it was your first trip away with Robert; it's one of his most treasured memories. He goes all misty-eyed whenever he talks about it.'

'He does?'

Dee nodded. 'And you can't even remember it!' There was a silence but she hadn't finished. 'When was the last time you surprised him with a meal out? Or took him to an art gallery?'

Paul felt on solid ground here and firmly explained, 'But I don't like going around art galleries.'

Dee raised her chin and took a step towards him. Her voice quivered with emotion and her tone deepened. 'I am very fond of you, Paul, but you really are the limit. You may not like art galleries but Robert does!' In a calmer voice she explained, 'In a loving relationship, actually in any relationship, it's necessary to give the other person some attention.'

Paul tried to process this novel idea.

'When was the last time you complimented Robert on his looks?'

Paul flushed but quickly thought of a way out. 'It's that Jim Stuart, isn't it? I knew I didn't like him! He's been making a play for Robert, hasn't he?'

Dee snorted. 'Don't try to blame Jim for your actions or lack of actions.'

It would be a major understatement to say that there was a bit of a strained silence between Dee and Paul as they transitioned from dissecting Robert and Paul's marriage to moving the apple-bobbing sink with minimal water spillage.

The All Hallows' Eve party was in full swing when Emily, Tristan and Victoria arrived. They could hear the welcoming sound of happy chatter and the squeals of overexcited children as they approached the hall. Light spilled out, inviting them into the party.

Once inside, Emily shed her coat and put it on the rail provided; there seemed to be children running in every direction. She watched the children and surmised that it was an elaborate game of chase and wondered how long it would be before a diminutive sugar plum fairy was tripped up by a mischievous American Indian and tears ensued. She also noted that a central circular table was in grave danger of having its towering arrangement of orange Chinese lanterns and the surrounding plates of biscuits sent crashing to the floor by the two spacemen and one mermaid who were tearing round and round it.

Not my problem, thought Emily philosophically.

What was undoubtedly her problem was the way Victoria seemed determined to hang on to her arm and act as if they were BFFs.

Emily reached to pick up a glass of white wine that was on

a table near the entrance but Sophie from the deli appeared. She was smiling and with her fair hair hanging loose rather than in her usual ponytail she looked too young to have an adult son. She had taken her work apron off but was wearing her usual well-fitting jeans but instead of her normal crisp white shirt, she was in a more luxuriant cream silk blouse.

She proffered a tray. 'Try one of these, they are delicious even if I say so myself – mulled apple juice, just the thing for a cold night like tonight.'

'They smell delicious,' agreed Emily.

'The ones on the right are just apple juice but I recommend the ones on the left.' She winked at Emily. 'They have a shot of a little extra something.'

Emily just had time to pick one up when Victoria started to drag her towards the back table that was arrayed with carved pumpkins, all lined up and flickering with candlelight.

'Come on – there's Justine and Oliver.' She nodded towards a suave couple who were admiring a particularly jolly pumpkin made to look like a hedgehog with masses of prickly toothpicks sticking out. 'They're great friends of Mummy and Daddy, but of course, you wouldn't know them. He's the current Lord-Lieutenant.'

Tristan had been intercepted by Jake, and Sophie's son, David, so there seemed no escape for her. She did note that Jake, tall and lanky at the best of times, looked unhealthily thin and pale and she felt a stab of anger towards his father and especially towards the anonymous blackmailer who had caused so much stress for the boy.

She didn't have long to dwell on this as Victoria was determined to drag her away from Jake, David and Tristan and towards the Lord-Lieutenant and his wife. However, once Victoria reached her exalted friends she lost all interest in Emily and far from doing any introductions, she stood with her body blocking Emily from them.

Emily mentally shrugged and stood admiring the variety of ideas for carving the pumpkins. There were lots of smiling faces and one that she thought was especially clever with the dove of peace skilfully carved on it.

Amelia walked up, also with a steaming glass of mulled apple. She was wearing a corset of a warm old-gold colour over a flamboyant silk shirt with pirate-style sleeves and thigh-length tan leather boots under a very short skirt.

'Wow you look amazing!' exclaimed Emily who was extremely relieved to see a friendly face. 'But I would have thought given it's Halloween you would have gone all-out Goth.'

Amelia laughed. 'If Josh was here he would say that you are Goth culture-stereotyping, which in his book is only one step down from the crime of stereotyping his Korean heritage. Actually, I don't really like all the skulls and occult bit – I find it a bit dark. Let's check out the competition cookies.'

They walked over to the cookie table.

Emily smiled. 'Lots of autumn leaves and hedgehogs.'

Amelia nodded. 'Well I think the competitors are a bit limited for the subjects as the vicar will have a fit if they sneak in a spider's web let alone a ghost. Are you okay?'

Instantly on the defensive, Emily stiffened and said, 'Yeah sure, why wouldn't I be?'

'You're rather pale.'

'Just a slight headache.'

'Oh, I thought you'd had a row with Tristan as he's not looking quite himself.' She smiled good-naturedly. 'Perhaps he's got a headache, too.'

Emily smiled back and felt somehow a little better. 'How's uni going?'

'Great. It's reading week so no lectures,' laughed Amelia. 'Actually, this term is proving to be really interesting; I'm doing a module on narcissistic personality disorder.'

Emily was about to ask her more but she was jostled by a scruffy-looking man. The man hadn't left his coat at the rail but was still wearing his rather unattractive grey mac.

He was reaching across to snatch a giant cookie with a smiling hedgehog on it when Amelia said firmly but politely, 'Excuse me,

Mr Charter-Fox, but they are for the competition, not for eating. I think you can buy them after judging.'

Winston Charter-Fox scowled at Amelia. 'I thought we got food.'

Amelia's charm was totally undented. With a smile, she explained, 'We do – the most delicious bacon baps –and judging by the heavenly smells coming from the kitchen they will be ready any minute.'

'What? A bacon bap? Is that all we get for the money? That's downright robbery!' he exclaimed in disgust.

Amelia refrained from pointing out that it was Dee not him who had paid for his ticket, instead, she said, 'There are bowls of crisps to keep you going – look, here's Vivian now with an overflowing bowl.'

Neatly, Amelia got Vivian and Winston Charter-Fox together; it was hard to tell which of them was most outraged by the introduction but it gave the girls a chance to slide away.

'What's he doing here? I wouldn't have thought it was at all his sort of thing.'

'I'm afraid that's Granny's doing. She had some quaint notion about welcoming him to the village. She said something about being so pleased he accepted the ticket. She really is incorrigible. Look there's Alex, let's go say hi!'

Emily looked over at the entrance where Alex in her large electric wheelchair was getting a little mermaid to help her hang up her coat.

Alex's face lit up when she saw Amelia and Emily walking up to her. They exchanged news and were just moving on to talk about a proposed quiz night at the Flying Pheasant when Zara interrupted.

She was wearing a burnished brown wrap dress with a pair of tan-heeled boots – it was a colour combination that suited her saffron hair and porcelain skin. 'Sorry to butt in but I'm needed out here to clean up some juice the little darlings have spilt.' She brandished some kitchen roll. 'Alex, could you please take over my job in the kitchen? I was in charge of ketchup. They are a bit frantic in there as the bacon baps are just about ready.'

'Can't we help in the kitchen?' asked Emily.

'Or clean up the juice?' Added Amelia.

'That's very kind of you but Alex knows her way around this kitchen from all the village dos she's helped at.' Alex nodded in agreement. 'And I'm quite pleased to have an excuse to be out of the kitchen. I'm finding Vivian annoying – she keeps coming in and complaining how many times she's had to go to the storeroom to get more crisps.'

Alex headed for the kitchen and Zara was soon on her hands and knees by the cookie table, leaving Amelia and Emily at a loose end. Paul came over to talk to them. Emily was struck by how good-looking he was, with his military bearing and chiselled features but he didn't seem really to engage with the girls. He asked Amelia some vague questions about her course but all the time his eyes kept drifting over to where Jim and Robert were standing and laughing by the pumpkins. Eventually, he made some excuse and strode over to his husband and the village newcomer.

Tristan was the next to approach them, his smile strained and his eyes nervously fixed on Emily. She felt an empty pit in her stomach and looked at the ground. So great was her discomfort that she was relieved when Victoria marched up and took him firmly by the arm without giving him the chance to say anything.

'Mummy and Daddy are here and they are simply longing to see you,' Victoria announced in a tone that demanded instant compliance. 'You don't mind do you?' She flashed something that was more of a snarl than a smile at Emily and Amelia.

As Tristan was frogmarched off, Amelia observed Emily and quickly decided it was better not to make any comment about what had just happened. Instead, she suggested, 'Let's go and see how Granny is getting on with the apple-bobbing.'

Emily nodded enthusiastically. 'That sounds great fun – I haven't done any apple-bobbing since I was a kid.' She glanced around the hall. 'But where is she?'

'Miles away,' said Amelia. 'They've put the apple-bobbing in the storeroom off the back passageway by the kitchen; it was the only place they could think of where it wouldn't matter how much water was spilt. Come on, I'll show you!' She led Emily through the throng of people and children. 'I'm surprised all these kids aren't lining up to do apple-bobbing.'

'Perhaps they don't know where it is,' suggested Emily as they reached the passage.

Amelia nodded. 'You're probably right. I'll ask Granny if she wants us to drum up some customers.'

Vivian was by the storeroom door. Amelia noted that she was unusually flustered and presumed she was wearing that enormous plastic apron to ensure that not a drop of bacon fat got on her cashmere and tweed.

'You wouldn't believe how quickly we're going through the crisps. At this rate, no one will have any room for the bacon baps. This must be my tenth trip to the storeroom to get more supplies,' Vivian said sourly.

'Here let me push the door open. I can't imagine why Granny has shut it,' said Amelia reaching for the handle.

She pushed the door open and screamed.

There was Dee, her back to them, slumped over the half-empty bowl of water with half-a-dozen apples floating in it. She was soaked with water, as were all the towels on the floor. Amelia took in her grandmother's wet hair and, more significantly, the presence of Winston Charter-Fox. He was still in his grey mac; with determination his bony hands firmly gripped Dee's shoulders.

Amelia screamed again with gusto.

Chapter 18

Vivian leapt into action; she was the embodiment of a ninja warrior with a love of lipstick and pearls. Using her sturdy crisp bowl as a weapon, she began violently hitting Winston Charter-Fox over the head while shouting, 'Unhand her, you villain!'

He released Dee and swung around to face his assailant. Zara took this as an opportunity to launch herself at him and as he was dazed by Vivian's blows, she had very little difficulty in flattening him, face-down, onto the ground. While remaining both modest and elegant, as only a FitzMorris lady could, she straddled his back and quickly secured him in an arm lock. The force of her hold elicited a moan of pain from Charter-Fox.

In all this fury Amelia reached for her phone and dialled 999. She was put through immediately and shouted down the phone, 'Help! A madman has murdered my granny!'

All attention was focused on Winston Charter-Fox so it came as a shock when Dee said, 'No, dear! Actually, I'm okay, just a touch winded.'

Everyone looked at Dee who sat back on her heels; she was soaked through but undoubtedly still breathing.

Winston Charter-Fox wriggled and spluttered. 'It wasn't me, I—'

Zara silenced him with a sharp flexing of the arm lock, which resulted in another gasp of agony.

Amelia calmly readdressed the dispatcher, 'A madman has attempted to murder my granny, but she's still alive.'

Her screams had alerted all the people in the hall and kitchen and a crowd now pressed in the passageway and around the doorway, creating a claustrophobic atmosphere. There were general murmurs of, 'What's happening?' 'Who screamed?' and

'Can you see anything?'

Then Paul, in his most commanding parade-ground voice cut across the hubbub. 'Ladies and gentlemen, I can assure you that everything is in hand and if I can ask you to all please return to the hall as the vicar will make an announcement in ten minutes.'

Robert, who was standing beside Paul and could see no more about what was going on than Paul himself, could only admire his calm command of the situation. As if by magic or sheer force of command, his words worked and people trooped obediently back into the hall.

This allowed both Paul and the vicar to approach the storeroom unimpeded. He quickly assessed the situation and politely suggested that Zara get off Winston Charter-Fox as the man seemed to be having difficulty breathing.

He then turned his attention to Virginia; his voice was unhurried and his body language gave the impression of total calm as he said, 'Get on the stage and say, "There has been an incident but there is nothing to worry about." Then tell everyone to stay until the police arrive. I suggest you serve the bacon baps as that will calm everyone down.'

Virginia's wide-eyed stare was flitting between a drenched Dee who was sitting among the wet towels with both Zara and Amelia embracing her and a clearly disoriented Winston Charter-Fox who was slumped against the back wall with Vivian guarding him by fiercely brandishing her crisp bowl.

She wrung her hands together. 'Er … I … Um …'

Paul snapped at her, 'Pull yourself together, Vicar, show some leadership and get out there.'

Virginia instantly straightened her spine and murmured, 'Yes, my parish needs me!' She strode out and successfully delivered calm to her flock, as well as that well-known panacea of agitation – bacon baps.

As was to be expected, it took hours for the police to take statements from everyone. The astronaut and mermaid were utterly fascinated by it all and acted as close shadows of Nicholas.

Eventually, exasperated by their constant, high-pitched questions, he asked Josh to reunite the little dears with their parents. The octopus did not fare so well, and as the hours went on, began to sob with exhaustion.

Virginia was doing only slightly better. With all hope of the cookies being judged having been lost now, she positioned herself by the table they were displayed on and steadily started to eat her way through them. Occasionally she could be heard muttering, 'Of all the things I was worrying about with this party, it never occurred to me that there might be an attempted murder over the apple-bobbing.'

Robert took pity on her drooping shoulders and forlorn look and offered her yet another cookie by way of consolation.

Josh reluctantly left the cookies to the vicar and sidled up to Amelia. He maintained his professional façade but whispered, 'Nice outfit.'

She grinned. 'Thanks.'

Tristan's only thought on hearing the scream had been Emily. As the first note reached him he abandoned his companions and ran in the direction of the cry. The relief he felt when he saw her was immense. There was no colour in her cheeks but otherwise, she looked unharmed.

He felt a surge of attraction and protectiveness. 'You okay?' he asked anxiously. She nodded and didn't shrug his arm off when he placed it over her shoulder in an attempt to shield her from the upset.

A couple of days later they were all still trying to come to terms with what had happened.

Nicholas called in at Dee's cottage to discuss matters and was delighted to be greeted at the door by Zara. She was wearing her casual wool dress and what he couldn't help thinking of as her sexy boots.

'Nicholas, how nice. Mother will be delighted to see you.'

Dee's expression when she saw him confirmed her daughter's prediction. Zara settled him down in an armchair next to a welcoming fire. The room was cosy, there was an attractive smell of burning wood, beeswax and lavender. The crackles and pops of the blazing logs were soothing. Dee's collection of lush pot plants added to the air of serenity.

Cat regarded Nicholas with disdain; she didn't like policemen and with dignity, she stalked off, intent on visiting Winston Charter-Fox's bleak home.

Zara went to the kitchen and soon returned with a teapot and some heavenly-smelling ginger biscuits. With a flirtatious smile, she told Nicholas, 'Good news for us – Mother has been stress-baking. These are still warm from the oven.'

Dee grinned back, she was looking decidedly relaxed in her dark jeans and oversized cashmere sweater. 'I don't know if it was so much stress as having a sudden longing for ginger biscuits. Either way, Nicholas, do help yourself.'

Nicholas liked the way Dee lived, he liked the touches; a proper teapot, loose-leaf tea and a sparkling silver strainer, homemade biscuits and a roaring fire. He settled back in his comfy chair to relish every element.

The two women allowed him to enjoy his tea and half of his biscuit before Zara fixed him with her brilliant green eyes. She arched an eyebrow and said, 'So?'

Nicholas suddenly remembered that he was here on police business. He reluctantly put down both the biscuit and teacup and took up a serious expression.

'I really came to see if Dee has remembered anything else.'

Dee looked apologetic. 'I'm so sorry, but it was like I told you that evening. I was just leaning over the tub to see if Billy's missing tooth was in there. He'd just been in, very upset as he'd only just realised that he'd lost a tooth – he's at that age, all happy smiles. He'd been in earlier and had successfully managed to bite into an apple. Anyway, he was distressed as he didn't think the tooth fairy would deliver if he didn't have the tooth as evidence to put under his pillow. We'd had a look together in the water and hadn't found it but I didn't think there could be any harm in my checking again.'

'I wondered what the going rate for a tooth is now?' mused Zara.

'Bound to be a fortune. It was sixpence in my day,' said Dee.

'When Amelia was little it was 50p but with inflation, it's bound to have gone up.'

Nicholas cleared his throat. 'If we could stick to the point.'

'Of course, Nicholas,' said Dee, looking totally unrepentant. 'Would you like some more tea? Another biscuit?'

'Dee!'

'Well, as I was saying, I was leaning over and the next thing I knew I was being held under the water.'

'It makes me shudder every time I think about it. You certainly won't catch me bobbing for apples anytime soon,' interrupted Zara.

'Nor me,' agreed Dee. She looked thoughtful, then added, looking at Nicholas, 'Or do you think it's a bit like riding a horse where if you fall off you must get straight back in the saddle? Perhaps, Zara, you and I should set up the washing-up bowl on the kitchen floor and give it a go? I'm sure I've got some Cox Orange Pippins in the fruit dish.'

'If we could get back to the incident,' sighed Nicholas, 'do you have any idea who it was? Or an impression of what they were like?'

Zara threw back her head, outraged and interjected, 'We know who it was! We caught him red-handed! We saw Charter-Fox with his evil hands entwined around Mother's fragile white throat!'

Dee looked at her daughter speculatively. 'Darling, have you been reading some of Lavinia Lovelace's Gothic romances again?'

Nicholas tried to take charge. 'Mr Charter-Fox insists he went in to see if he could get an apple as he was starving. He was surprised that the door was shut and when he opened it he found Dee slumped over the bowl. He claims he only got hold of her to save her.'

'What a load of piffle!' exclaimed Zara.

Dee thoughtfully sipped her tea. 'It is possible – I had water in my ears so couldn't hear a lot, and people had been going up and down the passage and Vivian had been in and out for crisps – there was so much noise and confusion I'm not sure exactly what happened.'

'Let's go back to you being held under the water. Did you see their shoes, say? Could you tell how big they were?'

Dee shook her head again. 'No, I struggled for a bit but it was obvious that they were a lot stronger than I was, so I went limp and played dead.'

'Good thinking, Mother,' enthused Zara. 'I've always admired your mental agility in a crisis.'

Dee blushed, 'Thank you, dear, that's so sweet of you.'

'Of course,' continued Zara with some asperity, 'I would prefer it if you didn't keep putting yourself in these life-threatening situations that require mental agility.'

'Darling, that really is a bit unfair. It's not as if I deliberately go around asking for people to try and kill me.'

Nicholas, sensing that a family fight was about to ensue, spoke. 'So after you went limp, what happened?'

'I'm not sure. Everything is a bit hazy.'

'You know, Mother, if only you'd been a bit more observant I'm sure that ghastly Winston Charter-Fox would have been in prison weeks ago. If you'd spotted him with his matches at the bird hide or sneaking out of Jim's home, it would have saved us all this trouble.'

'There is one good thing about this,' said Dee.

Nicholas and Zara looked at her in surprise.

'What in the name of all the heavens could be good about a man with dubious fashion sense trying to drown you?' asked Zara.

'Darling, Nicholas has just been saying that it might or might not be him.'

Zara harrumphed. 'I still don't see what's good about it.'

Dee looked complacent. 'Whoever is doing all these terrible things must really want to get rid of me. Attempting to kill me in the village hall in the middle of a party is a real act of desperation! It's much more dangerous than just cutting my brake lines.'

'I'm with Zara; I don't see what's good about it either,' said Nicholas.

'Don't you? They are obviously really keen to get rid of me so we just have to wait until they try again then we can catch them.' Dee was exultant.

Zara exclaimed, 'Mother!'

Nicholas was certain that Zara was about to castigate her mother so he contently sipped his tea and waited for Amelia to firmly explain why this was a bad idea.

But what Zara actually said was, 'Count Amelia and me in!'

Nicholas rolled his eyes to the heavens and reached for another biscuit.

Christopher might have been released from hospital but he was as uneasy as Nicholas about what was happening.

Propped up in bed, with Bramble sitting devotedly on the floor beside him, he took advantage of Vivian bringing him a cup of tea to voice his concerns. 'I say, old thing, nasty business with Dee.'

Vivian didn't look at him or acknowledge his statement, she just adjusted the shade on the bedside lamp. Bramble picked up on Vivian's hostile aura and tried to make herself as small as possible; she was fully aware that she wasn't really allowed upstairs. Vivian remained silent but moved on to plumping up a cushion on the armchair.

'Actually, I don't like any of it,' continued Christopher. 'The blackmail and poor Sebastian, Jim nearly drowning, Jo and that awful fire.'

'So what?' said Vivian. 'The police have got that awful Charter-Fox where he belongs – behind bars. The case is closed.'

She had her back to him and was rearranging things on the mantelpiece.

Christopher toyed with his duvet cover and muttered, 'You know old thing, I really don't mind not being Lord-Lieutenant.'

He saw his wife's back stiffen. Bramble slunk under the bed. Very slowly Vivian turned around, she regarded him coldly for a full minute and Christopher could feel his heart beating and his palms sweating then in a slow careful speech she said, 'Don't be ridiculous.'

Chapter 19

How did this happen? How on earth did I end up in this position?

Emily looked at her reflection in the swish changing room mirror in a smart London boutique.

Am I imagining it or does this dress look like a reject from an amateur dramatic production of The Sugar Plum Fairy?

Emily regarded herself again.

An X-rated version!

Victoria's voice called from outside the curtain, dripping with cloying Southern syrup but with a core of total command. 'How does it look? I bet it's just the sweetest thing on you!'

Emily hesitated and scanned the serene white changing room.

Why is there never an escape window when one needs it?

She could see herself legging it down South Molton Street in her microscopic pink costume. She'd only brought trainers. They looked striking under this dress with the expanse of white leg showing between the frothy skirt and the sturdy footwear.

Why didn't I think to bring heels to try on ball gowns with?

She knew why – she didn't own any.

Still, the trainers will give me an advantage in running to the nearest red London bus.

'Don't be coy! Come on out and show me. If you're not coming out, I'm coming in!'

The very thought of Victoria barging in and witnessing the debris of her discarded ropy old bra and vest was enough to propel Emily out of the sanctuary of the cubicle and into the glare of Victoria's scrutiny.

Victoria stepped back. She slowly looked Emily up and down then a smile spread across her face and Emily experienced a whole new level of discomfort.

I thought I couldn't feel any less confident than when I first clapped eyes on Victoria this morning but this is way worse.

An hour ago Emily had felt self-conscious in her jeans and an old waterproof when she had met Victoria outside Bond Street tube station. That week, like every other week, she'd gotten behind with her laundry, what with too many anal glands and not enough time to push her hoover around and wash her smalls. So when that morning had dawned, instead of reaching in her chest of drawers and finding her new figure-fitting jeans washed and pressed, she'd discovered them crumpled under a pile of equally dispiriting garments on her bedroom floor. Looking for the jeans had made her late so she had given up her frantic quest for her sumptuous red cashmere cardigan amid the chaos on top of the bedside chair. She had grabbed the nearest clean top – shame about the Donald Duck logo on the front. *Perhaps people will think it's an ironic nod towards my profession - sort of 'vet humorous chic'.*

It was only when she was three stops away from home on the tube that she remembered that she had actually hung the red cardigan up in her wardrobe.

Naturally, it didn't even occur to me to look there! What I need is, a) more respectable clothes and the funds to pay for them, and b) a better system for household chores or alternatively the guts not to care about what I wear.

Emily regarded Victoria with despair.

How does she do it? That effortless trendy-but-chic look? Is it the way that simple dress is styled with that little leather jacket? I bet she doesn't store that dress and jacket under a pile of old t-shirts on the floor. Mind you, it could be the hair ... or is it the makeup? Of course, as she would have saved hours in knowing where her kit was, she'd obviously had time to wash her hair and put her makeup on. I'm not even sure I managed to brush my teeth.

I think I hate her!

Emily swallowed and felt a bit sick.

Or is it that she is Victoria Pheasant and I'm just Emily Laddan?

Emily's feelings of inadequacy were only intensified in this little boutique – it was Victoria's natural habitat.

Whereas my natural habitat is squeezing dogs' anal glands in Clapham.

She felt a surge of anger towards Tristan as she remembered why she was in this situation. Victoria had walked into the Plovers' kitchen in Little Warthing just as Tristan had been talking about the Michaelmas Ball.

'Hey Victoria, Emily needs something to wear for the Michaelmas Ball. Shopping isn't really her thing and you have such brilliant taste.'

Before Emily had had time to stammer out, 'Really, that won't be necessary,' Victoria had her 'tiger going in for the kill' smile and was saying, 'Why, Tristan, I'd just do anything for you!'

Now with Emily wearing the dress for the Michaelmas Ball, Victoria's eyes were shining and she exclaimed, 'Emily Laddan, I do declare you are going to be the belle of the Michaelmas Ball!'

Emily stood awkwardly. 'You don't think it's just a little … tacky?'

Victoria tinkled out a laugh. 'Why as if anything you wore could be thought of as tacky!'

'There is quite a lot of … cleavage.'

'I bet you just can't wait for Tristan to see you in this little number!'

Emily could visualise Tristan's expression if he saw her like this. She could hear his hilarity and imagine the jokes that would haunt her for years to come.

'Now don't you move a muscle; it just needs a little finishing touch. I saw the dearest pink silk peony in the front part of the shop. I'll just pop out and get it for you – it will look so striking in your hair!'

'Er, Victoria?' stammered Emily.

But Victoria just called over her shoulder, 'No need to thank me. It's my pleasure.'

Emily felt both naked and over-dressed.

Does the fuchsia pink from my blushing face clash with the baby pink taffeta?

In her moment of crisis, Zara FitzMorris emerged from a nearby cubicle. Unlike Emily, she looked demure and elegant, wearing a long sheath dress in a rich caramel colour, with tonal heels and a neat bolero jacket.

She had obviously stepped out of her changing cubicle, intending to observe the overall effect of her outfit from a distance; there was a long mirror on the far wall for this purpose.

The sight of Emily in her pink fairy kit stopped her in her tracks. 'Emily?'

Emily wasn't sure if Zara was querying her identity or her sanity.

Zara's eyebrows were drawn together and she made eye contact with Emily, which was quite an achievement as she was trying to examine the carpet by her trainers.

'Are you shopping for the Michaelmas Ball?' Zara's voice was both alarmed and concerned.

'Is it suitable?' asked Emily anxiously.

Zara blinked, swallowed then very gently said, 'Well it's not so much its suitability, it's more …'

Emily wondered which bit was causing Zara's brows to furrow. *Is it the short length? The plunging neckline? Can it be the colour – a cross between baby pink and bubblegum pink? Might it be the trainers – with socks – mismatched? That reminds me, I must do a load of washing.*

'It's just that it doesn't strike me as being your style.'

Emily's shoulders slumped as she muttered, 'Why? Because it's not a sweatshirt?'

Zara regarded her for a moment before saying, 'Oh dear! I think you need a cup of coffee and some chocolate cake! Tell you what, I'm going to get this!' She twirled in front of the long mirror and smiled at what she saw. 'It's perfect for me. I'd set the whole day aside for dress shopping but as it's only eleven o'clock and I'm sorted, let's devote the rest of the day to getting you the perfect ensemble. After coffee and cake, of course.'

Hope flickered into Emily's heart and across her face.

Zara looked at the pink monstrosity again. 'I'm just a little curious, Emily. What exact aspect of this dress made you try it on?'

At that moment Victoria drawled, 'Why, honey, isn't this just the perfect finishing touch for your dress?' She marched in holding an enormous bright pink flower before her but halted at the sight of Zara.

'Oh! I see. That explains a lot,' said Zara coolly. Then in frosty tones, calmly and with a neutral expression she added, 'Victoria, how lovely to see you.'

As Zara and Victoria squared off against each other Emily watched with fascination. It was rather like one of those wildlife documentaries where the alpha elephant faces a younger adversary for supremacy over the African Savannah. Emily could almost hear David Attenborough.

And here we have the established alpha female, and doesn't she look magnificent in her bright plumage? But her challenger has youth on her side. Who exactly stands to win in this epic clash of wills?

'Zara, are you dress shopping too? I was just giving dear little Emily a hand. Tristan simply begged me to help.'

Oh, dear! That was a weak opening for the young contender – too obviously patronising. And I think this alpha female's body language shows she knows that this Southern Belle is no match for her.

'So I can see!'

Ladies and gentlemen as you can see there we have it, the knockout blow.

We will just replay it for you, it was so quick you may have missed the finer nuances. So the tone is all-important – totally unemotional, far more effective than a raised voice. And I'd just like to draw your attention to the relaxed shoulders and the eye contact: it's all about eye contact.

Victoria's smile was stiff, she was distinctly deflated and it was blatantly an excuse when she said, 'Oh, Emily darling, you really must forgive me – I have to run – urgent work call.'

As Emily watched her leave, David Attenborough's soothing

voice resounded in her head.

And there you have it, despite her youthful vitality and new outfit she was no match for seasoned experience. And as the contender retreats to a cab outside we can see a touching moment as the alpha female and her young friend exchange a smile of victory.

It wasn't long before Emily felt her sense of equilibrium returning. Zara was easy company. They talked of inconsequential things as they walked along the bustling London street that was full of noise from people and traffic. They paused to look at inviting shop windows that called out for attention.

Zara chose a coffee shop that served French pastries. She requested and secured a window seat. As they took their seats she said, 'Don't you just love people-watching? London has to be the best place to watch the world go by as there are so many different folk, and this table is ideal.'

As Zara settled herself at the table Emily had a chance to notice that under her camel coat, she was wearing a simple dress; it was of a similar colour to the evening gown that had so suited her in the boutique. Emily was most taken with Zara's neat handbag in the shape of a small old-fashioned trunk. *Could it be time to upgrade my Tesco bag for life to a proper dedicated handbag?*

While they waited for their coffee to come they observed people passing on the outside pavement and Zara threw out warm, happy comments.

'Isn't that dachshund delightful?'

'Aw, what an adorable toddler!'

'I love how that lady is all in black but her lipstick and nails are scarlet.'

Their coffee when it came was strong and black; Emily tamed hers with cream and sugar, but Zara took it neat, sipping and savouring it.

'It's so important to stay hydrated when shopping,' smiled Zara as they quenched their thirst with refreshing water, infused with bright slices of lemon.

The pastries were small works of art displayed on simple white plates. Zara's choice was a rounded *Religieuse*, and she took a delicate forkful with suitable reverence. Emily had gone for a *Tarte aux Fraises* and they both cooed over the bright and beautifully arranged strawberries.

Once more, Emily heard David Attenborough's commentary. *Let us just observe this tender moment as the alpha female takes the younger female under her wing and feeds her cake.*

Emily was not sure how they got onto the subject of clothes and Victoria.

Zara put her cake fork down and with her jade cat-like eyes regarded Emily. 'I'm sorry, can I just clarify – you allowed a girl who got you to dress up as a cat to help you choose a dress for the ball?'

Emily dropped her eyes and pushed a strawberry around her plate. 'The cat thing was just a joke and Victoria is a very old friend of Tristan's.'

Zara was silent and when Emily looked up she was still looking at her intently. What Zara saw was a very pretty girl, with a fresh complexion, an attractive mass of blonde curls and far too much naivety for her own good.

'It wasn't a joke, it was an act of war aimed at coming between you and Tristan. And what Victoria was or is to Tristan really doesn't matter, all that matters is what you are to Tristan. You are his fiancée. He is the man you've chosen to spend the rest of your life with and as such you have a duty of care towards your relationship and him.'

'I'm not … I mean he's not …' Emily mumbled.

'Not what?' asked Zara, deliberately sounding casual so as to coax more information out of Emily.

'We're not engaged. Actually, we're not even going out.'

There was a long silence and when Emily looked up her friend was smiling. To Emily's surprise, Zara didn't scream, 'What? *Why?*'

Instead, Zara enthused, 'How romantic! It's like something out of a Lavinia Lovelace romance; a handsome hero with a tragic past falls in love with a beautiful, spirited heroine. Shame we're not living in Jane Austin's era – your curls would look wonderful in a bonnet.'

'But Tristan isn't in love with me,' Emily blurted out, fighting back tears.

Zara patted her hand. 'I think you'll find that he is. More importantly, though, how do you feel about him?'

She shrugged. 'I don't know.'

Zara was about to insist, 'Don't be ridiculous! You must know!' Then she thought of a certain police inspector. How did she feel about him?

So she side-stepped the issue. 'Well, however you feel about him we need to get you a stunning dress.'

Emily rolled her eyes. 'Do we have to? I really don't like shopping.'

'That is only because you've never been shopping with me,' beamed Zara confidently. 'And on the Victoria issue, if you have a dog that comes into your surgery and tries to bite you, what do you do when it's booked in for another appointment?'

'Take precautions,' stated Emily as she thought of a particularly vicious little terrier that she'd had in the day before.

Zara smiled. 'So in your future encounters with Victoria, think of her as one of your more aggressive clients and take all necessary precautions to protect yourself.'

Emily thought of elegant and assured Victoria, all lip gloss and expensive sweaters, and then she thought of that terrier – muzzled – and suddenly she didn't feel so intimidated.

A further pleasant surprise awaited her once coffee and cake were completed: Zara was right, shopping with her was fun rather than humiliating. For a start, they went to a large department store where Emily felt quite at ease. Her confidence grew with each flattering dress she tried on.

Eventually, she heard David Attenborough speak again,

This, ladies and gentlemen, is why it is good that the established alpha female is still in command – just look at the way she is coaxing her protégé into that stunning understated red

evening dress. And ... yes the trainers are coming off and I think
we can all agree that those heels are magnificent.

It was only as Zara was going home on the train that her thoughts
turned to her conversation with Emily.

Poor child, it's hardly surprising that she's confused about
her feelings for Tristan. Love and relationships are so nuanced.

She looked out at skies that had turned bleak and grey and at
the rain that streaked the windows.

It's hard to believe that it's coming up for ten years since
Freddie, my husband, died in that car crash.

She had to check herself as the shock and confusion flooded
back.

At the time I don't think I really grieved at all – anything I felt
was totally overshadowed by Amelia's devastation.

She smiled as she thought of how Freddie had been when
they'd first met, so young, so hopeful. He'd introduced himself as
another FitzMorris and joked that they should get married as she
wouldn't have the bother of changing her name and three years
later they did just that.

With Freddie, we'd both been ridiculously young and passion
spilled out in physical affection and in fights. It had been magical
but would I really want that now?

Her mind turned to waltzing with Nicholas, then to that
evening of salsa and finally to the tango. She swallowed. *One*
would want some passion in a more mature relationship. She
swallowed again. *Just not that raw unbridled passion of youth.*

Her thoughts turned to their time in the garden centre. *Perhaps*
it would be an idea for Nicholas and me to have a meeting – purely
to discuss the case. After all, if Mother is going to offer herself up
as bait for whoever is plaguing Little Warthing, we should at least
be prepared. I'm certain it's Winston Charter-Fox but if Mother
and Nicholas need concrete proof, I'm happy to help.

She fished her phone out of her neat trunk handbag and look
at her calendar.

It will be difficult to find a date as I'm rather tied up with

Jim's development project, but I'm sure I'll manage.

She peeked at her new dress wrapped in tissue in its exquisite box and bag. *And of course, there's always the Michaelmas Ball.*

Nicholas paused to watch the men putting up the marquee for the Michaelmas Ball. Expertly they moved around Christopher's lawn with guide ropes and hammers. It was like watching a slow but well-choreographed dance.

I had hoped to have everything sorted by the Michaelmas Ball but everything is still so nebulous.

His call on Christopher and Vivian had been his last stop. He had hoped that by revisiting all the victims, something fresh would occur to him or that they would suddenly recall some previously forgotten clue, but it had been a pointless exercise.

All he had learnt at Dee's was that she made exceptionally good ginger biscuits. Sebastian, slightly dazed, had been surrounded by packing cases in his great echoing hall; his son Jake, and Amelia had been providing energy and direction for the removal men, but Nicholas left none the wiser.

Jim Stewart had also been packing but in a less dramatic way, he had two neat suitcases ready to go by his front door. He explained that once the Michaelmas Ball was over he was going for an extended holiday to Italy, but he had nothing new to say about the attempted drowning. It had been good to see Jo out of hospital and preparing to go back to work. Their talk about the fire was extremely unsatisfactory; she had struggled to remain unemotional and had no new information.

Now here he was at Christopher and Vivian's home and once again, his questions had elicited no new information.

As he let his mind wander over the few facts he had, Nicholas continued to watch the work going on with the marquee. Christopher, still pale from the food poisoning but getting better, was pushing a wheelbarrow along the path behind the lawn towards his kitchen garden and Bramble was trotting by his side with her tail wagging. Vivian strode out too but her objective was the marquee foreman and not the kitchen garden. Nicholas was too far away from him to be able to hear what she was saying but judging from how her hands were thrust on her hips and she was leaning into him, Nicholas felt only pity for the poor man.

He turned to go and caught sight of Winston Charter-Fox. *Perhaps I shouldn't have released him*, thought Nicholas. Winston Charter-Fox had obviously, like Nicholas, been taking an interest in the marquee going up but the sight of a policeman had sent him scurrying off. *But then I really couldn't hold him much longer as there isn't any evidence. We searched his house from top to bottom but all we found was Dee's cat. It would have been useful if there'd been something flammable, the same as the accelerant used to start the fire in the woods, or better still a note confessing everything.*

Nicholas had left his car parked on the road. As soon as he got into it he spotted that the immaculate interior had a sprinkling of something sticky and crumbling on the passenger seat. *How many times do I have to tell Josh not to snack in my car? That boy is always eating!* He tried to gather up the crumbs but they stuck to his hands, which made him even more determined to have some serious words with Josh about his unsavoury dining habits.

It was only as he was driving towards the police station that his thoughts left Josh's sticky crumbs and his mind returned to the happenings around Little Warthing.

Perhaps I should have a chat with Zara – she's always a good person to bounce ideas off. The thought filled him with warmth but it was short-lived. *No! Probably better not – Dee let slip that they are coming up to the tenth anniversary of Amelia's father's death so probably not a good idea to bother her, besides which Jim mentioned that she is very involved with some new development of his so she's bound to be busy.*

He spent the rest of the drive sunk in melancholic thoughts that got him nowhere.

Chapter 20

Jo woke up in a positive mood.

Today is the start of something new. I'm going to look forward. Considering what happened, I'm in pretty good shape.

She was alone in the house but she was used to that. The boys were at school and she had insisted her husband go on his business trip which had been in the diary for months.

As she headed to the bathroom she ran through her day's activities. *So I have a meeting at the village school at eight-thirty – Dee's finally getting her way about the library and we governors just need to sign off on it, and then from ten I have meetings back to back with all the key managers for the hotels and restaurants to bring me up to speed about what's been going on in my absence.*

She'd scheduled the afternoon after three o'clock to be devoted to going through all the figures with the company's accountant. *That's when I really get to grips with what's going on!*

She dressed and did her makeup with extra care; it was like putting on her armour before going to battle. It was only as she was leaving the bathroom that she remembered Vivian's calcium pills.

New start and I'm going to make more effort with my health, beginning with looking after my bones.

She got the bottle out of the medicine cabinet and checked the label; she was supposed to take two daily but a glance at the size of them made her decide to only take one. She swallowed it down with some difficulty, checked her watch, grabbed her car keys and left for the village school.

Dee was feeling emotionally buoyed up. *So kind of the governors of the village school to invite me to their final meeting about the school library. It will make such a difference to the children and it will be such fun to have all those new books to explore.*

She smiled at a knot of teenagers waiting by the bus stop. *They grow so fast – I read with each of them when they were at the village school. What is the girl's name? Jane? Janice? Anyway, whatever her name is, I do hope she doesn't catch a cold – that skirt is really little more than a belt.*

Dee liked the village at this time in the morning; it was both busy and sleepy with shops gently opening and dogs being walked in a moderate manner. There was none of that frantic, caffeine-fuelled desperation she'd seen in London at this time of day. She approved of the way Little Warthing's businesses eased into life. *It's rather the same as how I begin each day with soothing yoga stretches before my Taekwondo forms.*

Passing cars had their headlights on. *Yet another sign of winter,* thought Dee as she tucked her scarf in.

As she turned into the side road off the high street which was aptly named School Road, she recognised the sleek navy shooting brake that was also turning in.

How wonderful, Jo is back in action.

She waved and smiled, but the driver was obscured by the glare of the car's headlights. Dee waved again, then felt a shiver run through her body. She scrunched up her eyes, squinting to try and see Jo behind the wheel. She could hear the whoosh of the car's tyres against the wet tarmac and the thrumming of her own heart as she realised that something was wrong.

The car was moving slowly but erratically, its bonnet pointing towards the school gates where a crowd of mothers with pushchairs were chatting, while toddlers muffled up in bright hats and scarves played with the big children in their smart navy-and-red uniforms.

Time split, speeding hideously fast towards disaster and at the same instance moving agonisingly slowly.

Dee started shouting, screaming, 'Jo! *Stop! Help!*'

As she screamed she started to run beside the car, her heart pounding now from both fear and exertion. She seemed to be taking on multiple images from all angles: Jo slumped over her steering wheel, mothers and children staring immobile at the impending arrival of the car in their midst. *Why aren't they moving?* She remembered a picture of a visit she'd made to Pompeii where the people – mothers, children and babies – had all been frozen for eternity in their last horrifying moments.

Someone other than Dee was screaming. It broke the spell. Everyone was screaming now, scattering, running, crying.

Dee wrestled with the cold door, her gloved hand slipping.

'Jo!' she screamed feeling as if her lungs were exploding but her friend remained a deadly unconscious mass squashed against the wheel.

Dee realised she was praying, a desperate inarticulate cry for help.

With a click, the door opened. She lunged her body across Jo's back, reaching for the handbrake. It was one of those modern half-handles and her hands slipped through, It was no use – she couldn't stop the car.

Before her mind thought it through, her hands reached for the steering wheel. She gripped it and with all her strength turned it hard, wrenching the car from its course into the schoolchildren and mothers and into the unyielding and just as deadly stone wall that ran alongside.

She saw the wall, right down to the little cracks in the sandstone where lichen was trying to grow. She even registered a garish red and gold sweet wrapper that some child had wedged in a gap between the stones.

Then came the impact. She seemed to be watching it from far away, her body tossed like a rag doll. The noise of crunching metal and fractured stone echoed, harmonising with a Greek chorus of cries. Then her head hit something hard and all went black.

Chapter 21

Jo lay in her hospital bed in her private room. Technically it was different from the one she'd been in before but in every detail, it was the same. The walls were painted an unobtrusive pale colour, there were endless plug sockets for unknown equipment, and there were the same harsh fluorescent lights and a large windowpane looking out on nothing of any interest. The smell of disinfectant was barely masked by the generous flower arrangements sent by well-wishers. The sounds were identical too; soft shoes hurrying along echoing corridors, people speaking in hushed tones, the rattle of a trolley and distant bleeps. Even the staff seemed familiar; their name tags might be different from before but in essence, they were the same people, smiling cleaners and tea ladies and the calm, efficient nurses who were kind but kept a professional distance.

Jo disliked the scratchy sheets, the sharp pinch of the IV going in but most of all she detested this feeling of utter helplessness.

Dee adored her garden in winter when each twig, leaf and delicate spider's web was silvered by frost. It looked magical in the rays of the low golden sun. Her breath came out as billowing clouds. *Had it been Amelia or Zara who had loved to pretend they were dragons on frosty mornings like this? Perhaps it had been both of them.*

She moved stiffly towards the bird feeder. Every bone and muscle ached but the doctor had instructed her to keep moving. Cat followed in her wake, ever hopeful that some tasty garden bird would forget itself and drop into the feline's mouth.

Dee was finding it difficult to focus on even the most mundane of daily tasks. She fumbled with the top of the feeder and the fat balls filled with seeds but paused, distracted by her thoughts. Her head was tilted to one side and she bit her bottom lip, then drew her eyebrows together and addressed Cat, who was winding around her ankles. 'It's all wrong, I don't believe that the toxicology report came up with nothing. All those suggestions that Jo was simply overwrought and trying to do too much too soon are utter twaddle.'

A robin waiting on a nearby branch reminded Dee of what she was meant to be doing.

She put five fat balls in the feeder but her mind refused to stay on the task at hand; it kept going back to the accident. It wasn't the facts of what had been going on that so troubled her, it was the suffering of her friends; Sebastian, dear, noble, deeply flawed old Sebastian and poor young Jake, Jo always so vibrant and bright and now reduced to being a silent patient in a hospital bed, Jim being forced to relive his childhood trauma and then there was bumbling, harmless Christopher.

'We need to get this sorted,' she told Cat, who mewed in her annoyance that Dee was taking a long time to fill the feeder. As she thought of her friends, she took in a sharp cold breath and felt her eyes grow hot and tear up. 'If only I'd been more observant, I might have been able to stop all this from happening.'

She stared at a bush of frosted rosehips, the same red as the robin's breast, but she couldn't focus. Her head was starting to ache and she suddenly felt as if all her energy had been leached out of her. She shut and rehung the bird feeder.

She was less than halfway back to the kitchen when a family of noisy long-tail tits descended onto the fat balls, ecstatic at their largesse. Cat eyed them speculatively.

Sometimes Nicholas didn't like his job much; he'd gone into the police force imagining all the nobility of a character like Dixon of Dock Green, the hero of a TV programme he'd watched as a young child, but today he just felt like some grubby private investigator hired to get the dirt on an adulterous married man. It wasn't the sort of task he relished, especially as he had seen all those family photos at Jo's home. Most of the photos had been taken when the family had been on exotic holidays to palm-fringed beaches, and they depicted Jo looking beautiful and vibrant, her sons tanned and smiling and her husband, Tobias, always with a loving arm around Jo, with an azure blue sky and sea as the backdrop.

Nicholas liked Jo, he admired her intelligence and her no-nonsense approach to life. He dreaded the prospect of showing her that her loving family life was all a sham but that being said, he did not believe it any more than Dee had when the original toxicology report had come back negative. The cold, hard facts are that most murders or attempted murders are carried out by a spouse.

Spouses tend to murder their spouses for one of two reasons, either lust or money, and there seemed to be no shortage of cash so ...

Josh was asking questions of Jo's husband's secretary – were all these business trips strictly work-related? The secretary, blonde, neat and fearsomely intelligent, showed no sign of embarrassment and quelled Josh with a firm statement that her employer worked hard and certainly did not have the time or the inclination to indulge in extramarital affairs.

Nicholas question the couple's cleaner; she was young, thin, Eastern European and obviously disappointed that she was being interviewed by Nicholas rather than the beautiful Josh. She showed little interest in questions about what Jo and her husband's relationship was like but spoke with passion about what a mess the boys made when they weren't at boarding school.

At the Plover household, Vivian was alive with anticipation. She could not sit still; if she was at the kitchen table her foot would tap against the flagstones, wherever she was she kept looking at her watch, checking her lists and sending emails. She'd even started to bite her nails, something she had not done since she was a teenager. Her eyes had taken on a wild brilliance that disturbed Christopher; silently he left their home, followed by Bramble.

Virginia was surprised to see Christopher sitting silently in the empty church. He was so still that she would have missed him had it not been for Bramble sitting in the aisle by the end of his pew.

Virginia was late for a meeting with the Bishop and had only popped into the magnificent church to see if she'd left her car keys somewhere under its vaulted ceilings. There was something about the way Christopher was kneeling that reminded her of the stone carvings of long-dead knights in armour that dotted this hallowed space.

He didn't hear her approach in her sponge-soled lace-ups and was surprised when she spoke.

'Can I help?' she said softly.

Startled, he looked up and she caught an expression on his face of such desperation that it sent a shiver down her spine. For some odd reason, the contrast between Christopher's confident tweeds and his body's air of total defeat struck her as unbearably poignant.

'Is there anything I can do?' she whispered gently as the scent of incense hung in the air.

He looked at her with sad blue eyes and with a slight smile said, 'Thank you, my dear, but I don't think there is anything anyone can do.'

Chapter 22

By early afternoon, Dee found the stiffness was easing but the bruises still throbbed and she felt mentally deflated. *It doesn't matter how many times I run through everything in my mind, I just can't make any sense of all that's been going on. I can't see a pattern or discern a motive; if it wasn't for me being targeted it would be safe to say it was to do with the post of Lord-Lieutenant but as I'm not involved in that, why put so much effort into trying to get rid of me: cutting my brakes, setting fire to the birdwatching hide and then the apple-bobbing?*

She reflected for a moment. *And if it was to do with eliminating candidates for the role of Lord-Lieutenant, then the most obvious culprit would be one of the other contestants, but attacks have been made on all of them.*

She shook her head, then wished she hadn't as it ached. *Of course, Zara could be right and it could be Mr Charter-Fox bent on bringing down the establishment, but then surely he wouldn't have accepted a ticket for the All Hallow's Eve party from me only to try and drown me?*

She smiled, realising how ridiculous she was being, applying moral values to this scenario. *I think what I need is a cup of camomile tea and something to take my mind off all this.*

As she boiled the kettle she watered her impressive array of pot plants. *Gosh, these hyacinth bulbs are budding already. Oh dear, I must have forgotten to spray my ferns yesterday – they are looking a little brittle. Still, an extra spray today will see them right.*

The kettle clicked and she spooned camomile flowers into her glass teapot. She allowed the water to cool slightly before pouring it into the pot.

It's such a horrid thought, but it has to be faced that whoever is doing this must be local, someone who knows all of our movements – someone I see every day. Goodness, I've probably smiled at them and exchanged pleasantries about the weather!

With a shudder, she put the teapot, a favourite blue Spode cup and saucer and her silver strainer all on a tray and took them through to the sitting room.

She settled herself on the sofa and flicked on the television. *Good,* True Crime with Aphrodite Jones *is about to start. I do like the way she's so determined and forceful but still so feminine – I wonder what she's wearing today?*

She hadn't even finished pouring out her first cup of camomile when her attention was totally riveted by the TV's announcement, 'Today the true crime reporter is taking on the case of Dr Essa Yazeed and his wife Rosemarie, a case where the wife slumps behind her steering wheel and crashes. Was it a heart attack or foul play?'

Knowing Aphrodite Jones, Dee felt fairly safe in betting that it was foul play but the expression that struck her was the familiarity of that description, 'slumped behind her steering wheel'.

She watched as the sordid tale of Dr Yazeed's womanising unfolded, then came the relevant part – he had suggested his wife take some calcium tablets and he'd laced them with potassium cyanide and – here Dee could barely contain herself – this poison does not show up on routine toxicology screening tests as it requires a special test.

I knew it! I just knew Jo must have been poisoned! I knew something must be wrong with the negative toxic screening report. Leaping to her feet she started to scan the room. *Where's my phone? I must ring Nicholas!*

The doorbell rang. *Drat it! Well, whoever it is I'll just have to get rid of them quickly so that I can call Nicholas.*

To her surprise and relief, it was Nicholas on the doorstep. Dee was in too much of a fluster to register his neat suit and blue tie under his classic mac or his unfailingly shiny shoes.

He tried to say, 'I was just passing and I thought I'd call in to see how you—'

Dee didn't give him time to finish, but grabbed him by the arm and dragged him into the sitting room. 'Look!'

She pointed at the television where a dark-haired, good-looking woman was frozen mid-sentence.

Nicholas was confused, but then he so often was whenever he was in the company of any of the FitzMorris ladies.

'It's Aphrodite Jones!' Dee said in a tone that implied the information would explain everything.

'Sorry Dee, I don't quite follow.'

'You've got to do a special toxicology test for Jo and look for potassium cyanide. It doesn't show up on normal tests.' Dee's face was alive with excitement, her green eyes sparkling and her voice coming fast and high-pitched. She still grasped his arm.

'I have already requested it – the tests.'

Dee was laughing, 'That's a relief, so you've seen this programme? Isn't Aphrodite wonderful? Where would we all be without her to help solve cases?'

'Actually, Dee, I don't know who she is and I've never watched any of her programmes.'

She dropped his arm and looked at him with wide eyes. 'You haven't? But then how on earth did you think to ask for more tests to be done?'

Nicholas looked at Dee with a measure of exasperation. 'Usually, Dee, police officers do further investigations if they're not happy with reports. We should have the results in the next forty-eight hours.'

'Oh, good! Just in time for the Michaelmas Ball.' She suddenly went very pale and looked away from him.

'Dee? What have you just thought of?'

'Oh nothing,' she said casually, still not making eye contact.

'Dee!' said Nicholas sternly.

Reluctantly Dee looked up at Nicholas. 'I'm sure it's nothing – after all, it's ridiculous to think that they would do anything like try to poison anyone. Really, it's not worth mentioning.'

'Who and what are you talking about?' asked Nicholas firmly.

'Well,' Dee hesitated, then decided to tell the whole truth. 'Vivian gave Jo some calcium tablets – for osteoporosis or rather to prevent it. You see, Jo is going through early menopause and it's so important for a woman to look after her bones. You men are so lucky that you don't have to worry about these things but then I suppose we don't have prostrates to be concerned about so it all evens out in the end – sort of swings and roundabouts.' She finished with a smile.

Nicholas' eyebrows came together as he tried to untangle Dee's words. Eventually, he shrugged his shoulders and admitted, 'You've lost me, what has menopause got to do with anything?'

'You see, I was right! We all need a little help from Aphrodite Jones! In the Yazeed case, the husband – an extremely nasty character and a doctor to boot so he really should have known better – but perhaps doctors in America are different from doctors here—'

'Dee!'

'Oh yes! Well, he poisoned his wife by putting cyanide in her calcium tablets saying they were good for her bones, which they would have been, had they been calcium and not cyanide.'

The deli was busy and it was Sophie's son, David, who was in command. Tall, fair and possessed of the skinniness of youth, he surveyed the shop with his normal air of being not being bothered about anything. The large glass case by the till was well-stocked with cold meats. The separate cheese area with its large variety of cheeses all temptingly displayed, was also fine. A splash of red, green and yellow was added to a table where lemons, fresh fragrant herbs, glistening peppers and all manner of other fresh produce were laid out. The breadbaskets were running short, but they always were by twelve on a Saturday morning.

The new hire, a pretty girl from his college, was being kept busy filling crusty baguettes with whatever the customer asked for, from ham and homemade coleslaw to cheddar and pickle.

In the queue he recognised three locals. There were Julia Fryderberg otherwise known as Blossom Bim Bam and Ken Pilbersek, or

Joseph Popov, as he liked to be called in clowning hours, and next to them was the round, imposing figure of retired police chief Peter Wilson. The latter's ponytail and heavy metal T-shirt glimpsed beneath his overcoat were at odds with his booming voice and authoritarian stance. Finally, there was his prized MCC tie which marked him out as part of cricket's elite, but in his collarless outfit sat uncomfortably in the bulging folds of his neck.

Blossom and Ken were obviously either coming from or going to a children's party as they both wore full costume; Blossom's fairy pink gauze skirt sparkled beneath her pink faux fur jacket and she had a theatrical red dot on the tip of her pert little nose. Her mass of thick golden curls shimmered with a dusting of glitter. Her partner's sombre demeanour and austere attitude contrasted strongly with his rotating bow tie and oversized daisy buttonhole, not to mention his flipper-like red shiny shoes.

Inhaling happily, Blossom announced to the world in general, 'It always smells so delicious in here; it makes me feel hunger before I even see all the yummy food.'

Ken's sour look softened through his stage makeup and the twitch of an indulgent smile was just visible on his red-painted grin.

Peter Wilson grunted and said in the thunderous voice of a man turned deaf from listening to too much heavy metal, 'I just wish the girl would hurry up! I want to get home, have my lunch and have a nap. I was up half the night watching England play Australia – and what a waste of time that was.'

'The girl' couldn't fail to hear him and in her agitation dropped a spoonful of sloppy tuna filling onto the floor.

David decided to step in and distract his fractious customer to give her time to clean up the mess. 'Mr Wilson, Ken, Blossom, great to see you all.'

Blossom smiled at him. 'So, David, I see you're manning the fort today. No Sophie? I was hoping to have a word with her – we're overdue a catch-up. I wanted to invite her over to mine for a cupcake.'

David, though naturally shy, had become adept at charm

through practice and replied, 'Mum would love that – she always says you make the best cupcakes in the village – but she's busy getting ready.'

'For the Michaelmas Ball?'

David nodded.

Peter Wilson snapped to attention and with a decisive snort declared, 'Total waste of money. Did you see the price of the tickets this year?' He didn't wait for anyone to reply but ploughed on, 'In my opinion, some people have more money than sense.'

The professional actuary in Ken Pilbersek was about to agree but then he noticed Blossom had a faraway look in her eyes and her normally joyous smile was pensive.

Wistfully she said, 'Oh, I don't know, I've always rather fancied the idea of getting all dressed up and pretending to be a princess for a day.'

Overlooking her pink costume and twinkling wand, Ken grasped her free hand. 'Oh Blossom, I had no idea you felt like that.'

Straining to look up at him from her petite height she blinked into his small eyes above his red bulbous nose.

'Next year, my love. I promise to take you to the ball next year!'

Peter Wilson was not the only person aghast at the price of the ball tickets. In his cold, grey sitting room, Winston Charter-Fox was perched on the edge of his hard sofa with the nubile Comrade Smith from Putney and Comrade Hugh from Leytonstone.

They were sharing an unappetising lunch of white sliced bread and processed ham. Winston would much rather have popped into the deli and got one of their sumptuous baguettes, overflowing with honeyed ham and crisp lettuce, but he knew Comrade Hugh would have made some snide remark about him being bourgeois and then Comrade Smith would have tittered and looked admiringly at Comrade Hugh. Actually, he rather resented his brother-in-arms from Leytonstone being there at all; he'd rather hoped that after they had some impassioned debate about workers' rights he and

Comrade Smith might have spent the afternoon ...

But oh no! Comrade Hugh had invited himself along and what's more, had given Comrade Smith a lift in his red Ford Fiesta.

'The price of a ticket to that ball is outrageous! We should have a protest! Take direct action! Let everyone know that the whole notion of balls and Lord-Lieutenants and monarchy is unacceptable!' declared Comrade Smith, her eyes blazing and her voice full of ardour as she waved her limp sandwich in the air like a political banner on a march.

'Hear, hear!' cheered comrade Hugh.

Winston Charter-Fox thought of stern Nicholas Corman and the bleak local police station and wished his comrades weren't in Little Warthing this evening.

Comrade Smith stopped mid-gesture and stared at the window, 'What's that?'

Winston followed her gaze to where an opulently fluffy white Persian cat was mewing and pawing to come in.

He was about to explain that the feline representative of an overindulgent society belonged to his neighbour when Comrade Smith beamed and cooed, 'Oh, Winston you have a cat. Do let him in – I love cats. What's his name?'

'Lenin,' said Winston, hurrying to open the window.

Paul was in his black tie already; he just needed to fiddle with his gold cufflinks and he'd be ready to go to the ball. Robert was still humming in the shower and Paul suspected that he was happy in his own thoughts and not thinking of Paul in the slightest way.

Over the last few days, Robert had seemed to Paul to be quite content but somehow also totally detached from him. He was polite and courteous but also unaffected by either Paul's presence or his absence.

On the other hand, ever since the evening of the All Hallows' Eve party, Paul had been unable to think of anything or anyone else but Robert. He suddenly started noticing lots of little changes, from new boxer shorts to that shower gel he could smell coming from the bathroom.

Recent events had made him think about things and had led to him taking action. He carefully took out the small, discreet bag with its cord handle which he'd had hidden in his sock drawer and went down to the kitchen. In the fridge was a bottle of champagne he'd put there to chill when Robert had been elsewhere; now he took it out and found two champagne flutes.

He knew Robert would be down soon; he never took long to get dressed. Paul was surprised to realise that he had a slight pit in his stomach and had to ignore the faint nagging voice at the back of his mind that whispered, *'Too little, too late?'*

When Robert breezed in, still humming, he was taken aback to see the champagne. 'Aren't we a little old for preloading?'

Paul swallowed down his irritation – *I'm only fifty for goodness sake* – and with debonair ease popped the champagne cork. Mildly he said, 'Bollinger is hardly preloading.'

He poured two glasses of pale, bubbling heaven and handed one to Robert, making a point of looking at him directly in the eyes, just like he used to when their relationship was still fresh.

Paul noted Robert's raised eyebrow and the hesitancy in his voice when he asked, 'What are we drinking to?'

Without missing a beat, Paul replied, 'To us!'

They clinked glasses. Paul took a sip, as ever it was sublime. While Robert was smiling over the taste of the Bollinger, Paul handed him the gift.

Robert's eyebrows raised even higher and there was a suspicious note in his voice. 'What's this?'

'Just think of it as an early anniversary present.'

Tentatively Robert looked inside the bag, there was a grey box with the magical words *Jaeger-Lecoultre* written on the top. He put down his glass of champagne and glanced at Paul, who was looking decidedly smug.

He took the box out and rested it next to the champagne. He knew he was grinning; he gave a throaty laugh, as much out of surprise as pleasure. His fingers were trembling as he took the ribbon off and he could feel his heart pounding. When he opened the box and saw the distinguished lines of a Reverso Classic watch resting on its own cushion, he held his breath and just stared.

When he stared up at Paul he could see his head was tilted and he was watching Robert intently. With a thrill of happiness he realised, *He's wanting to see my reaction – he cares.*

'Will you put it on for me?' asked Robert, amazed that he felt shy.

Paul nodded and when his fingers brushed against the delicate skin inside Robert's wrist Robert felt a tingle of anticipation.

'This is just the beginning,' said Paul, his voice husky with emotion.

'It is?' queried Robert.

Again Paul nodded. 'I've booked for us to go to a wonderful place on the Amalfi Coast for two weeks. Our suite overlooks the sea and according to Conde Naste, their restaurant is the best in the area.'

Over at the Plovers' house, away from the scurrying preparations, Tristan was also nervously holding a valuable gift, a bag with the distinctive turquoise colour that proclaimed it to be from Tiffany's, the jewellery shop.

He was standing outside his room, or rather, he was rocking backwards and forwards on his toes, looking at his watch and running his sweaty hands through his hair. He was wishing that Emily would hurry up and be ready but at the same time wanted to put off his moment of truth.

He swallowed, he felt slightly sick; if she rejected him that would be the end ... of everything.

In Tristan's bedroom, Emily was feeling just as nervous. She was giving herself a final look in the mirror. She was simply sensational – what a difference there was in her appearance from the first time she'd come to Little Warthing. Her blonde curls gleamed in the mirror and she'd definitely nailed the whole makeup business.

Zara certainly picked out the right dress for me! she thought as she admired the way the red colour enhanced her skin and hair tone and really flattered her figure. She knew from the films that she really should make some grand entrance from the top of a tall staircase with Tristan standing open-mouthed in amazement at the bottom, but with all the comings and goings of the waitresses, not to mention Vivian, the stairs were definitely out of bounds.

Her only regret was that she didn't have a necklace; she felt a simple pendant would be the finishing touch with that sweetheart neckline, but still, it couldn't be helped and at least she had the diamond stud earrings her parents had given her for her twenty-first.

There was a faint knock and Tristan whispered, 'Emily? Are you ready? Can I come in?'

A sudden wave of nausea swept through her.

What if Tristan doesn't notice – or worse still, realises that I've gone to so much effort I must like him, and then he gives me some kind speech about how he's always valued me as a friend?

'I guess,' she murmured and Tristan opened the door.

He stopped mid-stride and simply stared at her, his jaw slack and his eyes wide. Emily felt a burning heat rush through her.

'Emily,' he stammered. 'You look beautiful.'

She was unable to speak, her throat seemed tight and she was finding it difficult to breathe, The only thing she was very aware of was his eyes looking at her.

After what seemed like an eternity he took a step closer to her, holding out in front of him a turquoise bag with a white ribbon handle.

'This is for you.' He had difficulty getting his words out.

She took it with trembling hands. She dare not glance at him. She took a neat rectangle box out of the bag and fumbled with the white ribbon.

Tristan realised he was anxiously wringing his hands, so in a futile effort to appear nonchalant rather than terrified, he thrust them into his trouser pockets.

Emily stared at the box. The room was very quiet but they could hear people busy in the marquee outside.

Eventually, Tristan could bear it no longer. His voice was husky as he said, 'Open it.'

She lifted the lid and unfolded the black velvet envelope and her breath caught as she saw a single dazzling diamond on a gold chain.

Bewildered, she glanced up at Tristan. His face was ashen, his lips trembling and she could see the tendons standing out on his neck. The pupils of his eyes were huge and very black, and she couldn't read the emotion behind them. *Fear? Hope? Love ...?*

'Will you put it on for me?' she whispered, looking up at him through her long black lashes.

He swallowed and nodded, unable to speak. Taking his hands out of his pockets he took the pendant.

Slowly, as if making a move in a choreographed dance, she turned her back to him. He took a step closer to her. She heard him swallow again. She could feel his breath on her bare shoulders and her skin tingled.

She could feel the warmth of his body as he leant over her and the diamond dropped against her décolletage. Her skin seemed alive to the slightest breeze and touch and when, as he fastened the clasp, his fingers brushed against her soft naked neck, she gave an involuntary small gasp.

He took a step back and Emily's body ached for the loss of his warmth.

She turned round to face him. He was flushed but still looked debonair in his black tie with his hands in his pockets and his mop of unruly hair falling over his forehead.

He was looking at her intently, then he moved closer to her. He very gently brushed a stray curl off her face then he cupped her cheek with his warm palm. She felt herself drowning in the intensity of his blue-eyed stare then he leaned towards her and she felt a kiss as soft as a fluttering butterfly wing on her slightly-parted lips.

It left her wanting more and when he leaned back, her arms reached around his neck and she pulled his mouth down towards her and kissed him hard. Feeling her response he clasped her around her waist and drew her body forcefully against his.

She closed her eyes and allowed herself to be carried away by their mutual passion. She ran her hands through his thick hair as they explored each other's kisses, giving free rein to their desire. His breathing was becoming heavier and he leaned into her, his hands sending electrical thrills through her body as they roamed down her side.

She flung an arm back to brace herself and accidentally knocking a picture frame off the chest of drawers. It crashed to the ground, breaking not only the glass but also the moment. Startled by the noise, their lips broke away from each other, but their arms remained entwined.

Now there was no mistaking the look in Tristan's eyes; it was pure lust with just a pleasurable hint of love.

Simultaneously they began to laugh; deep joyous laughter filled the room. She buried her head in his shoulder and he affectionately stroked the back of her head. When their laughter had subsided he held both her hands and gently kissed her forehead, saying, 'Come on, we have a ball to go to.'

Chapter 23

Jo sat at her dressing table putting on the finishing touches of her makeup. She looked at herself in the wraparound mirror. Without emotion she noted how tired she looked; her skin was dull and there were fine lines around her eyes. Her hair didn't hold its normal lustre, either, but hung dry and limp, shapeless despite her recent visit to the hairdressers.

She wasn't excited about tonight, she didn't feel anything much, just a sort of numbness.

She was wearing a black dress she'd had for years; it wasn't particularly special but it was reliable, the sort of thing you could throw on and you knew you would fit in.

She went to a lot of these black-tie dos, what with her work and her numerous charities, so it didn't make sense to buy new dresses all the time. Fortunately, Dee had put her on to an excellent dress-hire shop in Cheltenham; they had her measurements on file and she would pop in every few months to go through her upcoming events and wardrobe requirements. It was all the fun of shopping but without the eye-watering expense. She had hired a rather smart designer affair in a stunning green for this evening; it was cut to perfection and made the sort of unstated, stylish statement she loved but when she'd come to put it on she'd felt intimidated by its beauty and had zipped it back into its bag and reached for her old faithful black number.

The boys would all be home for Sunday lunch – a rare event these days. She could hear Tobias moving around the bathroom, his steps and movements were solid and familiar. He was going to be working from home for the next two weeks; he said some things had changed, a client mix-up, but she suspected he had arranged it so he could be with her more.

She glanced at her phone. She'd missed three unlisted calls, probably from Nicholas Corman wanting to ask her more inane questions. His sidekick, Josh Parks, had popped in and taken away her supplements in neatly labelled plastic bags. What would be next? Her toothpaste?

Jo had a sensation of dread, vague fear and a sensation of being out of control. Grappling with her tangled thoughts she wondered which would be better, that she was going mad or that someone had tried to poison her. She noticed from her reflection in the mirror that she was sitting rigid and very upright. She squeezed her eyes shut and was surprised to find tears trickling down her cheeks.

Without warning and as all-engulfing as a tsunami wave, Jo was seized by panic. She couldn't breathe. Quick, shallow gulps of air didn't help; she was suffocating. She felt dizzy and nauseous and wanted to run, but her limbs were heavy and unresponsive while her fingers and toes fizzed.

'Jo?' Tobias' voice reached her, calm and firm through the torrent of her emotions. He placed a warm, solid hand on her shoulder, anchoring her in the here and now.

In the swirling images around her, she tried to focus on his reflection in the mirror; his familiar heavy features, good-looking but tired. He was always tired; if it wasn't jet lag, it was overworking or overplaying.

Now Jo clung to his unwavering eye contact like a drowning man to a lifebuoy.

His voice was strong and decisive. 'Jo, breathe!'

She obeyed and the room stopped spinning. 'I can't do it,' she stammered.

'Can't do what?' he asked.

'Any of it! Tonight, the boys' lunch. I've forgotten to order a joint from the butchers,' she finished with a whimper.

'Oh darling, it's all going to be okay,' was all he said and he wrapped his arms around her and held her tight.

Dee was pleased with the dress she had hired from that little place in Cheltenham. It was vintage and a shimmering midnight blue.

Jim Stuart knocked on the door at the exact allotted time. He looked extremely suave in his black tie and presented her with a beautiful bouquet of golden roses. She reached for her wrap, took his arm and they walked towards the Plovers' house.

Zara was as pleased as her mother with the dress she was wearing. Amelia, in a figure-hugging tailcoat and well-cut tuxedo trousers, was both striking and attractive. The high-winged collar set off her elegant neck and her red hair cascaded in curls from a loose bun at the top of her head. Unlike Jim Stuart, their escorts did not arrive on time. Ten minutes after the designated time both Zara and Amelia received apologetic texts.

'Seems like our gallant lads in blue have been called away on urgent police matters,' sighed Amelia.

'Never mind, we can go together,' smiled Zara.

Virginia was also without an escort, but it bothered her more than it bothered Zara and Amelia. Actually, she wasn't very happy about any aspect of tonight. She just finished the most delightful Lavinia Lovelace novel, set in Regency times, where the blushing heroine had finally been swept off her feet by the handsome Marquis at the Grand Ball. Virginia looked at her sad reflection in the bathroom mirror. *I know I shouldn't be worldly but this navy pass-me-down of Cousin Vi's really is ghastly.* She sighed. *It would help if she was even vaguely the same height or shape as me.*

Emily felt like a heroine in one of Lavinia Lovelace's romances; here she was with the man she loved, going to a ball. She and Tristan dodged a rather flushed Vivian who was wearing a stiff bottle-green velvet dress and giving some poor waitress hell.

The marquee was magnificent. Vast and tall it reminded Emily of the church's vaulted ceiling. The dance floor was at the far end. Round tables all decked in white table clothes dotted this end of the tent. Amid their green arrangements, long flickering candles shone, their light reflected in the ordered silverware and cut-glass at each place setting. The three supporting poles that ran through the centre of the marque were decked with more trailing foliage and, against Vivian's wishes but at the committee's insistence, fairy lights twinkled like stars. The ambience was perfectly enhanced by the Glenn Miller Tribute Band, who were hired for the occasion, playing *Moonlight Serenade*.

Efficient waiters were weaving between the tables with flutes of champagne and Tristan secured one for Emily and one for himself.

'Here we go!' He grinned as he tucked her hand in his and walked towards a knot of people.

When he looked at her she felt total confidence in both his adoration of her and that she really was for once drop-dead gorgeous. Even the sight of Victoria Pheasant could not dent her newfound faith in herself.

Victoria was chatting with a cluster of people. Emily recognised Victoria's parents as well as the retiring Lord-Lieutenant and his wife, but the young man whom Victoria was draped over was totally unfamiliar.

'Let's get this over and done with,' whispered Tristan, 'then we can relax and enjoy the evening.'

Emily didn't really care what they did or who they talked to as long as they were together.

As they approached the group, they could hear Victoria's painfully thin mother exclaiming in her overly loud voice, 'Well, Justine, I guess this is a happy day for you! Your last official engagement as the wife of the Lord-Lieutenant.'

Justine beamed. 'My dear, I am practically doing cartwheels around the marquee.'

Victoria's nondescript father and Oliver, Justine's jolly rotund husband, both laughed. The broad-shouldered young man entwined by Victoria gave a half-smile that could have been a sneer.

When Emily and Tristan joined the group they were for the most part greeted warmly. Justine and Oliver both hugged and kissed Emily and commented on how delightful she looked. To Emily's surprise, she realised that she did actually rather outshine

Victoria who had opted for a black dress which would have been more apt for a matron twice her age.

She also noted that Victoria's python grip on the young man had intensified at the sight of Emily with Tristan. Now, with what she could only think of as an aggressive tone, Victoria declared, 'I don't believe you have met Jamie MacPherson, but of course, you will have read about him in the Financial Times.'

'Of course,' smiled Tristan giving him a strong handshake.

'Still no engagement ring I see,' said Victoria's mother with a waspish note.

Unruffled, Tristan smiled some more and lightly replied, 'No, but it won't be long now. Do please excuse us but there is Dee and we need to have a word with her.'

Tristan and Emily weren't the only ones who had spotted Dee and were making their way towards her, viewing her not only as a safe harbour but also someone who was guaranteed to be enjoyable company. Jo's panic had resurfaced in the car on the way to the ball and it was only the strength she found on Tobias' arm that had propelled her into the marquee. Dee was with Jim and it looked like they were soon to be joined by Emily and Tristan – all people that Jo knew she would feel safe with.

Jo and Tobias joined Dee, Jim, Tristan and Emily just as the band switched to the upbeat, "*In the Mood*".

Dee started to tap her toe and declared, 'I love this song and my, isn't the band good! We are certainly in for a jolly evening.'

They talked of this and that in a relaxed manner for about ten minutes until Vivian roared into the marquee. She was in unfamiliar disarray, her lipstick smeared, forming an ugly red gash across her face.

'Christopher? Have you seen Christopher?' she screamed, drowning out the band and causing people to turn and stare in silence.

Jo, Tobias and Jim, as well as Emily and Tristan, gaped at Vivian in amazement. None of them registered Dee's look of sad confirmation.

'Vivian, are you alright?' whispered Tristan, taking her elbow and continuing in hushed tones. 'Let's go and get you a glass of water somewhere quiet.'

'I don't need a glass of water, I need Christopher! The bloody man should be here to greet the guests – it's the job of the Lord-Lieutenant – greeting and being gracious.'

Jo began to say, 'But he's not the—'

Vivian cut across her. 'I have to do everything myself! I bet he's cleaning his shotgun or is in the bloody kitchen garden.'

Forcibly she shook Tristan's hand off and stormed out of the marquee in the direction of the house.

Tristan went to follow her but Dee caught his sleeve and with calm firmness said, 'It's better if I go. You stay here.'

'Are you sure? She seems to be totally losing the plot,' said Tristan, looking anxiously in the direction his godmother had gone.

Dee nodded and with great composure followed the route Vivian had taken.

People were beginning to talk again and their murmurs swelled as Dee reached the entrance to the marquee nearest the house. She was pleased to be joined by Zara and Amelia.

'I say, Granny, what was that hullabaloo all about? We've just arrived and I certainly didn't expect to be greeted by Vivian having a total meltdown,' exclaimed Amelia.

Zara nodded in agreement. 'I didn't have her pegged as someone who would let the pressure get to her like that. I mean, I know she wants Christopher to be the next Lord-Lieutenant and tonight's the big announcement, but really …'

'I'm afraid it's a bit more serious than that,' said Dee grimly as they reached the back door to the kitchen.

Vivian, still frantically looking for Christopher, approached the back corridor just as Amelia was excitedly exclaiming, 'No way, Granny! So Vivian, beneath all her pearls and tweed has been trying to knock off Christopher's opposition? Wow! That's awesome! I bet she's like the people I've been studying this term, you know driven by a narcissistic void.'

Vivian didn't hear Amelia add, 'I wonder if I'll get extra credits if I use her as an end-of-term case study?'

She missed Amelia's final words because she had tiptoed away and secured a key from Christopher's study, then with equal stealth gone to the gun safe, unlocked the door and taken out Christopher's shotgun. All she had to do now was to go a separate place where, for safety's sake, he kept the cartridges.

She returned in time to hear Zara say, 'The pity of it is that I don't think Christopher was ever in the running; it was always going to be between Jim and Jo.'

'Don't be ridiculous!' shrieked Vivian. Her eyes were bunched up and looked wild, especially when viewed peering down the two long barrels of a shotgun.

In her sensible black patent evening shoes and her unfashionably formal green velvet dress, she expertly raised the gun to rest against her shoulder and screamed, in a high voice, reminiscent of a toddler, 'Christopher *is* the next lord! I've seen to it and now I'm going to deal with you three!'

Protectively Dee stood in front of Zara and Amelia, using her body as a shield. She was surprised that Vivian's yells hadn't brought the caterers running but evidently, they were all fully occupied and Dee needed to rescue herself and her family. Her heart was pounding and her mouth was dry but she channelled her martial arts training and calmed herself.

She spoke to Vivian as if she was a frightened deer. 'Vivian, my dear, you've been under such a lot of stress; why don't we have a nice cup of camomile tea and—'

'Will you bloody well shut up? You've no idea how annoying your endless little bright sayings and cups of tea are. So bloody self-righteous and chirpy. You, Dee FitzMorris, are a detestable woman and the sooner I take care of you, the better.' She swung the end of the shotgun to the right of them, indicating a door that Dee knew led down to the wine cellar. 'But I haven't got time for this now – a gracious hostess should be with her guests – so you three go down there and I'll deal with you later.'

None of them moved until Vivian shrieked, '*Now!*'

The wine cellar was dimly lit with deep stone steps, worn shallow in the middle by centuries of use. Reluctantly, the three FitzMorris ladies made their way down the stairs, leaving Vivian silhouetted in the doorway.

A chill assailed Dee; she wasn't sure if it was fear or the climate of the cellar with its flagstone floor and mahogany racks of wine bottles.

It smelt damp and when Amelia spoke her words had the ring of an echo. 'Before you go, Vivian, can I just ask you a couple of questions?'

'Not now!' hissed Zara.

Vivian nodded. 'What?'

'You've obviously planned all this very carefully, Christopher's rise to power. You've been rather like some military general going into battle. You've gone to such a lot of trouble. Presumably, it was you who wrote those letters to Sebastian threatening him?'

'Yes! And I had a gentle word with him about the other chap who'd been caught doing the same thing; that just pushed him over the edge.' Vivian's voice rang down into the cellar; it was full of gleeful pleasure.

'Then Granny's brakes?'

'That was fun, in broad daylight, too. No one suspected a thing.'

'And the fire?'

'The only tricky bit there was carrying Christopher's fuel for his mower to the woods, but I managed and once again no one thought of me.' Her voice was ecstatic.

'Then there was Jim?'

They could see the outline of her figure move as she nodded vigorously. 'Odious man!'

'And then Granny again at the All Hallows' Eve party?'

Vivian giggled. 'Yes, and with all those people around.' She sounded proud of herself.

'And how on earth did you get the idea of cyanide in a pill?'

'Oh, some TV true crime programme. It was fortuitous timing; I saw it just before we went on holiday to the States and I thought it might be a good idea to get some when I was over.'

'You really think you are pretty clever, don't you?'

'Yes! Yes!' exclaimed Vivian eagerly. 'They always underestimated me – my mother, my sister – but not now. *Now* everyone will see how brilliant I am.'

'Oh, well done, darling, she's softening,' whispered Zara in Amelia's ear.

Looking rather like a slim petite Victorian gentleman addressing parliament in her tailcoat and high collar, Amelia went confidently on, 'Oh, I don't know.'

'Know what?' demanded Vivian.

'That your mother and sister weren't right.'

Vivian screamed, '*What?*'

'Well, let's face it – you've been pretty incompetent, haven't you?'

'*What?*'

Vivian was visibly shaking and Dee could imagine sweat borne of rage pouring off her and her finger slipping on the trigger.

'Darling!' Dee said to Amelia, hoping the one word would quell her granddaughter but Amelia was in full flow.

'Let's examine all your failures one by one.'

Vivian's silhouette stiffened.

Dee's intake of breath was audible.

'Not now, Amelia!' Zara said with a note of exasperation in her voice.

Amelia, like all FitzMorris ladies, was unstoppable once she had a goal in mind.

'Would you say you were clumsy with Sebastian or just plain inefficient? After all, he didn't kill himself, did he?'

There was a worrying silence from the lady with the shotgun at the top of the stairs.

'And Jo – you failed there with both fire and poison. As for Jim, he's still alive and well, and a strong contender for the role of

Lord-Lieutenant.'

Vivian spluttered.

Then with a final flourish, Amelia declared, 'And you couldn't even finish off my harmless little granny!'

'I'm not a failure!' screamed Vivian, steadying the shotgun.

Amelia finally seemed to realise that sometimes tact is sensible and, now pale and rigid, stopped talking. At the moment when both Dee and Zara were about to throw themselves between the possible gunshot and Amelia, Vivian started and glanced hurriedly over her shoulder. Evidently, someone was coming down the corridor.

Instead of giving Amelia both barrels, she slammed the heavy door shut and the FitzMorris ladies were left in the empty wine cellar.

After a moment, when they each allowed their breathing to return to normal and their pulses to fall, Dee put an arm around Amelia. 'Darling, I don't know what you intend to do career-wise after you leave university, but I'm not sure that working with people who are psychologically fragile is a good idea.'

Zara was more forthright. 'What on earth were you playing at?'

'We had a lecture last week on the fragile sense of self that someone with a narcissistic personality disorder has and how any criticism of them leads to an uncontrollable narcissistic rage. I wanted to see if it was true.'

'Very clever, dear,' said Dee patting Amelia's shoulder.

'I don't really think it was necessary,' Zara said tartly. She was wandering around the room, phone in hand, trying to get some reception.

Amelia clarified, 'I also thought that if I got her wound up enough, she'd let off that shotgun and someone would hear and come and rescue us.'

'Yes dear, but one of us might have been dead,' Dee pointed out patiently.

Amelia shrugged.

Zara sighed. 'There's no reception down here so I can't call for help and that door is so thick that if we pounded on it no one would hear; it would be a total waste of effort.' She switched her phone to flashlight mode and scanned the labels on the wine racks. 'I say, there are some excellent bottles of wine here; do either of you have a corkscrew?'

In the marquee, most of the guests had arrived and Tristan imagined that any moment now the Master of Ceremonies would ask everyone to take their seats.

He took Emily's elbow and said, 'Come on, let's check where we're sitting.'

They wandered over to where the board with the plan on it, telling everyone where they were sitting, was displayed. Having found their names, Tristan was just escorting Emily to their table when Justine came up.

'Tristan, I can't find Christopher or Vivian anywhere. They'll be so disappointed if they're not here when supper begins. I know Oliver wants to say a few words to them in his opening speech to thank them for hosting this do and the committee has got Vivian the most beautiful bouquet of flowers which they plan to present after Oliver has said his bit. Could you be a dear and run into the house and see if they're there?'

'Sure!' said Tristan. 'Back in a mo!' He smiled at Emily and went.

In the house, he didn't find Christopher or Vivian but he did find Nicholas and Josh. They were in the kitchen, both in black tie, but from their earnest expressions and the way Nicholas was conferring with a uniformed police officer, they weren't there for the party.

'What's going on?' he asked.

They looked up but didn't get a chance to reply as Christopher walked in through the back door. He had his shoulders back and his stance was very much that of a retired army officer. His black tie was immaculate and his shoes shone. Over his arm, he carried his shotgun, broken open in the accepted way to prevent accidents when walking.

He had an unhealthy pallor but his voice was steady when he said, 'They've come for Vivian.'

Tristan gaped from Christopher to Nicholas and then back to Christopher.

'I've taken care of her. She would have hated all the shame and publicity of a trial. Poor old thing – I wish I could have made her happy but at least I could do this for her.'

He handed the gun to Josh. 'You'll want this – as evidence.' For the first time, his voice faltered. 'Look after it; it was my father's.'

He swallowed, regained his composure and looking Nicholas straight in the eye said, 'She's in the vegetable garden. I thought it was the best place, she did so hate her kitchen floor getting messy. Besides which she's worked so hard for this party that she wouldn't want it spoiled by the sound of a gunshot. The dell by the veggie patch and those thick walls were all excellent for deadening the noise.'

'Christopher?' asked Tristan in disbelief.

Christopher gave him a sad smile and patted his shoulder. 'I'm sorry my boy but I couldn't let her carry on. When I saw her threatening the FitzMorris ladies with my shotgun I knew I needed to stop her.' He looked infinitely sad. 'It was easy really. She didn't suffer. I think her last moments were happy; I told her that Oliver wanted to have a quiet word with us in the vegetable garden about—' Here his voice caught and he swallowed again. 'About the procedure of announcing me as the next Lord-Lieutenant and she trotted along quite happily, never suspected a thing.' He sighed. 'If only I'd been more like my brother, none of this would have happened. She wasn't a bad woman just … deeply unhappy.'

Epilogue

It was in early spring that Dee walked into her kitchen to find both Amelia and Zara had let themselves in and were happily making tea.

The kitchen table was bright with a large jug of yellow daffodils and the windowsills boasted terracotta pots full of tiny narcissi and heavily-fragrant hyacinths.

'Kettle's just boiled, what would you like, Mum?' asked Zara who was looking very seasonal in a light cotton dress but with a warm cardigan.

Amelia, sitting at the table, was also embracing the season, in a pair of jeans and some sort of a floaty blouse – the only nod to her Goth identity was slightly heavy eye makeup and a studded leather choker and wristband.

'Camomile tea would be lovely, dear. I've just come from visiting Christopher.' She shed her tan leather flying jacket and put down her tote bag.

'How is he?' asked Zara bringing over Dee's tea.

'Surprisingly well. He says he loves the peace and quiet. I don't suppose being married to Vivian could have been very restful. They're still doing psychological assessments of him but he seems to be spending a lot of time working on the prison allotment. His only concern is that Bramble is alright.'

Zara sat down next to her mother with her steaming cup of red berry tea, 'I hope you reassured him that Bramble is as happy as he can be living with Emily and Tristan. Now they're living in Vivian and Christopher's old house I see them all the time out walking Bramble.'

Dee nodded. 'I did and he's so pleased Emily is running her vet practice out of the house. That house really would be too big for the two of them but with Emily opening her vet's surgery there and Tristan working from home, it's perfect.'

Amelia looked at the time on her phone. 'Must dash. Josh and I are going for a walk in Warthing Woods, but I thought you'd like to know Jake and the dogs are very happy in the cottage. He likes living in this village and in a small place. He says it looks like his dad, Sebastian, will be out of prison earlier than expected for good behaviour.'

'That's excellent news,' said Dee and she turned to Zara. 'How about you, dear, can you stay to lunch?'

Zara shook her head. 'No, I'm having lunch with Jo; I'm looking forward to catching up with her. She is so busy with work and with being the area's first lady Lord-Lieutenant.'

'But she's enjoying it?' asked Dee.

Zara smiled. 'Loving every minute.'

Virginia was wearing her habitual shapeless sweater and black rubber shoes and of course, her dog collar. She didn't have long as she was taking a lunchtime assembly at the village school but she just couldn't resist looking for yet another time at the website. Its inviting opening page read, 'Find love in Jane Austen's Bath!' There were several very appealing photos of beautiful young women in Regency costumes set against Bath's beautiful architecture. The webpage went on to say, 'Have you ever dreamed of being the heroine in one of Lavinia Lovelace's historical novels? Well, now's your chance! Click below and sign up for our all-inclusive package!'

What harm can it do? thought Virginia and she bravely clicked on the link, little imagining the dangers and turmoil she was committing herself to.

Books in the FitzMorris Family Mystery Series

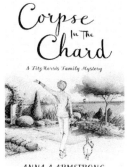

Corpse In The Chard

A Fitz Morris Family Mystery

ANNA A ARMSTRONG

Murder On The Isle

A Fitz Morris Family Mystery

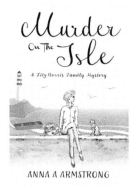

ANNA A ARMSTRONG

Season For Murder

A Fitz Morris Family Mystery

ANNA A ARMSTRONG

Printed in Great Britain
by Amazon

29721895R00131